MAFIA
QUEEN

paige press

MAFIA QUEEN

New York Times Bestselling Author
CD REISS

Copyright © 2021 by Flip City Media Inc.

All rights reserved.

CD Reiss is a trademark of Flip City Media Inc.

No part of this book may be reproduced in any form or by any electronic or mechanical means, including information storage and retrieval systems, without written permission from the author, except for the use of brief quotations in a book review.

This book is a work of fiction. I made up the characters, situations, and sex acts. Brand names, businesses, and places are used to make it all seem like your best real life. Any similarities to places, situations or persons living or dead is the result of coincidence or wish fulfillment.

Paige Press
Leander, TX 78641

Ebook:
ISBN: 978-1-953520-69-2

Print:
ISBN: 978-1-953520-70-8

Editor: Cassie Robertson at Joy Editing
Cover: CD Reiss

The crown was hand forged by Leonidas Moustakas of Adam's Forge. https://adamsforge.org/

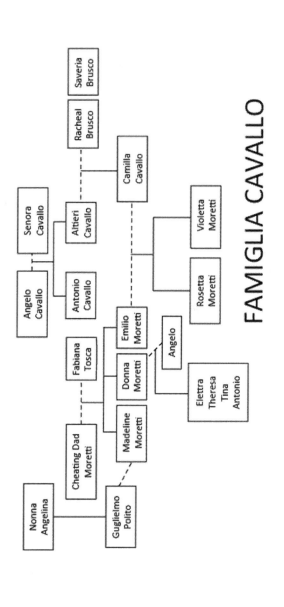

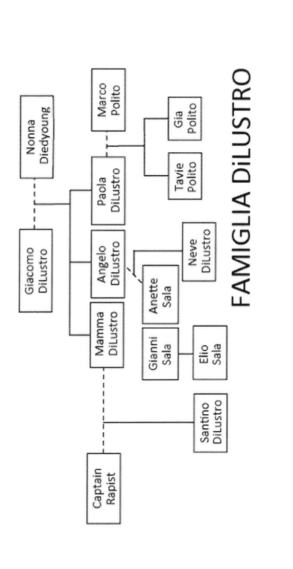

FAMIGLIA DiLUSTRO

Nonna, I didn't listen to a damn word you said, because I thought I lived in a different world. Mi dispiace.

Love is not just looking at each other, but in looking together in the same direction.

— Antoine de Saint-Exupery

ABOUT THE BOOK

An epic mafia romance trilogy from NY Times Bestselling author CD Reiss.

What doesn't kill you makes you a killer.

Santino DiLustro changed me. You can't spend time in bed with the devil without getting addicted to the heat.

Before him, I was a girl. Innocent and weak.

Now, I'm a woman. A fighter. A killer.

I'll burn the world down for him. Shatter the sky. But I will not break.

No. I will rise up and destroy whoever dares to threaten what my king has built, because I am forever his queen.

PROLOGUE
VIOLETTA

How long does it take to become a woman? How many moons disappear into the darkness? How many suns climb over the sheer face of the horizon only to collapse on the other side?

The journey to womanhood is not measured in suns or moons, but in decisions counted like money that can never be spent. The account is always at zero, because one choice leads to another, on and on—forever, and ever, and ever—until a girl is lost inside them, looking for her own edges.

Are you here, inside this foreverness of broken stars and cold space?

Santino, I told you to set me free, and you turned those words into your language and made it into a promise of forever. I hated you for it, but then I met you where you were, and the words you made me say in that church turned into the truth.

Lo voglio.

Because of you, I am who I was always meant to be.

Without you, I'm not sure I'll ever be free, or whole, or finished.

It's dark here, and heavy, and the pain goes on, and on, and on. You're supposed to be mine, and I am yours, but you are gone. I am unowned and all that I possess. I am my only companion, and I am a stranger to myself.

Lo voglio.

Lo voglio, Santino.

I do, I do, I do.

But I don't know what to do.

1

VIOLETTA

FIFTEEN YEARS EARLIER

I am five, which—as my sister has pointed out repeatedly—makes me too young to know how Mamma got a baby inside her. I'm also too little to make my own *pastina*, brush my own hair, or pour my own milk.

I'm not too little for any of those things. I'm just too little for them to let me.

Today, Raggedy Ann sits in my lap, sulking. The pastina is too hot, and Mamma didn't put in enough milk to cool it off. The blob of white is shaped a little like a cat. It pushes against the puddle of melted butter that has dots of salt indenting it and a streak of opaque fat in the center.

Normally, I'd feed Raggedy Ann half of my pastina, but it's too hot for even a doll. We live in a big house and have lots of food. Mamma just opened the milk, so there's plenty. Papà sells it at the store. But she put it away already, so that's that.

Raggedy Ann will have to go hungry or burn her tongue. Ever since I tried to brush the red yarn that made up her hair, and wound up pulling out half of it, she won't do anything that hurts even a little. So no pastina for her.

"Eat," Mamma commands from behind me, dragging a brush through my hair. My head jerks when she hits a tangle.

I swirl my spoon around the porridge. Sometimes I can get the butter and milk to make a perfect spiral, but not with my head being pulled all over the place.

"Where are my suede shoes?" Rosetta asks, coming into the kitchen from her room.

I remember this scene in English, even though I only spoke Italian then.

"How should I know?" Mamma quickly brushes knots out of the ends.

"Patricia Scotto's mother always lays out her clothes in the mornings." Rosetta slides into her chair. Lately, she likes saying things that make Mamma mad. I don't understand it.

"Because she's a bored *stronza*."

Rosetta gasps. I giggle. Mamma taps the side of my head with the back of the brush.

"Stop catching butterflies." Mamma yanks the brush down.

"Ow!" I exclaim.

"*Cazzo*," she growls at my uncooperative hair. My head's jerked around again, but in a different way.

"Mamma!" Rosetta exclaims.

With a final *snap*, my hair is in a ponytail.

"Don't scold me," Mamma says, dropping into the chair at the head of the table. "I'm in no mood for that, or Joanna Scotto, or you losing your shoes." She turns to me and points at the bowl. "And I'm not in the mood to hear you complain you're hungry later."

I eat a spoonful of pastina before Mamma starts feeding me like a baby.

She's been tired since her belly started getting rounder. She told Papà that carrying this baby's been more exhausting than Rosetta, but not as exhausting as when I was inside her. They laughed. Papino kissed the top of my head.

Mamma's been short-tempered since Papà got out of the hospital at the end of summer. Rosetta goes to school now, so she hasn't been able to play with me in forever. It's been lonely.

"Will Fiore come today?" I ask.

My best friend plays with me in the alley behind the grocery, and though Sal and Tomas are always watching us, they are more like ghosts, or furniture. They don't boss and get mad like Mamma does, and they don't kiss away my hurts either.

"Am I his keeper?" With the flick of a wrist, Mamma answers herself. No. She is not.

Just then, a movement by the stairs catches my eye.

"Papino!" I cry, jumping out of my chair. "*Buongiorno!*"

By the time I get to the kitchen doorway, he's already there, crouched down with his arms ready to fold me inside his warm embrace. His shirt smells like spicy things, and his moustache tickles my cheek.

"*Il mio soldatino*," he coos, calling me by my nickname: little soldier. He reaches out another arm and pulls Rosetta into his embrace. She's stiff next to me as if she doesn't love him anymore... which is fine with me. I have enough love to take her place as favorite.

After kissing both our heads, he stands. Mamma waits with a smile. He takes her jaw in one of his big hands and pulls her into a kiss.

"I can't find my suede shoes," Rosetta interrupts, and is ignored.

"How is my son this morning?" Papà puts his hand on Mamma's belly. Usually, you can't really tell it's changed unless you know, but when he does that, it's as if she's huge.

"Don't try to distract me," she says.

"How would I do that?" He goes in for another kiss, but she holds him back.

"Girls," Mamma says, "get ready. Violetta, put a jacket on. Rosetta, I don't care which shoes you wear, but both of you, be at the door in ten minutes."

We rush, leaving the half-finished pastina for Mamma's helper, Carlotta, to clean up when she comes in the afternoon. Rosetta yelps when she finds one suede shoe and gets lost in her deep closet to find the other.

"Come on!" I say to Rosetta, my doll and favorite hooded sweatshirt dragging on the floor.

"I'll be right there!"

I can't tell time, but it feels as though it's been too long. The sounds of shoes being flung around comes from deep inside the darkness of her closet.

"Ah!" Rosetta cries, as if she's found her second shoe.

There's yelling from downstairs. I panic. I don't like getting yelled at, so I run down, jacket dragging behind me.

Mamma and Papà are not by the front door. They're in the kitchen, where bowls of pastina are now too cold to eat, talking in that way that's like yelling but also whispering at the same time. They're standing close and touching. So that's confusing, because they look like they love each other, but they're also very mad at the same time.

"Santi's taking care of other business tonight," Papino says. "We can go out tomorrow."

"He's not even twenty, and you act like he's the only man you have."

"DiLustro fights like a dog. That's why I chose him for the 'mbasciata. Dinner can wait."

"You chose him to protect power." She points at him. "And you didn't consult me."

"This argument again? Over a dinner out? Come on."

"If you find yourself dead, I'm in charge and that deal is off."

Papà's voice gets smoother and softer. "I will take you to an anniversary dinner for the ages...tomorrow night." Tenderly, my father brushes my mother's hair off her face. "I swear on the crown."

Mamma scoffs, and a smile teases the corners of her mouth. Her anger seems thinner. "You can only swear on what's yours."

"I swear on you then." He brushes his lips on her cheek. "I swear on our children."

"You can swear on all the inventory I have to do today. That's yours. Then you can swear on dinner at *La Lavagna*. Tonight. Or you're going to have to find love with your right hand for a long time."

I don't know what that means, but it seems to break his resistance.

"Fine. Tonight. Happy anniversary, my love." He gets close again. I love when they're like this. I don't understand what they're saying half the time, but it doesn't matter. Their body language tells a story of love. "Sal can take the girls. Let's you and I spend the hour alone before..."

I don't hear the rest, because Rosetta's feet *clop-clop* down the stairs in suede platforms. Mamma turns and sees me standing there, then my sister approaching from behind me.

"Girls," Mamma says, shifting away from our father. She stands in front of the hall mirror and pins on a purple hat with a black ribbon. "Your father and I are going out tonight. Grab what you need to spend the night at Nonna's."

Rosetta stomps upstairs, personally offended at being pawned off. That's dumb. Spending the night with Nonna means hot chocolate and all the biscotti I can eat, even if it ruins dinner.

As I'm turning to follow Rosetta, I catch sight of my mother looking at herself in the mirror, and I have to stop, because she doesn't look like herself. She's different. Everything about her. I don't recognize her stone-faced expression, the matte sheen of her white skin, the chiseled nose. She's not a dead version of herself—she is a version that was never alive.

Her eyes shoot to me, and she's back to her flush, living self.

"*Sciò!*" She shoos me away, and I run.

By the time I get to the top of the stairs, I'm mentally deciding which pajamas to bring, and the strange mother looking in the mirror isn't even a memory.

2

VIOLETTA

NOW

"Is your husband dead?"

My mind is cluttered with the dead, but I'm an American woman, and in my culture, we learn about life and death from movies. There, the dead come back to the living and offer advice, comfort, or permission to seek vengeance. Sometimes you can see through them, and maybe they glow a little or their color is washed out. Sometimes they're just the actor in an unusual place, and their loved one wakes up inspired to do a new thing.

My education in the habits and power of the dead is a lie.

The Santino in my mind is just a product of my effort. It's not him, or his soul, or his will. The spell I cast is no more powerful than the imaginings of a desperate woman.

In my half-consciousness, I try to conjure my king with a prayer to the only god whose presence I feel.

Hail Pain
Holy Agony
Smile upon my sacrifice
And fire, fire, fire

I can't think in clear sentences, and pictures flip through my mind as if Zio Guglielmo is doing his best to make me crazy with the TV's remote control at the end of a long day. It's after dinner, and he's in the recliner, too tired to make a decision. Too wired to go to sleep and let me watch *Supernatural* in peace. It's a ball game, the news, paper towels disappearing a red splatter, one of the *Law and Order*s, Santino's smile, reciting every step of our plan, Gia looking up at me from poolside, my husband thrown back from an impact to the chest, swallowed by cool, clean water one final time.

"Mrs. DiLustro?" The same urgent voice from the other side of a long, dark tunnel. "I need to know, is your husband dead? Santino DiLustro? Does he still walk the earth or no?"

Walking. Falling back. Splash. Swallow.

"He swims," I say, but I'm not sure if the words make it past my lips.

A part of me wakes up and separates itself from the sleeper, the groggy, the mind moving as if it's underwater, and that part has questions.

Who's asking?

Why do they not know?

Why do they care so much?

Why do I smell incense?

The left side of my face is bursting. The nerves on the surface stretch from the fluid gathering underneath the skin, screaming for release. The pressure is too much.

I'm going to throw up, and that's when I become more conscious than unconscious, because a person can choke on their own vomit, and I'm not ready to die.

Knowing that is new.

Was I even conscious of a will to live a moment ago?

When I open my eyes, the dim light only enters one. The other is swollen shut, but through the fog, I can make out a blurry, dark blob in the center of flickering yellow light. A head. A man. The voice.

I am sitting. My wrists lay on the arms of a chair. I can't move them.

"Mrs. DiLustro." He has the voice of an old man, and his breath stinks of fermented plaque. "I need to know—"

"Who are you?"

"Father Alfonso." His reply is slow and drunken. "I officiated your wedding to Santino DiLustro."

"Asshole." I blink hard. Breathe in the incense. Scratch a sudden itch on my nose and cheek with an overly rough right hand, then lift my left off the arm of the chair.

Okay. So my arms are weak. Not tied down.

Itches attack my face. When I try to scratch my left

eye, it tingles then explodes in pain like an afterthought.

"I cannot commit a sin," Father Alfonso says. "Please. Tell me if your husband has died."

My mind is clearing slowly, but I cannot fathom what Santino's life or death has to do with a priest adding one more sin to a long, long list of them.

"He's dead." I scratch my jaw and rub a colony of itches from my right cheek. My hand feels rough as lace. "She killed him."

I point to some place to the left where Gia exists in my mind, and I'm about to say her name when I realize my hand is lighter than usual.

Father Alfonso leaves, hunched, touching surfaces and walls until he finds the door before he clicks it closed. When I'm alone, I sit straight in the chair. Hold up my hand. My one good eye is full of gunk. I blink. Blink. Blink. When it clears, I know what the candlelight will reveal.

A room with plaster walls.

A tiny, darkened stained glass window.

I can't see close. The world is crisscrossed by the net I'm caught inside.

But across the room...a thick wooden door. A cabinet with a small statue of the Virgin, surrounded by the unassertive yellow glow of candles.

When I scratch my face this time, it's easier to identify the roughness of my fingertips.

I'm wearing a veil.

Throwing it back, I see clearly and hold my left hand in front of me. My ring. Rosetta's ring. A meaningless assembly of rock and metal that my husband etched with a secret and gave to me.

It's gone.

MY CONSCIOUSNESS RETURNED moments after I ripped off the veil, and in the five minutes since, the pain in my face has grown with the itchiness I've been rubbing from my face and neck.

The door is locked from the outside.

...vasodilation...

I open the cabinet doors, trying not to think about why I'm having a histamine release.

The cabinet is full of church shit. Moving it out of the way, I peer into the back, find nothing, then sit back down on the floor. I don't even know what I'm looking for. Santino isn't in the cabinet, and what do I need besides him?

Has he even been fished from the pool yet?

My face itches where it hurts and hurts where it itches.

...a reversal of systemic dilation of cutaneous blood vessels...

Damiano hit me. The blunt trauma to the head wouldn't keep me unconscious more than a few minutes unless I was in a coma, which I wasn't.

I've been drugged with an opioid. It's wearing off, and the pain is just about hitting me.

The baby.

I rock back and forth, scratching my face like an addict denied relief.

Shit.

What kind of drug? How much of it? How long? I need the packaging and a Davis Guide, stat. Because I get to keep one, single remnant of Santino, and it's growing inside me.

Before him, a pregnancy would have been invasive and unwelcome. Catholicism aside, I would have considered the pros and cons of continuing. But I love my king, and this thing we started—this potential life that's the sum of the best and worst of us—is a product of that love, made real by the dreams we wove for it together.

"I'll take care of your child," I whisper to my dead husband. "I won't let you die twice."

He neither approves nor disapproves, because he's dead.

A shaft of light appears against the far wall with the sound of metal squeaking against metal.

My eyes adjust. The effect of the candles dims as the light from the outer hallway enters.

A woman comes in. She holds a tray, and her dark hair is a curly mane pushed back by a gold banana clip.

Her name is Gia, and she shot Santino.

I launch myself at her like a bullet, hands out, tingling face contorted into a growl.

She doesn't back away, scream, or protect herself, because the drug in my system is a knife driven between my will and my body. I can't move that fast, so I don't move at all. Chemicals have dislocated my spirit from my actions, proving that I am now and have always been just a piece of sentient meat.

"I'm listening," the man who opened the door says.

"If I hear anything—"

"Shush, Dami," Gia scolds.

The door closes, leaving us in the dimness.

"Violetta," Gia says softly, putting the tray on an ancient table carved with crosses.

"Fuck you." These are my first words to her, and they're not strong enough.

"Just stay still." She takes something from the tray and crouches in front of me.

"Santino. Our baby." There are no questions or statements attached. I'm just naming the things I love the most.

The painful half of my face is suddenly cold. She's put an ice compress on the swelling. The light behind her makes her look like a saint.

"That's not going to do shit." I push away the compress. "He broke the orbital bone."

"No, he didn't." She puts the cold wetness back on my face.

"I wish you weren't such a bitch, but wishes don't make truths."

She uses a single breath to laugh. "You were always so clever."

"Not clever enough to see you coming."

There are voices on the other side of the door, and we both look at it as if we can see through the wood.

When they fade out, I ask, "What did you give me? Which opioid?"

"Does it matter?" She shrugs it off like a passing grade she didn't study for.

How did I miss the sociopathy? Should I have seen

it when she focused on what marriage looked like rather than what it was? Or the first moments I knew her, when I cowered in a strange room as she stood over me, showing me wedding dresses as if it was fun?

"Hold this." She presses my hand over the compress and leans back to pluck a bottle of water from the tray. "The doctor says you have to be hydrated."

Mob doctors are the extended professional family of the mob priests and mob lawyers who already ruined my life. But if I want to kill this bitch and her man, I'm going to need my body and mind working at capacity, so I drain it.

"I hate you," I say, handing back the bottle. "I'm going to kill you." I shouldn't warn her, but the message isn't for her, really. I'm putting myself on warning.

"Your husband was going to start a war, Violetta. I thought you'd understand."

Santino wasn't going to start a war—I believe that from the bottom of my heart—but a war may have started anyway, and his intentions would have been irrelevant.

"You shot Santino. You brought Damiano to my house. You drugged me when you know I'm pregnant. What am I supposed to understand?"

"That I did what I had to do to be free."

The morality of what she's describing is broken, but the logic of sacrificing me or killing someone to escape is as clear as it is cruel. What I can't sort out is how she's acting as if the plan worked and she's free, when she's got me locked in an oversized, empty closet.

"How can you be free if Damiano is waiting right outside? If you're marrying him, you're not free."

She laughs, then covers her mouth to quiet herself. A square-cut diamond on her finger glints in the candlelight. She's wearing the ring. My ring. Rosetta's ring.

"I'm not marrying him." She scoffs with the absurdity of it. "You are."

3

VIOLETTA

In this same church, I was forced to marry Santino DiLustro so that he could collect my inheritance—the missing pieces of the *Corona Ferrea,* the Iron Crown of Lombardy, worn by both Constantine and Napoleon, inset with a nail from the One True Cross, and so powerful, even those few pieces compelled a warehouse full of men to kneel before the one who held it.

The crown's power should be filed with other superstitions. Like, if you go to mass on any nine consecutive first Fridays of the month, you're guaranteed a place in heaven. Also, if you're wearing a brown scapular under your shirt when you die, Our Lady of Carmel will personally pull you out of purgatory and deliver you to paradise on the first Saturday after your death, amen.

"I wore that scapular from first grade to third," I remind the tabletop statue of the Virgin, but not for her sake, for my own.

My zia made me wear it under my shirt. I was

orphaned in a new country where I didn't speak the language, and the feel of the brown felt was a comfort. I could see the ribbons and matchbook-sized rectangles under the thin white cotton shirts of the other kids at school. This was a key to making me feel as if I belonged, and for a few years, I thought I wanted to be a nun. Not out of devotion to the Church or love for God, but because—in my new world of St. Anselm's—they had all the power, and they wielded it like a coven of psychopaths.

This says more about me than it ever did about them.

"Gia should have been a nun," I tell myself, rubbing away a last itch from my chin.

I had been stolen from my life, and Gia had wiped away my tears so she could put eye shadow on me. She held up the train of my dress and placed the veil over my face so I could walk into Hell blind.

With her cheerful friendship, she'd somehow lulled me into compliance. I'm smarter this time. Tougher. So much fucking older.

Santino may be dead, but I can still make him proud.

I pick up the Virgin statue and slam it against the little stained-glass window. Our Lady of Plaster smashes against the tight lead web between the glass pieces, having no effect on the window itself, but magically transmutating into Our Lady of Ruins.

My disappointment is like a shot of adrenaline, and it's just as short-lived. I pick up a shard and run it against the length of my finger.

Sharp.

The Virgin might save me after all.

I open the top drawer of the cabinet and sweep the pieces and dust into it, then notice a long, clear plastic sleeve. Taking it out, I turn it over and laugh to myself.

It's ridiculously convenient, almost magical, that there should be a sleeve full of scapulars with a white SKU sticker proving they were shipped directly from the Sisters of Our Lady of Carmel in Colorado Springs, Colorado, USA.

Well, if I'm going to die today, there's no harm in hedging my bets.

I slide one out. A doubled brown ribbon about a foot long connects two rectangles. One has a picture of Mary sewn on, the other with the pale-skinned, blue-eyed Jesus with a thorny, glowing heart in his chest. The brown felt side has a little pocket for a medal that's going to stay empty right now. I loop the ribbon around my neck, under my shirt, placing the felt side against my skin.

There's a click from the door, and I quickly shut the drawer, putting the cabinet to my back so the missing statue isn't noticed.

It's Gia again.

"It's a beautiful day," she says, sliding my veil off the chair. "Did I interrupt something?"

"Just praying."

Either she knows I'm lying or she's not impressed by my devotion.

"Cool." She holds up the rectangle of lace, but all I can see is the ring. "Do you want me to pin this on, or are you going to let it just drape? Either way it'll cover…" With her nose wrinkled, she draws a circle around her own eye.

"The eye that Damiano hit so hard it's swollen shut?"

"You'll think that's funny when you see him." She already thinks it's funny. "You stuck a pin in his eye."

"I did." I indicate the veil. "Is this the one you brought from Naples?"

"No," she scoffs. "That's for *my* wedding, whenever *that* is. My mother's over on the other side with all that stuff. This is the one you had on when you married Santino."

I'm not sure if the repeat use is meant as a kindness or an insult, but I won't give her the satisfaction of either gratitude or anger.

"Drape is fine," I say.

She holds out the fabric for me to take, but I have a razor-sharp shard in my fist. I bow so she can lay it over my head. When I look up, I have the same view through the netting as I had when I woke up in the chair, except now the light's behind me and I can see the woman I destroyed everything to save. She looks just fine… as if she never needed to be rescued. All she needed was a little time to figure out how to fuck someone over before she got fucked.

"No dress this time." She shrugs.

"You held my train."

"I remember!" She smiles warmly.

"I'm going to kill you," I say with a flatness I don't recognize.

She squints, barely registering the threat, then chuckles and shrugs as if I must be joking.

"I mean it."

"Oh, believe me, we know." She fusses with my veil. "We ran up a thousand dollars in international phone bills planning for you to be super mad. But…" She steps back to look me up and down. "I think once we have the crown, it's not going to matter what you want or how you feel."

"Who's going to marry you? After all this?"

"Here's a secret, Violetta." She leans so close I can smell her flowery perfume. "When a man loves you, he loves you no matter what you do."

By the look on her face, I know she has a specific man on her mind. Maybe I know him. Maybe I can use it to break her confidence. But before I can ask who loves her that much, the door behind her creaks open.

She steps back, and I see my future husband in a simple, ill-fitting suit that makes him look like a football player borrowing his smaller brother's clothes. He obviously doesn't believe in the prohibition of seeing the bride before the wedding. He only gets one eyeful though. The other is poorly bandaged. I get no satisfaction from it, because his thick hands are clasped in front of him as if one holds back the other and I notice a glint.

Santino's diamond crown ring is at the base of Damiano's right pinkie.

I look away, unable to bear the sight of it. "You need to get that eye looked at by a real doctor."

"We gonna do this easy?" he asks me. "Or we gonna do this hard?"

I mirror the position of his hands, though on me,

it's not a threat, but a false submission, hiding the sharp edge that protrudes between two fingers of my fist.

"Easy," I say. "It's going to be real easy."

"Good." He reaches for me, but I curl back.

"On one condition."

"You don't get conditions."

Obviously, I have zero power in this situation, and he has no reason to give up any of his. But there is a ceremony to attend to, and I'll have plenty of opportunities to kill him later, so he may be pliable.

"I want to bury Santino," I say quickly. "Properly. I know you haven't. Let me do it. Then you can put me in the hole with him. I don't care."

"I can do that." He shrugs with the magnanimity of a kindly king. "I respect the dead."

4

SANTINO

In the waiting room of an Italian hospital, Camilla told Damiano and me that the numeric key was a lawyer's license number, and years later, a young woman named Theresa Rubino told her cousin that her lover, Roman, was getting an important and secret thing engraved inside Violetta's ring.

This whole drama... It was never about Damiano and Gia's *'mbasciata*, her father's debt, or the string of overlooked insults.

Gia didn't resign herself to a forced wedding for the sake of peace or the security of a marriage. The bride was never confused or moody.

I shouldn't be so surprised when she shoots me.

She always wanted to be free.

Time slows down into details without a story. Crystal-clear events shuffle like the *wht-wht-wht* of a deck of cards.

I stand at the pool and follow the sound of pounding fists up. I see Damiano holding her up against her window. Then—and only then—do I understand my mistake.

wht-wht-wht

Before the bullet, the error is the first ache in my chest. Then I see Gia, and the pain bursts through me. The heat. The pressure. The life pushed out of my lungs in a blast of air. I feel myself go flat and weightless.

wht-wht-wht

I am in a shroud of noise. It's everywhere, like God. Thick as all my sins against Him. Loud as the crunch of a footstep to the insect it's about to crush.

wht-wht-wht

Falling backward into the pool, the last thing I see is Violetta in the window with her mouth open. I can't hear her, but I know she's screaming from a different time, a distant place, tying the spaces between us with her voice. But then all I see is sky.

wht-wht-wht

When I see Gia pointing a gun at me in my own house, I understand their plan. In that moment between when I drop my gun and step back, it's so clear I could write a book on it.

If I'm dead before Violetta collects her inheritance, Damiano can marry her, and he will have access to it.

wht-wht-wht

I go down with empty lungs. Face up. White foam closing off my route to Violetta.

Though I know what's happened, who did it, and why, my body takes a breath before I shout to my wife.

Wait for me.

I'll be there. I'll come. I'll swim. I'll crawl. I'll fly on wings of fire.

My lungs fill with water. It's excruciating. My limbs jerk, but my mouth forgets and breathes and breathes. The water sucks me down into solid silence, and I breathe liquid because I have no choice. I will die unredeemed.

My last thought is that Violetta was right.

This all could have been avoided if I'd outlawed *'mbasciata* the moment I saw her cry.

IT ALL FLASHES before me so fast, I have time to remember everything.

My mother is sad, then she is happy. Her hair is tied back, but half of it has escaped already. I follow her up a mountain. Vesuvius. She's going to heal herself at the opening of a dead volcano. It's been days uphill, grasping at rocks and scrub, and we're barely a quarter of the way. I am hungry.

Paola visits me in a place with many children. She promises to take me home one day. Then she keeps that promise.

Mario sleeping on the couch. Fighting with his wife about how much I eat.

The street. Damiano. The oranges. Mario blames me for the mess.

I open my best friend's face. Blood everywhere. I'm in trouble, but my uncle stops yelling. He pats my head.

Emilio pats my shoulder. He says I have a certain something, then he steals it for his own purposes. I will marry his daughter to protect his interests. Then I am at his funeral, and I have to keep the promise he made for me. I've been sold for it, and I know I'm worthless because Emilio is a stingy man.

Violetta in the hallway. Part of me shifts. I never understand what it means, because Rosetta is crying. The boy cries when I kill him. Rosetta cries in relief when I give her the ring. I've made someone happy and soon—dead.

I can't stop thinking about what I stole from the girl in the hallway, then I marry her, and I fuck her, and I love her. I protect her. Shield her. I make her life about me and what I can do for her. She won't understand. She fights and resists. But she loves me anyway.

And now there's light everywhere, and I know I am forgiven.

I am clean. My God, I am clean.

This is what they mean when they say your sins are wiped away.

I wish Violetta could know this. I'm not a devil. I'll never be good enough for her, but I have a chance to not be bad for her.

And God says I will tell her one day, but the devil laughs from far away and says, "Enjoy sainthood while she's getting raped, *coglione*."

The shock of the devil's truth turns me away from heaven and back to Earth. I see my body from above, flat on my back at the edge of the pool, one leg dangling in the water. A man in wet clothes crouches nearby, pulling Emilio's ring off my finger.

"I told you there wasn't no blood," he says nervously, his voice close to me even though I'm a mile overhead. He pulled me out for that fucking ring.

"So shoot him," says the man standing a few feet away.

I know the voice. He's Lucio. From Lasertopia. Cosimo's man. The one who acted as if he didn't speak English. This man is a threat to everything I love. From the moment I saw him, I could tell he'd committed murder more times than he could count on his fingers.

Emilio's ring comes off. It is meaningless. It's not what draws me back. The increasing need to save Violetta pulls me through the thick space, against a tide, like a fish on a hook.

The man holds the ring up to the sun—to me—as I speed back to earth. He is Calimero Tabona. This is where Damiano is getting his strength—from the few Tabonas left after they tried to take Violetta. They are based on the other side of the mountains, in Green Springs, and now they're here. Calimero starts to put the crown ring in his pocket.

"That's Dami's." Gia's words come from somewhere out of my vision, which has folded like an envelope.

Calimero shrugs and tosses it in the direction of her voice.

I spin through space with the ring. Vengeance unhooks me from Heaven, and when she catches it, I drop back to Earth like a stone, meeting my body on the pool's edge. Breathing into motion, everything is everywhere. I'm facing every direction, seeing through closed eyes, and I know the backstabbing *stronzetta* leaves without another word.

She's unfinished business. Her and others. Damiano. Marco. Maybe Loretta. Eventually Cosimo.

I can't die until they pay for what they've done to

Violetta, what they intend, and what they're going to do. My soul takes back possession of my body as if blown into the fingertips and toes by the breath of vengeance—I'm going to kill all of them.

Animated by that sudden expansion, I take Calimero's legs from under him, sweep up the gun he drops, and shoot in his direction. The pop of the gunshot is drowned out by the whooshing in my ears. I hit his thigh.

A shadow alerts me to Lucio's movements. I point the gun at his chest, praying for a lucky bullet, and blow his face into a blackened hole of meat.

My vision is still swimming and my chest hurts. I expel two bullets in Gia's direction before I bend and retch a lungful of pool water. It washes away a streak of blood on the tiles. Like a drunk committed to the inevitable, I heave again, coughing up the contents of my chest.

With a slam from the front door, Gia walks out of my range. For now.

A man sobs. It's not me. Holding myself steady against the table, I look around. The green of the trees is shockingly vivid. The pool water is so transparent I can perceive the brushstrokes in the concrete's turquoise paint. And the man dragging his bleeding leg as he crawls is cast in shadow as dark as the sun is bright.

I am here.

For whatever purpose God or the devil let me live, I have my own reasons for not letting death take me.

Wobbly for the first few steps, I intercept Calimero's path to Lucio's gun. He stops and looks up at me, his leg gushing on my patio. He won't last long.

"Please," he says.

"You need a tourniquet." I crouch in front of him.

"I have a wife and a son."

There was a time I wouldn't have been moved by those words at all—except to extend his suffering for the insult of assuming I'd take on his personal problems. I'm surprised to find my understanding has expanded. I do care about wives and children.

"So do I." I check his gun for bullets and snap it closed. "And you're going to tell me where to find them."

I press the gun to his forehead.

"I don't know."

This is a man who is either not getting the message or who's been threatened with more than death.

"How old is your son?"

Calimero groans in pain, eyelids clamped shut. He's losing consciousness. "Fourteen."

"Ah, a nice age." I drop into the nearest chair, where I can watch the path of blood behind the crawling man. I want a cigarette, but they're soaked, and my lungs still feel half-filled with broken glass. "When I was fourteen, I swore an oath to the Cavallo family. My father was dead, and the man who took me in…wasn't much of one. So. You get the family you get, no?"

"I can't… I don't…"

"Your wife though. Let's make a deal."

"Don't." Lucio's gun is out of reach, but he grabs in that direction.

I lean my heel on his wrist. "If my wife is dead, I

take yours."

"I don't know where she is."

"You'd better tell me something, Cali. The hand of God pulled me out of death. What will you say when you meet Him? You didn't tell me what I needed to know—what God Himself sent me back to Earth for—because you were *loyal*?"

In his weakened state, the superstitious logic gets through. He swallows hard. Blinks. Starts to answer, then stops.

"It's Damiano," Calimero says.

"Tell me something I don't know."

"And Cosimo. His father. Bankrolling. Paid us all."

No surprise. Cosimo's lusted after the crown since the day it was pulled from the devil's warehouse.

"What's in it for you besides a paycheck?"

"A place. Under the crown." His energy flags. The river of blood from his leg flows into the pool.

"Where is she now? This is your last chance."

"Don't know. Tomorrow morning…church." His eyes close, and his body goes limp.

I slap his face until he's half-conscious. I'm trying to stay calm and failing. "Then what?"

"Marry her. Claim crown…"

Dami's intentions with the crown may be to rule himself or give it to his father to expand his territory here. He may want to jerk off on it. None of it will matter. He'll kill Violetta after God and the devil used up a miracle to save me from death.

"Where is she *now*?" I ask again.

But the light goes out from his eyes, and I drop him to stand. The blood stops flowing from his leg. He didn't know. She could be anywhere, suffering in a thousand different ways.

"Fuck!" I shoot him in the head.

Bone and blood and brain spray like paint. The bullet leaves a hole in the patio tile. No blood flows. He was already dead. Can't turn back time and kill him. Can't turn it forward.

Tomorrow morning.

I pace into my house, turn corners, sweep the pictures off the mantel, the garbage statues and clocks off the tables. There's an entire house to waste time destroying because she's out of my reach. I fall back onto the couch. My chest hurts.

How many hours to blow a hole through this town? Burn down every house she isn't in until I find her? Leave them a place to run? To go deeper into hiding?

Out of habit, I reach for the pack of useless cigarettes, but they're not there.

Not in one piece, at least. My pocket is full of soaked tobacco and paper sludge around a misshapen, dented Zippo, and I understand everything.

The bullet hit my chest hard enough to send me into the pool, but the lighter's steel casing kept it from piercing me. When I laugh, my chest hurts, but I laugh anyway. Neither Heaven nor Hell saved me, but my purpose is both holy and damned.

Gia's already telling them I'm dead.

Good. When I come for them, they won't expect it.

Violetta and our child will live. Whether or not I die a second time is not up to any mortal.

God help them, and God help me.

I will kill them all.

5

VIOLETTA

Through my headache, I remember a thing.

Last night, or a few hours ago, or last week, Gia brought two guys into the room. One was the size of an old oak. He had no neck and a hairline behind his ears. The other was young—around my age—with full lips and big brown eyes as tender as undercooked meatballs. Behind them came a balding man with a round, clean-shaven face. I recognized him as Alina Farina's father...a doctor from our little hospital.

He'd rooted around his bag and asked me how I was but didn't listen to the response. He took out a needle, and I said, "No. No drugs. I'm pregnant," but Gia sighed. Oak Tree and Meatball Eyes held me down so he could give me the shot. He either didn't say what it was or I lost consciousness before I heard it.

"I respect the dead," Damiano says again, but more softly.

Under my veil, I nod—not because I agree, but

because I'm out of stall tactics, and nodding makes my head swim.

Clutching the plaster shard, I decide to die rather than be forced to marry again.

"You're going to do fine," Gia says.

Oak Tree and Meatball Eyes lead me down the marble hall, through the bronze door, and into the narthex of St. Paul's.

From inside, an organ plays. It's deep and melodic. Almost a little sad. It sounds like my soul's song. A message, maybe, from beyond—from Santino—to tell me he's with me.

A bolt of sickness crawls from my guts to my throat…another message from the embryo struggling to grow inside me. The man who planted it inside me may be gone, but it still needs me.

I commit to living for Santino's child. The last thing we made together.

The suits part to let me inside the nave. Through the veil, I see the length of the long aisle lined with enough pews for an army of the devoted. Gia waits at the front, centered in the width of the aisle, all perspective pointing to her where she waits for the moment she doesn't need Damiano and she can be fully free.

Behind her is the altar. No bridesmaids, no best man. Just an ancient priest and Damiano with a poorly-bandaged eye and an ill-fitting suit.

I don't know who shoves me forward, but I go.

From the transept, the Virgin watches me for a second time. Neither she nor God are coming to my rescue.

The protruding edge between the fingers of my

right hand grazes the palm of my left as I walk down the aisle of St. Paul's for a second time, until I can see Father Alfonso's cataracts.

No matter what happens, I have to live.

Heading up the carpeted path to the altar, I lose my footing up the steps. Meatball Eyes catches me and gets me on my feet, grabbing me by the wrist. Despite his soft gaze, he's rough, treating me like a plaster statue that almost fell when he bumped into the table. I keep my fist around the shard, sneering at him from behind my veil. He holds up his palms as if no harm was meant, but he's a liar—harm is definitely intended. He isn't innocent. None of them are.

I get to the altar without help and face Damiano's one unbandaged eye.

"Let's get this over with," he says.

Through the veil, I see his fear. His weaknesses. It's as if I've known Damiano Orolio since I was a child, and I see that boy in front of me. He's finally conquering Santino, the man who scarred his face, yet his one free eye darts from man to man, soldier to soldier, unsure of their loyalty.

Maybe it's the diminishing opiates in my blood or the benevolence of the scapular, but I know that what I see as clear as day in Damiano is what Santino saw through his own eyes.

"Marriage brings us here today, to be witnessed by God," Father Alfonso creaks, his voice old and warbling.

I close my eyes, breathe deeply, and focus on the priest's voice.

I can get through this. Santino's spirit is here with

me. He gives me strength. Even in death, he is my courage. My vision.

Father Alfonso clears his throat before asking, "Do you, Violetta Antonia Moretti, take this man to be your husband?"

I open my eyes. Damiano stands over me expectantly, his one eye narrowed. He can't see my face through the veil. I lean into him, and he takes me by the upper arms.

"Say it," he says, jugular pulsing.

"I do—" My hand juts straight for his throat on his blind side, seeking the pumping vein with the Virgin's shard. "Not."

I'm grabbed, and there's a shuffle I can't keep track of, but I wave my fist with the sharp porcelain jutting from between my fingers, looking for a body to cut. When I find resistance in a dark suit, I slash left and right, up and down, screaming, "*Non lo voglio!*" Blood splashes on my veil, dotting it with black. I scream as he drops to one knee with one hand over his throat.

This is exactly as it should be. It is correct. His blood is payment for a debt, and every drop reweights the scales of justice.

I am righteousness and law. I am power and fire.

Slashing at the top of his head—at any bit of flesh I can find—I am no longer who I was.

The gunshots come from deep in my lungs as a primal death scream, and I fall on him, punching down with the plaster edge jutting from my fist as he bleeds and bleeds.

The cracks of gunfire are my soul shattering.

They're the blood jets opening under my thrusts. His wrists, his forehead, his choking mouth.

The *pop-pop-pop* is my rage clicking into my ecstasy with every cut, and the gunpowder is the smell of that union.

I am in a dream state when I'm pulled off him, screaming curses, flailing to cut him open again and again, until I wake enough to really see the man below me, and it's not Damiano.

It's the boy with the meatball eyes, widened to darkening headlights.

A voice I know and love reaches through the rush in my ears, and something I've lost and not had a moment to grieve for is found.

"*Forzetta!*"

6

VIOLETTA

St. Augustine said that to sing in worship is to pray twice, and Father Alfonso DeLuca takes that to heart, canting every singsong word of the ceremony as the boy twitches in an ever-growing pool of blood.

"Have you come freely and without reservation to give yourselves to each other in marriage?" The priest does not stop a sacrament. Not even matrimony, with the groom sputtering and bleeding at his feet, and my husband—who I swore was dead—in front of me.

"How?" I ask, though that's just curiosity peeking out from behind tentative relief and joyful disbelief.

"Where did he go?"

He can only mean the man who kidnapped me and tried to force me to marry him. I point at the man on the floor making the burbling sound. We both know that's not him, but I point anyway.

Santino shouts to someone outside the tunnel of my attention. *Find him.* Someone shouts back. *We don't know.* And *Where?* And they swear they checked everywhere from the front door to the sacristy to the basement. All the while, I watch the boy's bleeding slow with the beating of his heart.

I should feel something about this body. I don't. I only feel relief that my husband is here, but I'm too deep in shock to move toward him.

Santino takes a corner of the veil and pulls it off. Even with the lace grid gone, he's still blurred when he gasps at the condition of my left eye.

"Damiano did this." His words are flat and emotionless, as if he's speaking through a cinder block wall he's erected for my protection. "He's going to have more than a bandage on his eye when I'm done with him."

"I'll be fine," I say, pushing his hand off the bruise and pointing at the man I cut open.

But him? That's what my pointing finger asks. He will not be fine, and he's not who should be there.

"*Will you honor each other as man and wife for the rest of your lives?*" Father Alfonso goes on, rocking back and forth, blind or indifferent to everything around him. The vows are a chanting backdrop to what I've done here.

Santino looks at the man clutching his throat, choking up blood that seeps and squirts through the fingers, and through the bright red mask painted on his face, are two matching eyes—unbandaged, unwounded by a cameo pin—both as big and soft as meatballs.

In the scuffle, I lost sight of who I was attacking. The shard drops from my fingers.

"Santino," I say, still in shock. "That's not Damiano."

"This? No. This is Arturo Tabona." He lays his hand over the one pressing the jugular.

I could do something. Stanch the wounds. Take him to the hospital to be sewn up. As long as there's pressure on the arteries, he might even survive long enough to get to the ER, but not long enough to avoid starving his brain.

My living husband crouches by him.

"*Will you accept children lovingly from God?*"

"Ke-ke-ke..." Each attempt is a cough.

"Shh, now." Santino reaches into the boy's pocket and takes out his phone. He presses the bottom circle to the owner's thumb, and it opens. The wallpaper is a sunset scene of a happy couple. "Ah. Anna Silvio. I'll visit her and offer condolences."

The tender eyes go wide with an expression of terror. Arturo already knows what it's taking me a moment to figure out. The condolences aren't benign. They're a threat, and he's going to be dead in a few minutes—unable to protect his family or girlfriend—because I killed him.

"*And bring them up according to the law of Christ and his church?*"

That's Father Alfonso's last chant as he's led away. The king doesn't move.

"Where is Damiano Orolio?" he asks the dying man. "Where did he run?"

"*Dh-dh-dh. Nuh-nuh.*"

Santino takes the pressure off the wound I inflicted, letting it spurt life in a jet. There's no last gasp. No audible last breath of life. Just a silence so deep I have to look down to make sure Arturo's still lying there—and I see it. Clear as words on a page. His eyes go from living to dead. Full of fear to fully empty.

His skin contracts against the muscle by a fraction of a hair.

Last summer, I attended in the ER during the wildfires. A fireman died on the table, and it wasn't like this. Maybe because we were trying to keep him alive. Or because he had no last words. Or maybe I hadn't felt as if my own soul was being sucked away when he died because I hadn't killed him.

The silence from the now-absent priest couples with the departure of a soul, and the sounds echoing inside the church drown out everything.

There's only Santino, but outside of that, I'm distracted and small, stuffed into a padded box and sealed inside. This is over, but I can't digest what just happened or what's going to happen. There's only this man who rose from the dead and came for me.

Back from the dead, staring down at me, reaching into his jacket pocket for a pack of cigarettes. He opens it with one hand, thumbs one free, and bites the filter to pull it out.

"He got away," I say, stating a fact, expressing fear, and looking for reassurance in just three words.

"I'll find him." Santino goes back into his breast pocket and comes out with his steel Zippo. It's bent, and he has to use two hands to open it. "Then I'm going to kill him."

He lights up. I've never smoked, but when I smell the raw, unburned tobacco, I realize how much I want to.

"We checked everywhere, boss," a man says from outside the width of my connection with Santino.

"Get the car," my husband replies.

The men—maybe half a dozen of them—take off out the transept door. Gas cans litter the ambulatory, about twenty feet away, and the white linen altar cloth is soaked piss-yellow.

"The fuse ends at your feet," he says.

With a *scritch,* Santino spins the flint and hands me the flaming Zippo. I take it and get a good look at it for the first time. The steel bends in the center around a bullet-sized indentation.

He had this in his jacket pocket when Gia shot him. Smoking saved his life.

"Do it now before the fumes catch."

I look down. There's a wet, twisted rope of fabric on the floor. A tide of blood from the man I killed soaks it pink. I touch the flame to the end, and it blossoms into heat and light. The church will burn, and I have no will to do anything else.

Santino leads me down the aisle, away from the fiery altar, and out into Secondo Vasto.

The clarity of the afternoon sun is merciless, taming the slightest breeze into submission.

The fire crackles, looking for fuel. I blink away the burn.

Santino can't take his attention from my black eye. "He'll die for doing this to you."

Damiano's failure to kill my husband doesn't change the fact that he tried, and who knows what he would have done to me if he'd succeeded in marrying me. Santino's rage is justified.

There will be more death. The murder I committed, that I haven't even digested, won't be the last. Was that one also defensible? I was blank with anger and raw intention. Not a single neuron was firing when I cut into him. How can murder be justified when the killer didn't have a thought in her head?

"The blood," is all I can say.

My husband takes my chin and makes me face him. He inspects my expression and makes a sharp *tsk*.

"No," he says. "You did what you had to do."

"I'm still a murderer."

"Yes."

He leads me to the curb where a black Mercedes is pulling up. He opens the back door for me. I assume he's disturbed about the same thing that's weighing on me. His *Forzetta* committed murder and should feel guilty and traumatized. I should pray for my eternal soul and make reparations to God and Arturo Tabona Meatball Eyes's family. I should spend the rest of my life mortifying the flesh in penance.

But all that seems pointless. It's impossible because nothing after this moment will ever happen. My senses are frozen in horror, and my heart barely feels as though it's beating. I don't want to feel bad. I don't want to be sorry. I've never prayed much, and I'm not starting as I run from a burning church, but an unwelcome awareness tugs at me. I don't know what to think or what feelings to put in place of the ones I refuse.

Santino joins me in the back of the car. I take his hand and hold it so tightly my knuckles pale. He puts his remaining hand over the doubled fist, and I lean into him, comforted. In all the thick, unthinking guilt—in all the gray dullness protecting me from what I've done—he is the only reality. He is my anchor.

"She's not in the trunk," says the driver, an older

guy with a receding hairline. He slaps the back of the passenger's head. "Tell him why, *stunad!*"

"Fuck you, Gennaro." The passenger is a younger guy, but probably older than me. Tightly waved dark hair. He turns around to face us, but averts his eyes.

"What happened?" Santino asks. I feel as if I'm seeing all this and reacting through him, because I'm wrapped in a hundred layers of gauze.

"She was crying."

"Oh, boo-fucking-hoo," Gennaro mocks.

"Is this true, Carmine?" Santino's tone is soft. Almost inviting. "You let her go because she *cried?*"

"She's Gia! Our little waitress!" Carmine defends himself with the obvious notion that a woman you know is a woman who's harmless. "She was scared, so she started kicking and twisting all around. What was I supposed to do? Hit her?"

"Dami and Gia." Santino rubs his eyes. "We lost both of them."

I don't know enough about his business to know what resources he has to find her, but there's one thing I do know for sure. If Gia was ever a powerless victim of cruel traditions, it was before I met her. She's neither helpless nor powerless now, and she will not hesitate to kill anyone between her and what she wants.

"Next time," I interject, but it's someone else talking. Some other Violetta with a strong, definitive voice. "You show her a little respect."

Gennaro—stopped at a light—twists around to look at me as if I've argued Carmine wasn't gentle enough, but that's not what I'm saying at all, and my husband knows it.

"You underestimated her," Santino says. "That was your second mistake. Your first mistake was losing sight of what she did to my wife. Gia's going to cry again. I promise you that."

SANTINO'S HOUSE always seemed impregnable with its front gate and men walking the ramparts, but the castle was breached, and I don't know if I'll ever see it again.

"Gia has my ring," I say softly as the car twists up the road. "She can find the lawyer."

"She just likes the stone."

"I'm sorry, Santi. About that and something else." My hands don't know what to do with each other, lying in my lap like helpless fish pulled from the water. "Dr. Farina was there. He gave me at least one shot. He didn't tell me what was in it, but I was unconscious for a few hours, and if there was something else… I don't know, but…whether it was just one thing or more, it's not safe for…" I stop because I can't say baby yet—not to him and not while the situation is so delicate—and I can't say any of the other words to define this thing that's still so small and means so much to me.

Tears burn my left eye and fall painlessly from my right.

"It's going to be okay." He kisses the top of my head.

Am I talking to myself in his voice? I feel him. I know he's here. But my heart refuses to believe it. It's locked against relief.

"I don't have the right to worry about the baby," I whisper. "Not after what I just did." I hear myself dancing around painful words, and I'm angry at myself for playing mind games with my own conscience. "To that kid."

"Ah," he says in realization. I expect him to excuse it. Tell me it wasn't my fault. Tell me I had to. Offer forgiveness I won't take for myself. But he doesn't.

He just says, "It changes a person."

Santino puts his arm around me and kisses my head. He doesn't say more, doesn't tell me it'll be all right or to hush. He just gives me something to lean on until I'm strong enough to fight again.

He holds me close as the car heads down a familiar road. I recognize the green house to the left and the copse of oaks.

"Where are we going?" I ask.

"I'm taking you home."

Home? I don't have a home. I was taken from my parents' house, then to my aunt and uncle's in America, which I was forced from.

None of those places are home to me. Home is with Santino.

But when the car makes the last turn and stops at a familiar gate that guards a modern house filled with gold-painted furniture, I freeze.

There's a pool behind it, and that's where I watched him die. I can't sleep in a bedroom overlooking it. It's a murder weapon.

"No," I say.

"No?"

I get out of the car and walk to the gate, the gravel crunching under my feet.

This house. It has too much inside it. Bad memories. Bad decisions. Not just him dying in the pool. But me crying in the corner. Gia beaming over my wedding gown. The look on Santino's face when I put a gun to his head.

I hear his footsteps on the loose rocks behind me, and when he puts his hands on my shoulders, I relax, but not enough.

"I can't go here," I admit.

"I thought you'd prefer it."

I turn to face him. "Prefer it to what?"

He nods slightly and brings me back to the car, and I follow, trusting I'll never have to spend another night in that house.

SECONDO VASTO IS A TRIANGLE. Two sides are tucked into the mountain range, and the river—with its single bridge—is the hypotenuse. The shape of the horizon has always oriented me, even now, heading up the foothills to a fortress I've only ever seen from below.

We stop at a set of cast-iron gates at the highest buildable point of the mountain. Stone guardhouses stand on opposite ends of the gate, each flat on top and big enough for two men and their guns. One is built into the sheer rock face. The other is attached to a wall that drops off the steep end of the earth. The day Santino took me to Loretta's home, this was the house he pointed toward on top of the hill. The one he said his men watched from.

The gates open, and we take a driveway that cuts through a pristine lawn. On the dropside is the back of a white house with a cupola atop the roof—like a watchtower over the world—standing against an expansive view of Secondo Vasto. Five smaller buildings are built into the rock-wall side.

"Welcome to *Torre Cavallo*," Santino says. "Your grandfather built this for his American mistress."

"She must have been something else to need this kind of protection."

"They say it was to protect her from his wife." He shrugs. "But he died badly, and his mistress died old."

Good for her, I guess.

"When we were kids, we told each other no one lived here," I say, looking out the window. "Rosetta went to school, and the kids told her Altieri Cavallo haunted it to make sure his mistress never had another man. To punish him, when she died she wouldn't let him follow her to the land of the dead, so he's stuck here."

"I haven't seen him."

"When I found out my mother's maiden name, I asked Zia if this was her house, and she laughed. She said that was a different Cavallo family. She said I shouldn't read anything into names, and I believed her. My father was a grocer. You know?" I look at him, and our eyes meet. "I always thought of you as more of a Cavallo than me."

His arm tightens around my shoulders. "I'm as much of a Moretti as you, but not by blood."

That sounds right. Emilio Moretti was more of a father to him than to me. I didn't even know him.

We pull up, and Carmine gets out to open the gate and close it when Gennaro drives us through. Santino helps me out of the back. A handful of men rush out the front door, barking news in Italian. I learn their names from listening. Vito is the tall one. Florio with the brown suit. Remo, whose handsome face matches something already in my brain.

"Remo Priola?" I say, still rattled but trying to find an anchor in the chaos, and this guy is it. "From St. Anselm's? Third base?"

"Hey." He smiles. "When they said Violetta, I kinda figured it was you." He glances at Santino and puts up his hands. "I played baseball."

"You were good too."

My husband nods at him, then brushes a lock of hair from my face. "You can walk? Or should I carry you?"

"I can walk."

"*Bene, allora.*" He offers his arm.

Silently, the men part like a sea of reeds, making room for us to pass into the house—as much my property as it is Santino's—arm in arm as if we're king and queen returning home.

The entrance is gilded, carved, painted, and inlaid with intricacies of stone and wood. A naked woman holding a pitcher rises in the center of a waterless marble fountain set in front of the curved staircase.

"Wow," I say dryly. "Altieri's mistress and your grandfather went to the same interior design school."

Santino scoffs. "It's fine for business."

He leads me upstairs, and as I peer into the rooms we pass, I notice there are no pictures on the walls or decorations anywhere, and the sharp-edged, clean-lined furniture is as much a mismatch here as the gaudy, overdone furniture in Santino's glass-and-stucco house. There are double doors on each side of the hall. One set is open to reveal dark wood and warm light.

"That's my office. Like at home."

"You should keep the doors closed if it's off-limits."

"To you, it's not."

He takes me across the hall. There's a narrow, twisting staircase in the center. Bright light filters on the steps from above.

"The cupola." I stop to look.

"I don't want you up there," he says as he opens the double doors to the bedroom.

Before I can ask why, something inside me twists. I bend and cringe, but it passes as quickly as it came.

"Violetta?" He shuts the door. "Are you all right? I'll call you a doctor."

"No doctors." I don't mean to be this definitive, but I can't bear the thought right now. "I think I'm hungry."

"Celia's making something for you." He puts a hand over my jaw, brushing his thumb along my bottom lip.

"She's up here?" I have never been more delighted.

"*Sì.*" He says it absently, running his fingers over my forehead, my bruised eye, my jaw and throat—touching me as if he's rediscovering something he lost.

I find myself mirroring his appreciation in the same way. I touch the shape of him. The body I thought was cold and dead is warm and alive. The unattended beard on his cheeks, down his neck to the hair on his chest, and the shape I can feel through the shirt.

The way we trace each other isn't sexual. Not at first. Initially, we are exploring in silent appreciation of everything we love and almost lost. It's the first moment I've had to take in that the vacuum his death created is now full again.

"I want you to know something," I say, unbuttoning his shirt so my fingers can discover what my mind is only now accepting.

"What is it?" he whispers, efficiently pulling off my T-shirt and leaving the scapular sticking to my skin.

He's here. He's really here. Somehow, I still can't believe it. I won't let myself. Even when I run my fingertips over his face, I'm afraid to accept it. My fear won't let the facts stick.

"I don't know when I stopped wishing you dead," I say, gently touching the bruise over his heart. "But when I lost you, my life felt thinner...like someone had shaved half of it off. That was what it was like before you came. I was half a person, and I'm never, I swear it, never going back to that again."

"You won't, Violetta." He takes my chin between his thumb and the crook of his index finger, holding it so tightly it hurts just enough to stab through the lingering sadness. "You won't see my back the rest of your days." He brushes my nipples with the backs of his fingers. "I'm only walking toward you or standing by you."

"Or lying in bed next to me."

A smile creeps up one side of his mouth. "Or

making you scream to heaven." He undoes my pants and slides them down, kneeling in front of me.

"Take me there."

I don't have to ask twice. Kissing as we pull off each other's clothes, we're two people with the same goal, falling onto the bed in a knot of limbs, exploratory grasps, and hungry strokes, like lovers at it for the first time. My legs wrap around his waist. I want every bit of my skin to touch every bit of his. To be so close we can't be pulled apart. His erection slides into me as if we were always one body, temporarily separated.

"My violet," he whispers into my shoulder. We're on our sides, rolling across the bed, locked together chest to chest. "No one can take you. You're mine. Only mine."

"Yes." The pent-up emotions of the last days have no name. They've been blended into a mass of pressure in my heart and their release sends tears streaming down my face. "Only yours."

"Mine." He exhales a short breath that cracks as if he's also moved.

The power of his vulnerability pushes deep inside me, and I am engulfed in it. Overcome. The orgasm is a tsunami that's beyond physical. It's the inverse of every fear, every cry of despair, every ounce of rage I've been through, forced outward.

It's exactly the heaven he promised, and it's real, but when I come down from the overwhelming pleasure, Santino is still a ghost to me, and I am living in a world I don't believe in.

7

VIOLETTA

Santino—or the ghost of him—takes me down to the kitchen and helps me into the nook as if I can't do it myself.

The sight of Celia stirring a pot of soup is comforting. "They didn't give me time to get much from home. Just a few pans and knives. I dumped all my spices in a bag. And what did I come into?" She waves her hand around the room. "An upstairs kitchen for a skeleton crew that came in and out. Men. Paper plates and a drawer full of soy sauce. The microwave...you should have seen it. Looked like something was murdered in there."

She takes a bowl from the rack. Just washed. Then I notice boxes of new plates.

"And the one in the basement? Worse. Right next to a coal furnace. The smell." She wrinkles her nose.

"Can you feed her instead of complaining?" Santino says.

"Cheese?" she offers.

"Please."

"Anyway, I got it all figured out." She opens the fridge for the parmesan. It's stocked. "Armando got everything in no time."

"Armando?!" I exclaim, looking from Santino to Celia and back. "He's here?"

I haven't thought about that warm, gentle, armoire of a man in days, and now his presence in the world is the exact news I need. I miss my prison of a home, where I was trapped by the man I fell in love with. I miss the ugly furniture and the big windows. I miss the pool and watching Santino swim in it. I miss my husband being my only problem.

"He's around somewhere." Celia sprinkles cheese on the soup.

"Who?" a voice booms from the doorway. It's Armando himself with a paper bag from Giordano's Pastries.

Celia grabs the bag as I rush to hug him.

"I'm so sorry," he says when we separate.

"For what?"

"Violetta." He takes a moment to sigh. "I was supposed to protect you. I let you get in Marco's car. I should have known. I should have seen it, but…I was distracted. And there's no excuse. My head wasn't in the game."

"They had cherry!" Celia exclaims with delight as she dumps biscotti into a container. She plucks one out and lodges it in her teeth.

"Tell her why you were distracted," Santino commands. Whatever it was, my husband isn't happy about it. He gestures for me to return to my seat at the table.

"When Gia came home, I was going to tell her I loved her." He's gone from looking at the floor to rubbing his eyes as if he can't stand the sight of anything in the world. "And Re Santino too. I swear."

The king does not respond.

"Maybe he can pay for his crime with more cherry biscotti," Celia says, chewing on her cookie while ladling out soup.

"It was a betrayal of Santino," Armando admits with downcast eyes.

"Enough," Santino says firmly with a look to each of them. "My wife doesn't need to hear about this today."

Celia puts the bowl of soup in front of me. Its surface is dusted with cheese, and nothing has ever looked this good.

Santino is still cross-armed and stern.

"Gia Polito is—," I say, but stop short. If Armando loves her, he'll hear the word sociopath as an insult or scold. "Not right in the head. You know that now, right?"

"Yes, but—"

"She fooled all of us," I say with a definitive jab in Santino's direction.

"I take responsibility when I fuck up. I should be dead already for what I did."

"No," I say, picking up the spoon. There's been too much death today. "Celia needs her biscotti. And none of it would have happened if we didn't sell our daughters."

As I try to eat, my hand shakes, splashing the soup

back into the bowl. By the time it gets to my mouth, it is empty. Celia glances from me to Santino.

"I'm fine," I lie. I'm not fine. I'm speaking strongly and clearly, but a part of me is still uncontained.

"Out," Santino says with a short wave of his arm.

Celia and Armando leave us alone. Santino sits diagonally from me. He has to be here. Celia and Armando wouldn't leave me alone at a time like this.

Stop it.

Just stop sabotaging your own happiness.

"I'm just a little uncoordinated." I make excuses even though he can see right through me.

Only the real Santino can do that. He's here. Right here. It's just me and him. My guard drops. I am exposed and raw all over again. The terror returns, but it's lessened. Maybe half. I wonder if it'll be halved forever, always getting smaller but never getting to zero.

Santino holds out the spoon, cupping his other hand under it so it won't spill. I eat it.

God bless Celia. It's perfect.

"You're safe," he says softly. "I'm with you."

He's not lying. If anyone came for us here, they'd be seen and dealt with, and that's exactly what brings the waxy smell of incense, the impact of the fist in my face, and the sight of blood on church marble into my mind all at the same time. When my thoughts are quiet and relaxed, I see Santino fall into the pool, over and over, overriding the fear of being forced into another marriage. It blocks out being hit by a man three times my size. The utter desolation of waking in that room knowing Santino was dead is what's making me shake uncontrollably.

He's got his elbows on the table, leaning close enough that I see every hair of his beard, the errant eyebrows, every fleck in eyes that can seem bottomless. I was so close to him twenty minutes ago, but I feel as if I'm seeing him for the first time. I can't live like a newborn every day.

"Open your mouth." He takes a spoonful with a meatball and vegetables.

Finally having a complete mouthful is a shock to my system, but chewing brings my appetite around. By the time I've swallowed, Santino has another ready for me. I take it and speak around my food.

"We just had a whole conversation, but inside? I still can't process it. That you're here." I swallow, touching his resting hand.

He feeds me more without losing a drop.

"And all that other stuff that happened after you... died? That room. The shot they gave me. Gia being so dead inside." I shudder then open for more soup. "The replay of our wedding, and going crazy—killing that kid—it all had this hopelessness."

"Hush. Eat first."

Once I obey the second command, I disregard the first. "There's a part of me that's convinced that if I stop touching you, you'll turn into a ghost."

"Tell that part my ghost is still attached to my body." He uses both hands to hold the bowl and scrape up the last of the soup.

I resist the urge to touch him again. When I swallow, I close my eyes and try to feel his physical presence, but all my mind sees is emptiness, and all I sense is the sinking vacuum of death.

"It's not listening." I reach into the darkness. My hand lands on his arm. It's real and physically present, yet I don't believe it. I open my eyes. He's here. Right here.

"Do you want more soup?"

I don't want more soup.

Down to bone and blood, I want to know he's alive. I want to be convinced, and there's only one way to do it.

"I want to be normal again." I push away the bowl. "I want you to take me. Like you do. Now. Hard."

"You're in no condition." He sits back.

"I said now."

"And I say when you're well enough."

He's really going to refuse me—not because he doesn't want to do it, but because he's afraid he'll hurt me or something.

He has to hurt me. That's the point.

My right hand gets the message half a millisecond after my brain decides to send it, shooting forward and slapping him in the face as hard as I can.

I can't tell if it hurts, or if he even has a reaction. He doesn't budge. Maybe he looks a little curious, which isn't what I'm after, so I swing harder, aiming for the same spot on his cheek. He grabs my wrist an inch from his face.

"What are you trying to do?" His grip is tight, but not hard enough.

"Make me believe you're here."

"I am here."

"Prove it." We're locked in a gaze crackling with questions and demands. "I can't live with this doubt. I won't be able to sleep, or think, or trust my own eyes ever again. I need you to rip me apart. Pretend I was at that altar because I wanted to be."

His grip tightens, and his eyes burn with new intensity. That's it. I've found the big green button to push repeatedly.

"Stop it," he growls. "This is a dangerous game."

"Play it for me. Tell yourself I couldn't wait for my new husband to—"

"I'll destroy you." He yanks my wrist and pulls me off the chair, flings me to the floor, and puts his foot between my shoulder blades. I can barely breathe from the pressure. "Is that what you want?"

"Yes."

My head jerks back when he pulls my hair, then he removes his foot so he can pull the rest of me off the floor. I never get my feet under me as I'm thrown over the table, with the corner digging against my lower back. The soup spoon clatters to the floor. The hand that had pulled my hair is under my chin, ear to ear, forcing my throat to stretch.

"You're going to know I'm here by how I break you."

Is he past the point of no return?

He needs to be.

"You were almost too late. I almost sucked his dick."

"No more talking." With his palm on my throat, he puts two fingers in my mouth. "This opens when I want, and you take what I put in it."

He probes deep, blocking my airway. There's no

more verbal agreement necessary. I'm pulsing with arousal, and he knows his every word swells the flood of my desire.

"I'll let you breathe when I see your tits."

Wiggling, I yank up my shirt and bra, exposing myself to him.

When he pulls out his hand, I breathe. He puts his spit-covered middle finger in his mouth and sucks my saliva off, eyes coursing down to my hard nipples. He takes one in his wet fingers and twists, turning me into his arch-backed *puta*.

"Look at you, waiting for my cock." I'm locked in place by his eyes, and it's not until he steps back and says, "On your knees, that I'm able to move…but not quickly enough. He pushes me down violently and undoes his fly, digging his erection out of his pants.

"Open your mouth, and suck a dead man's cock." I open up, and he guides himself in, pushing deep and holding me against him by the back of my head. "I am not dead. I never want to hear it again. How many holes do I have to fuck to make you believe it?" He pulls out and I gulp air. "How many?"

"Three."

"*Va bene, allora.*" He spins a chair to face me and sits in it, propping his cock up at the base. "It's not going to suck itself."

Holding back a smile, I crawl the short distance to him and take him in my mouth, but Santino does not ever give up control. He pushes me down and holds me for a moment, then lets me breathe before pushing my face onto him so deep my nose is against his skin.

"What man could die when a woman like you spreads her legs for him?"

I shrug—lungs tightening, throat clenching.

"Not me." He pulls me off.

I gasp, chest heaving, spit dripping from my chin.

"Prove it."

"Take your pants down."

I tug on the elastic waistband. I don't get to finish before he takes me by the back of the neck, pulls me up, and pushes my face to the table. He has complete control over me, and every drop of fluid in my body rushes below my waist.

"Who owns your cunt?" He unceremoniously sticks three fingers in me, and that alone is enough to push me close to orgasm.

"You do."

"It doesn't matter if I'm dead, Violetta." He bends his inserted fingers and twists his hand at the wrist like he's trying to screw it inside me, finding sources of pleasure I didn't know were there. "You're mine."

"Yes."

I grunt when he takes out his fingers and kicks my legs wide open before commanding, "Show me."

I look over my shoulder, watching him spread my lips and ass apart. He fingers both like a man who can't decide which new car he wants, biting his lip as he edges my asshole with his thumb, then pulls my clit. The pleasure is agony.

"All yours," I say to urge him on.

"This is so wet," he says with a flick, "and so tight." He runs the head of his cock along my seam. "And all mine."

With that, he fucks me where I'm wet, thrusting so hard I'm lifted to my toes. He pushes again, twisting to wedge himself deep as he pushes me down by the back of the head.

"Put your ass up, sexy girl." The pressure of him is so great, I feel as though I barely move, but he groans and closes his fist on a handful of my hair. "You think I'd leave you a widow." I'm yanked back by the hair. "When I can fuck you like this?"

"Yes. Like this."

He pulls so hard my chest comes off the table.

"You're a toy for my cock." Reaching around, he puts one hand on my clit, and with the other, he handles my breasts as though he owns them, finding the hard nipples and pinching them. "You still want me to use you like this?"

"Please. Yes."

I'm half standing, partly crouching, getting pounded against the table while his dick holds me up. From my tits, his hand moves up to my jaw, then tightens around my throat, choking me.

"You'll crawl for my cock." He rubs my clit harder and tightens his grip on my throat, pressing my arteries while he drives into me. I put my hand over his, but don't pull him away. "Now show me how much you like it when I use you."

A gentle blackness crawls at the edges of my consciousness, pushing out thought and reason, and suddenly, in a rush, I awaken in the throes of an explosion of pleasure, shuddering endlessly in his arms.

But he's not done. I'm barely through the orgasm when he pulls my pants all the way down, lifts my ankles, and flips me onto my back. He rips off the pants and spreads my legs, pushing my knees until they're almost touching the table. I'm exposed and helpless, and in realizing that he can hurt me, that he will hurt me, and that I want him to hurt me, the resistant part of my brain clicks into submission.

"Beg me to fuck your tight little ass." He slaps the sensitive folds between my legs where I'm still swollen, and I yelp with the sting.

"Please fuck my ass."

"Open it. Show me."

Every command lands inside a desire to please him, this living man, who rose from the dead to come for me. He's alive. I reach down and open my cheeks to expose myself to the danger of him. The risk is real because he is.

He snaps a flask of olive oil from the counter and drips it on my stomach, my pussy, my stretched-open asshole. Then sends the flow to his thick, hard cock.

"I'm going to come in your ass," he says, putting down the bottle. "But first, you come again." He kisses the drops of green oil on my belly, running his tongue down to my clit. He sucks off the oil.

"I just came... It's too much."

In answer, he slides a finger into my ass, and with a careful flick of his tongue, I'm ready again, writhing on the table as he sucks my clit and adds another finger, stretching me so I can take his cock.

"Good girl," he mutters between flicks and sucks. "Open for me. Show me what your ass does when you come."

He sucks again, pulling an orgasm out of me while

digging his fingers deep. My muscles pulse around them, squeezing in a rhythm I don't consciously intend.

Standing, he wipes his mouth with his wrist, then drops more olive oil on my ass.

"You ready?" he asks, putting down the bottle.

"Yes."

"Do you believe?" He circles my anus with his cock.

"Maybe."

He pushes in. I stretch for the head.

"Maybe?" He lets it slip out. "Does a ghost fuck you like this?"

Pushing harder, he gets the head in, and he groans, and I know he doesn't care about my answer. He's past the point of no return. When he thrusts deeper, it hurts, and it's awe-inspiring, exquisite, irrationally gratifying.

He shoves forward and buries himself, taking me all the way back to reality.

8

VIOLETTA

Santino rolls up a towel and puts it on the bath ledge behind me so that I can lean my head back comfortably. The waterline of scalding heat cuts across my chest. Bubbles pop like rice cereal. I am sore and satisfied, but most importantly, I'm alive, and so is Santino. When I close my eyes, I still feel that fist hitting me, I still smell the incense and see the growing pool of blood in the church…but none of it is accompanied by the same grief.

He is here with me, and I'm never losing him again.

Downstairs, men stomp their feet, bark in conversation, and even laugh as if their boss wasn't just saved from a bullet by a cigarette lighter. I haven't counted the guys in the halls, but it seems like a couple of dozen. Enough to run a business in a small town, but not enough to win a war for it.

I open my eyes to find Santino naked, standing over me with a nasty bruise on his chest that—from the dark center to the blue flames radiating outward—is not much smaller than a dinner plate.

Even wounded, he is a work of beauty. Sword and shield. Warrior and protector. Attacker and armor.

Who else would accept me with my bloodstained soul?

"Why are you looking at me like that?" I ask.

"Like what?"

"Like you're mad."

"Someone hurt you." He eases himself into the tub. Water and bubbles splash over the side as he settles across from me. He can't lean back with the faucet behind him, so he sits with his back straight and my legs draped over his thighs.

"So you're not mad at me?"

"Why would I be?" He runs his hands under my knees and clasps my hands.

"Because I killed someone, and I'm sad about it, but I needed to do it. I wanted to. I think..." A part of me runs in front of my words, palms out, screaming *don't say this, even if you mean it, never say it*. But I mean it. "I enjoyed killing him."

Lifting my hands above the waterline, he inspects the blood embedded in my fingernails.

"And this should make me mad?"

"It's not what you wanted in a wife."

"For half of my life," Santino starts, running a little brush against the top of the soap, "I didn't think I'd marry a woman. I was set up to marry a crown. A position." He scrubs the blood from under my nails. I can barely stand to look at it. "Maybe I married a fight for territory and respect. But the woman?" He shrugs.

"Irrelevant. Emilio gave me a girl to keep the crown in his family." He switches hands. "What I wanted in a wife didn't matter, so I didn't want anything. That place was empty, and now it's filled with you, whatever you are. Whatever you enjoy." He checks my nails, running his thumb over them one by one. "If I'd been free, I would have had nothing in common with the woman I married. But I wasn't free. I was yours, and now we share the same sins." He shows me my clean nails and lets go of my hand. "*Bene.*"

"How do I look?"

He considers me with cold probity, as if he has to pause to recognize his own wife. "Beautiful."

This compliment is not a compliment. Somehow, the subject changed. I just told him I liked murdering a man. That should have sent him running. Instead, he made up a story about being unhappy with a clean, innocent woman. He's lying to himself or me.

I feel ugly and broken, used as a pawn, thrown from frying pan to fire, wrung out and exhausted. He needs to say nice things to me, and my question is a blinking neon sign on a dark road, but he doesn't even see it.

"I want to kill them all. I don't want a war, but trying to take what's mine is a suicide mission. No truce could settle what they did to you." He focuses on my left eye. "All of them will be ghosts before I rest."

A fire burns behind the darkness of his eyes. It casts no light. It will consume everything, including me, and I'll be in my finest and most perfect state—a woman-shaped pillar of charred carbon. Beautiful, whole, used as fuel for a fire that burns the world.

"What is it, *Forzetta?*"

I'll be his link to the crown. I'll stay by his side while he fights to keep it, because I am from this side of the river.

But what then?

Who will we be in a kingdom consumed by fire?

"Do you need the crown?" I ask. "To kill them, do you need it?"

"If I have it, Secondo Vasto will follow my lead. Some of Damiano's men—not all of them, but enough—will abandon him. And when I beat him into the earth, his strongest will follow me instead of trying to take his place. I won't have to kill them."

This is the trajectory of my life if he wins this war—from this moment to the point where it disappears over the horizon. My eventual, inescapable intimacy with death. My embrace of the unacceptable. I am already a murderer, and if I continue down this road, I will become harder and harder. I will die brittle and heavy with the bitter taste of borrowed power on my tongue.

"What if we didn't get the crown?" I say.

He looks at me as if I didn't hear a word he just said. But I did. I heard all of it.

"What if we just…did a different thing? Made a different choice? What if we didn't assume it was inevitable? What then?" I lean into him. The bathwater swooshes around me and splashes to the floor. "What if you and I just drove away? As far as we could go…just went. And what if we stopped somewhere and had this baby and a couple more and just…lived?"

"And then?"

How can he not get this? It's so perfect.

"The war Damiano's bringing to Secondo Vasto is only a war if he has an enemy. What if we opt out? We leave the crown at the lawyer's. He can steal it or find some other way to get it. We don't have to care. Let him have it. We'll be ten hundred million miles away. We can never think of the stupid crown, Gia, the Orolios, or any of it ever again except when we tell stories about how it brought us together. We can play with our grandkids in an old house, and one day, we'll die from something old people die of." I lay my hands on his face the way he's done to me so many times. His eyelashes are wet from the bath steam, gathered into black blades. "Imagine it. We can be normal."

My body floods with elation. The unglamorous possibility of the ordinary mixed with the frightening probability of his volatility is a powerful drug.

"Me?" he says, taking my wrists and putting my hands against his bruised chest. "With *me*?"

I take a deep breath.

It's more than bringing Santino into harmony with the modern world. There's salvation for both of us in normal. Normal people don't kill their enemies, watching the life go out of their eyes. Normal people aren't forced into unforgivable sins.

"We'll be free," I say. "Really, really free."

He rubs his eyes as if he has to clear out the junk. They're bloodshot when he's done, and yet…he still can't see what's right in front of him.

"In this life you made in your head," he says, "who will I be? *What* will I be?" He presses his fingers to his chest, thrusting his head forward. "I can't crawl out of my skin and into this TV show you imagine."

Why is he not jumping on this? What's the holdup here? I'm presenting him with a treasure map, and he's disputing the value of what's under the X.

"I don't understand how what I just described is unappealing."

"No, Violetta. Of course I want a quiet life. I don't reject your version of normal. It rejects me."

He's terrified. By suggesting a life far away from his world, I've struck fear into his heart. Maybe I'm going too quickly, but it's not like I have a choice.

"How do you know?" I ask. "Is the king of this little place really all you are?"

He looks away. I'm hurting him, and I don't know how to stop.

"Please, Santino," I plead. "This is our only chance. You rule me. Always. Please. If we get that crown and you win, I don't know what I'll become. I don't know what *we'll* become."

He settles his hands on my knees. The plopping water and softly cracking bubbles relax me into the pause between. I want this moment to last forever, with the hands I thought I'd never feel again, and the echoes of the voice I thought I'd never hear again. I want to sit in silence with the things I thought I'd lost forever, because I know it won't last, and I'll grieve over and over.

When he touches my belly, I put my hand over his and hold it there.

"I'm scared something bad happened," I say, looking at the ceiling.

Now that Santino is here with me, the questions I

couldn't ask come flooding in like a test I've been cramming for.

How vulnerable is the pregnancy this early?

What's the chance I can carry it?

Will the baby be broken?

What will be the effect of having a murderer for a mother?

Is it my fault?

Is this why I want to run away so badly?

"Violetta?" Santino calls me from the other side of guilt.

"I don't know anything." Opening my eyes, I clutch his arm as if I'm in danger of falling. "We might not know until it's born, and what if it's bad, Santi? What if it's hurt forever?"

"They didn't teach you in school?"

"I was second year. It's not like I finished."

Reaching over me to the counter, he blocks the light above to pick up his phone. "You know where to look it up?"

"Yes." I look around for a towel to dry my hands so I can search for the possibility of congenital defects caused by maternal opioid use. Then I'll drill down to non-addictive, single mass dose. Then check to see if the mother murdering a man in a church becomes the burden of the child.

The colorful boxes of Santino's home screen stare back at me.

All I have to do is tap it and all the knowledge of the universe will be available to me in stark, impersonal language. I will interpret it as it relates to my own situation and adjust my life and expectations from there, adding in the fact that I have killed the second man who kidnapped me and may spend the rest of my days running away from consequences of that.

"I feel like I failed you," I say, still trying to get the courage to tap the web browser. "There was no blood in the pool, but I let myself believe you were dead. They put drugs in me that might hurt our baby. I thought I'd lost everything, then I killed someone." I scrunch my face to keep the tears inside. "I didn't think about it enough...what it would mean...because I didn't want to. I didn't want to talk myself out of it. I chose it. I know where the arteries are, and he didn't protect them because he thought I was harmless."

"You are not harmless."

"I'm not, and I'm scared."

And all I have to do is look up the effects of maternal opioid intake on fetal development, yet I can't. I have to know, but I don't want to be told by a study or a data set. My heart is too brittle, and I'm too frozen over, too distant, too blank, to hear the truth shouted over the cold expanse of space.

Santino takes the phone from me and puts it to the side, then looks right through me from two inches away. "You had no choice."

His excuse is too easy. It's the reasoning of madmen and thieves. There were a hundred options that didn't involve murder, yet that's what I chose.

"I didn't do what I *had to* do," I admit not just to him, but myself—reigniting that rage with every word. "I did what I *wanted* to do."

Santino leans back onto his knees, and the water swooshes, displacing into my belly. He's not trying to get farther away. I know this much. He's listening. Taking in the whole of what I'm saying.

"I wanted to kill Damiano, and it wasn't over the crown or being forced to marry again. His life offended me. His breath. His heart beating on this earth while yours wasn't."

There's more, and I shouldn't say it out loud, much less to a man I need to love me—a man who prizes gentle femininity. Speaking the rest is a mistake, but I can't stop. I can't live with him not knowing I have this inside me. The burden would break me.

"I'd do it again, Santi," I continue, despite my better judgment. "I killed the wrong man, but if Damiano was in front of me...for real this time...I'd make it last longer. I'd watch him suffer. You're right, I've changed, but I've always been terrible and broken. You should leave me. You should send me away. Far away."

Santino's eyes drop, looking down, chin to bruised chest, and I fear he's disappointed, or worse. It's possible I've killed more than one man. I may have left our love for dead.

"If it's hard for you to love me now," I add, "you need to be honest with yourself. Nothing's going to fix that. And I won't act like it didn't happen."

He picks up his head and touches the tops of my hands, gradually tightening around them as his gaze locks onto mine. "Neither will I. When I say you're mine, I mean all of you. The violet that heals, and my *Forzetta*, who kills when she has to. And when she wants to."

"How are you not disgusted by me?"

"You want me to be honest?"

"Sure."

I don't really want to hear it. I want him to forget it entirely. Pretend it doesn't exist so that I can avoid any honesty that comes with the word disgust attached. He makes it ten times worse by sliding to the other side of the tub.

"I don't know," he says with amazement in his voice. "I should be...something. Disappointed. Maybe disgusted, like you say. You're not what I see in the wives of other men. You're who I want, but also, you're who I was given. And you're more. More..." He looks around the room as if the right word will appear on the walls. "I am more in love with you now than before. *L'amore governa senza regole.*" I understand the words, but he translates anyway. "Love rules without rules. You are outside expectations. Bigger than the law or tradition. A filthy sinner like me can never reign over a woman like you."

"The only place I want to be reigned over is the bedroom. And the bath."

Smiling, he stands, slick with wet, patched with bubbles sliding down to gather around his erection.

"This, I can do." He holds out his hand for me.

We get out of the tub together. He snaps a thick towel from the cabinet and covers my shoulders.

"We'll have to get the crown," I say as he carefully dries me from fingertip to under my arms.

"Yes." He gets on his knee to dry my feet, moving upward. Over my breasts and collarbones, his touch is reverent, soothing, healing.

"Today. Before Gia does."

He pats my face dry with gentle taps, then gives

himself a quick toweling. "She can't walk in and take what's yours. The lawyers... It's not a *camorra* firm. The genius of your father's *consigliere* was using outsiders, so it's not like what you call a 'mob priest' or a 'mob doctor.'"

He's playfully mocking what I've said before, but with the mention of a mob doctor, a lump rises in my throat.

"No." I try to swallow the lump, but it sticks, reminding me that I need to be looked at. I can't avoid it too much longer. "I want to see an obstetrician. A real one. Not Dr. Salafia—the one who checks to make sure brides are virgins."

"He died last May." He hangs up the towel, not getting it.

"Not Farina. He's no doctor."

He *tsks* a no. "There's a doctor on Tamino Avenue. Aselli. We can go tonight."

"Not here. On the other side of the river. A real doctor with no loyalties. I think I can still use the student clinic. You need to take me first thing in the morning or I'll go myself."

He holds up his hands to stop me, then puts them on either side of my face. "We go together. Always. Everywhere. Together."

I believe him. God help me, I believe him, and inside that box of faith is a prize—a shining truth.

Trust. I trust him.

"Thank you," I whisper. "I'll call tomorrow and make sure they can see me."

"No. I'll call them and tell them when we're coming."

Santino leans down, picks me up in his arms, and carries me to the bedroom, where he lays me on the covers.

"It's too early to sleep," I say, even though I'm completely exhausted. "We haven't even had dinner."

"Just relax." He stands at the side of the bed, body fluid, bruised, ready to get dressed and walk out of the room to whatever business awaits downstairs.

My cells and bones react to the thought of him leaving before I fall asleep. No. He can't.

"You going to feed me this?" I reach for his cock, wrapping my hand around the base. He leans over and parts my legs.

"Again?" He kisses inside my thigh. "You're insatiable."

In answer, I pull him into me and wrap my legs around him. He kisses the unbruised side of my face, and I turn so his lips touch the broken vessels and still-swollen skin. He pauses, then gently kisses where I'm hurt.

I sigh. It's exactly what I need.

Mostly exactly, but I want more.

Pushing into him, I press his erection on my seam. We kiss as he slides along the length of it. I moan into his mouth, jerking faster as all the pain and worry flow between my legs and transform into pleasure.

"Please," I whisper. "Don't make me beg."

"I won't, my violet." He pulls back and realigns at my opening. "Maybe tomorrow."

I'm so wet his massiveness slides in without friction, stretching and filling, but so slowly I'm taunted by every inch. He is unyielding but shaped for me, fucking with gentle force that asks no questions and tells no lies. In it, I am safe, but not from him.

Someday he's going to destroy me, but not today.

Today, I am filled but not overflowing. Broken but not shattered.

He holds me so tightly, I am powerless.

"Be still," he murmurs in Italian. "Just open your legs wide, so I can feel your sin from the inside."

I am still.

He fucks me to the depth of my sins, and loves me for them.

9

SANTINO

I hold my wife, wondering if I can ever make her happy.

When I stole her and forced her into marriage, she was the signature at the end of a contract. I didn't care if she was miserable, content, anything. All she had to be was breathing.

When I started to love her, I didn't doubt I could be everything she needed.

Even after Damiano stole her, I was convinced she only had to be rescued to be content.

But this plea to be normal? I can't pretend to misunderstand what she means. It's not four children in an Italian-speaking house with *due cucine* and big Sundays. It's not the normal I know. Her normal is barbecues and July Fourth. There are lawnmowers and garden beds. Husbands working behind desks all day. There's more to it, I'm sure, but I can't picture it in the real world. It's all television, but a different channel than the laughable mob movies where tough guys say *capeesh* without any irony.

Maybe we can blend the two.

Once this is over, maybe. Once everyone who tried to take her is dead, and I've won her safety, we can try some version of happiness.

Maybe I can meet her between her normal and mine.

When I'm sure Violetta is asleep, I slip out from under her, dress, and go to the office down the hall.

Damiano and his alliance with what's left of the Tabonas needs to be dealt with. There's a list of people who are going to die with or without a war. They hurt my violet's body, which is bad enough, but the torment in her heart is intolerable. They're all going to pay for it.

My rage isn't wild or reckless. I am in control. The procedure is clear. I am a surgeon, cutting away flesh to get to the people who hurt Violetta, then to the man who ordered her hurt. When they're dead, I'll drop the scalpel, pull away my mask and scrubs, and leave the body for the rats.

We'll go to her doctor over the river, then to the crown. Just the two of us. Three men will scout ahead to make sure it's safe, but otherwise, I don't want to be seen. I don't want to announce our intentions by making a show of moving men around to secure the area again.

Once I have the pieces of the crown, I'll solidify the loyalties of everyone in Secondo Vasto. There will be nowhere for Damiano or his allies to hide.

My wife wants a normal life, but this is my normal.

I've had it easy up until now. I've been lazy and complacent, letting so many of the Tabonas live as long as they left Secondo Vasto, believing Damiano would be satisfied with friendship. Too many years in America made me soft.

That's over. They say taking a wife makes a man weak, but Violetta's forced me to get stronger.

It's the dark time of day that's both late and early. We've been in my office for hours, trying to come up with a way to destroy Damiano and his crew. Carmine's fallen asleep in his chair with his head back and his mouth open. Gennaro's fidgeting like a kid catching a third wind just as the pastries are coming around.

"Marco knows," I tell Gennaro. "He knows where his daughter is. We find him, we find Gia, we find Damiano."

"We gonna get it out of her the hard way?" Behind his words is a cringe of discomfort.

"We'll do what we have to." I sound more confident about beating information out of a woman—my young cousin especially—than I am. I don't like it. "We'll make sure Tavie's far away."

Gia's brother came to Torre Cavallo yesterday and swore allegiance, but when push comes to shove, he's unlikely to act against his family.

There's a knock at the office door before it opens a crack. It's Tavie himself, who looks more awake than anyone else in the room.

"Speak of the fucking devil," Gennaro says.

"Who?" he asks. "Me?"

"Are you the devil?" I ask, then wave off the answer. "What is it?"

"Yeah, uh…" Tavie runs his fingers through his dark hair. "You told me to tell you if anyone came to the gate?"

"I did."

"There's this guy, Dario Lucari?"

That is not a name I expected to hear.

"Send him up."

He runs off, and Gennaro shakes his head at the boy.

"He's so disgusted with his old man, makes me feel sorry." Gennaro tries to act flippant about it, but he does feel sorry, and that's disappointing. Bad enough I have to deal with Marco—the man who rescued and raised me because he loved my aunt. "All he cares about is Gia."

I should have listened to Violetta while it was possible to stop the *'mbasciata*, then taken out Damiano. He was the poison in the well.

"Tavie can stay on small tasks for now," I say. "Like Remo. Running messages between the gate and the house. Getting coffee."

I remember Tavie running around in diapers while I played hide-and-seek with Gia. I fought off school bullies on their behalf. Now everyone I grew up calling family is motivated to betray me.

Tavie isn't guarded enough to lie with his mouth and his face at the same time, and both tell the same story. He has no idea where his sister is. But a boy who cannot hide his emotions is a boy who could break when we drag his father up the mountain and beat his sister's whereabouts out of him. That's going to have to be dealt with, because I need Marco—right now—before everything gets rearranged.

Maybe Dario Lucari can help with that.

A moment later, the man himself comes through the door wearing a pressed shirt and smelling as fresh as a virgin's underpants. He opens his arms so I can see inside his jacket.

"I got nothing on me," he says. "I come in peace."

"We frisked him," Tavie says.

I stand and shake the man's hand. "If Dario Lucari wanted to get in here with a loaded gun, you wouldn't even know it." I indicate a chair across my desk. "Sit."

He sits, crossing an ankle over his knee. Gennaro shakes Carmine awake.

"Nice place," Dario says. "New?"

"It came with the job." I wave. "*Andate via.* All of you."

Gennaro, Tavie, and Carmine leave.

"They seem like good kids." Dario jerks his thumb toward the door behind him after it clicks shut. When he turns, I can see the tops of his ear ends in a straight line.

I rub my eyes, suddenly as tired as I should be. "They're so good"—I stand and go to the side bar—"they should all be priests."

Dario laughs. "The men on this side don't have hair on their stomachs."

He should know. He runs a huge chunk of the Cavallo operation in New York, and the city is big enough for three families to wet their beaks without stepping on toes. Unless they want to. And someone always wants to. No one man can be king, and no man can rest.

"Drink?" I ask, opening a bottle of Strega. He nods, and I pour us both a short glass. "They're good with people. Everyone likes them." I hand him his cup. "They're the men you want in peacetime." We tap our glasses and I bring the bottle back to my seat. "So, you came all the way from New York to sit in my office and shoot the shit?"

"Well, I didn't come for the Strega." Dario pours the rest down his throat and puts down his glass. I pick up the bottle, and he nods. As I fill his cup, he leans forward with his elbows on his knees, rubbing his palms together. Blue eyes. Part Northern.

He and I are equals. I am the sole capo of a small territory, and he has a piece of a much larger pie that's harder to defend.

"I heard you were dead," he says.

"I was."

"How was Hell?"

"Hot." I offer nothing else. I'm not going to ask him what he's doing here again.

Smiling, he pushes his weight back. "I'm lying low. Trying to draw some people out."

"Did you die too?"

"Not yet. But it's getting tense. Very tense..." He takes a barely perceptible pause. "With the Colonia."

I practically spit my Strega.

"You want to draw out the Colonia?" I put my elbows on my desk. If I'm six inches closer, maybe I'll hear him right next time. No one wants to draw out the Colonia. The world is in balance as long as they stay underground.

"It's safer than going in to get them," he says as if it's obvious. "So since you were dead, I figured I'd come around and see if you had guys looking for a change of pace. Guys too loyal to work for whoever put you under. Guys who wouldn't mind paying four grand a month to live in a broom closet."

"But I'm not dead, and you're still here."

"Paying my respects."

"Sure." I polish off half my drink. It burns going down. "You come halfway across the country to pick over my carcass and decide to have a drink instead? Going home empty-handed is no problem? Come on. What do I look like?"

"That a rhetorical question?"

Fucking Northerners and their fancy ideas. I don't even know what he's talking about.

"You still need guys," I say. "You need faces no one over there recognizes."

"Could be."

"And you're supposed to be someplace else. Prison?" When he smirks, I know it's not that. No one would believe Dario Lucari went to prison. "You still have that thing in St...." I snap my fingers, trying to jog the name loose.

"St. Eustatius." He says the name of a Caribbean island so obscure I can't even remember it a second after it's told to me.

"*Grazie*," I say. "They think you're there. But no.

You're here to pick meat off my bones. Then you come home early...with an army."

He shrugs as if I'm a genius who somehow got him, but it was all too easy. I may be partly right, but if I guessed every nuance of his plan against the Colonia, he'd try to kill me in my seat.

"You want a piece?" he asks. "I could use you."

Ten years ago—maybe even five—I would have restored order here and flown to New York City to take him up on it. Now, though, that would mean leaving Violetta. I cannot leave her behind any more than I can dash her hopes that I'll give her the normal life she dreams of. Once this is past us, I might see it her way.

First, this has to be over.

"Thank you for the offer," I reply. "I cannot. My wife is delicate. She might worry."

This is an act. She'll worry, and then everyone in her sights will find out what a lie her delicacy is.

"I heard you married." He lifts his glass. "*Tanti auguri.*"

"*Grazie.* But, to business. You still need men. Good men. That's why you're here. Right?"

"Yes."

"I have them to give. But not until my business with the Orolios is finished."

"*Ti ringrazio.* How long do you think this business is going to take?" he asks.

"Depends. You pay for the men with a certain favor, and it could be done before a single leaf turns red."

Dario puts his elbows on the desk, ready to hear my proposal. "I need to be in New York by the eleventh."

"The sooner I find Damiano Orolio, the sooner you get the men you need and get home."

He lifts his glass and I lift mine. We drink on it, and I tell him where to find Marco Polito, the closest thing to a father I ever had.

THE SUN IS HIDING JUST behind the horizon when she groans in her sleep. Her brows knot and she curls into a tight fetal position.

"I'm here," I whisper too low to wake her, but she groans again and curls into herself. I can't see her like this, chasing demons in her mind when I'm right here to slaughter them for her. "It's just a dream."

I stroke her cheek. Her eyes open, then go wide. Wakefulness hasn't chased away the bad dream.

"I'm here," I repeat.

"No."

"You were having a nightmare."

"No," she repeats, throwing the covers off her.

There's blood everywhere.

Violetta turns on the light. The black shape under her becomes a violent red.

I've seen a lot of blood in my life—and I've seen more than this come from a person's body. She must be shot or stabbed, but I haven't slept. No one came in. And she's not acting wounded. So this shape soaked into the sheets—I'm shocked by it, and I'm not sure I should be. Women bleed. But how much blood? And shouldn't they stop when they're pregnant?

"Is this—" I'm going to say *normal,* but a bark of pain comes from my wife.

She buckles at the waist. She's in pain and I have nothing, nothing to say or do about it.

"What?" Loretta once said I only knew a woman's body to the length of my dick. I knew she was right and didn't think there was anything I needed to do about it. Now I wish I'd learned something, anything that would help Violetta now. I'm afraid to touch her and afraid not to. I'm like a runner on the first day of work for a new boss. "What do I do?"

She takes one hand from her belly and points toward the bathroom. "Help me."

Given sudden purpose, I leap off the bed and pick her up in my arms, rushing to the bathroom in seven steps. Once there, though, my purpose is gone. I don't know what to do. Still in my arms, she reaches over my shoulder, turns on the light, and motions to put her feet on the floor. She looks down at herself. Her panties and the bottom of her T-shirt are soaked with red.

"Oh, God." She's distressed and overwhelmed, and all I'm doing is standing here like an idiot.

I get on my knees in front of her and put my hands on her hips. "We get these off, okay?"

She nods. I lower her blood-soaked underwear over thighs dripping with it. She steps out, flips up the toilet lid, and crouches on the seat, bent at the waist with her elbows on her knees.

"You don't have to stay," she says, eyes closed. The bruised one looks swollen all over again. She's been through so much, and I can't do anything.

"I want to."

"It's bad. It's going to be bad. You can…" Her face crunches like dough being kneaded, and she lets out a long *mmmnnnn* through clenched teeth. Beneath her, water splashes on and on. I put my hand on her knee, and she grabs it, tightens, and her deep groans turn to a series of squeaks. She's in pain, and I can't kill someone or cut it out of her.

"This is the baby?"

"Yes."

"It's coming out?"

She nods, sniffing as if she's going to cry. Selfishly, I hope she doesn't, because I won't know what to do with my anger.

"Is there something I can do?"

She shakes her head. "Just stay."

I stay with her, making a mental list of who deserves to die for this. "I'm sorry, Violetta. I'm so sorry."

"Not your fault."

"I shouldn't have made love to you. It was—"

Her laugh dissolves into more groans, more splashing. She bends so deep her forehead touches the top of my hand as it rests on her knee. Her shoulders shake.

She's still laughing.

"What's so funny?"

"You," she says into her thighs. "You backward *paisà*. They don't teach you anything." She looks up. I can't tell if the white part of her black eye is more bloodshot than yesterday. "It was the drugs they gave me. Or the stress. Or it just wasn't a good egg. But it wasn't your dick. That's not how it works."

I can't pretend to know how any of it works. All I know about a woman's body is where to put my dick, my fingers, and my mouth. I know I'm stupid enough about the rest to ask if I'm hurting her. I've never had to deal with pain I didn't cause and couldn't stop.

"I'm sorry anyway. *Mi dispiace.*"

Her face crunches, and she nods, bending again. "It just hurts."

"Is there something I can get for you?" I squeeze her hands. It's all I have. I'm out of my depth. "Anything? I'll kill an animal for you to eat. I'll bring a river if you're thirsty. If you're cold, I'll set the world on fire to keep you warm."

"You're sweet." She sobs into her knees, and I want to put the world into a shredder to make her stop.

"You want normal? I'll give it to you. Barbecues and a house. Like they show on television. We'll get in the car and drive anyplace you want. The ends of the earth. The middle of nowhere. The moon. California."

"Calif—?" She cuts herself off, and I think it's to cry until she lifts her head. "Don't try to be funny."

"I'm not trying to be funny. I don't like winter."

Her face twists like dough. "Ow. Sorry. Me neither." She bends again, putting her lips on our clasped hands. "Ow."

"Whatever you want," I whisper, repeating the promise over and over, wishing for some way to fix this disaster.

"I want my mother," she says into our hands. "And two Advil."

She doesn't let me get up for the pills for a few minutes.

As far as her mother goes, even the king can't raise Camilla Cavallo from the dead. But I can bring her the comfort of women.

CELIA BROUGHT Advil when I texted for it. She stood in the doorway, saw my wife on the toilet with blood everywhere, and knew what to do. She stripped the bed, brought us a stack of clean towels, and readied a hot water bottle.

Women must be taught these things while men are killing animals and moving rivers, and since Violetta isn't hungry or thirsty, I'm useless once I carry her to a fresh bed.

"I'm fine," she says. Her eyelids droop, then she cringes and groans again.

"Is the Advil not working?" I ask Celia, realizing my cook is not enough. She has a job. This is not going to work.

"Go," Violetta says. "Move a mountain or whatever. I'm fine."

I let Celia hustle me out, but once I'm in the hallway, all of the threads of the coming war tighten around me into a trap. If I don't do something for her, I'll go crazy.

This insanity isn't new. When Rosetta died, I couldn't figure out why it happened or who to blame. Outside my territory, I couldn't threaten my way to an answer. I couldn't break the doctor or midwife without exposing myself and thus Violetta, who was a sitting duck on the other side. I didn't know the right questions to ask, and I didn't believe the answers anyway. Rosetta was a good girl. I didn't want her, but she'd been given to me, and when it turned out I had another, more noble reason to marry her, I saw it as a gift. I would raise the ill-conceived child as my own and make the best from the worst.

Then she died. A hole opened in the earth, and I fell into the gaps in my knowledge. An ectopic pregnancy is still a baby... Or is it not? And does it matter? Was it preventable? On purpose? Who did it? I was a wild man, trying to close the gap with assumptions and old wives' tales.

Here I am again. I recognize this helplessness. This ignorance.

Out the window, I see Secondo Vasto, but also the houses built into the mountain below, and I know what to do.

I hustle downstairs. This time, I will do something. I will not leave Violetta with no one to talk to.

LORETTA DOESN'T KNOW I'm coming. If she's home, I'll talk to her. If she's not, I'll wait. If Damiano's there again, all the better. This will be over sooner than I thought.

"So," Tavie says as he drives. "We getting her for leverage? 'Cos of her and Damiano?"

"No." I don't explain further. My cousin doesn't have to know my reasons even if he knows Loretta's history. Dami would let her die to get ten centimeters closer to the crown.

The road down to her place can be as treacherous as the conversation I am forced to have with Tavie. He drives the Mercedes around the curves with confidence. If we all get past this, I decide this will be his job.

We're halfway to Loretta's when I have enough signal to call the Politos.

"Pronto?" Guglielmo answers the phone.

"It's Santino," I say. "I need Madeline to come to her niece. Have her pack a bag."

He grunts, and there's a muffle over the receiver. Words spoken in whispers. Then her Zia Madeline comes on the phone.

"Where is she?" Her voice is stiff. Something isn't right, and I decide not to answer the question.

"Just be ready."

"Is she up the mountain?"

"You'll know when you know."

"I can't come, I'm sorry," she says quickly and hangs up.

I'm left looking at my phone. Something is wrong.

"What happened?" Tavie asks.

"We'll pick up another car and go there next," I say more to myself than him, counting how many men I think I'll need. "Someone's there."

"Gia?" he asks.

Maybe. Maybe not. But now I know I have to deal with the problem in front of me. Tavie.

When someone is sent into exile, I personally tell the family why. When men are killed, I tell the family how. I promise vengeance if it's appropriate and let them know when it was delivered. I have to do this every time, in person, or the whole city would erupt into amateur killing hour. It's a terrible thing, to tell young parents their son was murdered. It's worse when they're older. They think it's time to rest and let their children move forward, then I come to let them know there will be no more forward motion. Everything they took for granted now stops.

Now I owe this boy the same respect.

"Your sister," I say.

"If I knew where she was, I'd go to her and tell her she's doing the wrong thing."

"Don't bullshit me, Octavio." I grab a handful of his hair and give his head a playful shake. "You'd tell her to run."

"I would not." He pushes my hand away.

"Don't lie to me. You'd give her your car keys and a full tank of gas so she could get out."

In a low Italian falsetto of my voice, he replays an incident from our childhood. "'Run, Tavie, before they get shoved up your ass! Run!'"

"How stupid do you have to be to steal strawberries from Emilio Moretti? Eh? Who does this?" I push his shoulder. "Men get killed for less."

"I was seven."

"You were eight. And that only means Camilla's the one to beat you. Or worse, I have to do it to prove I won't go easy on my little brother."

We drop into silence. He's not my brother, but he is as close as anyone will ever be.

"You would have gone easy," he murmurs.

"I did. I let you run."

"Yeah. You were a good brother to me and Gia."

"Tavie," I say, trying to tell him the thing I don't want to.

"I know, Santi."

"What do you know?"

"Gia. She… You're going to… You're really mad at her, and I don't blame you. She shot you."

"She did more than that."

"Don't say it. Whatever she did, don't tell me. It's not my business. But you should let her run away. Send her with nothing in her pockets if that's what you have to do."

He's pleading for Gia when what I wanted to talk about was his father. Give him the option to be far away when we drag the man onto the compound. But we arrive at Loretta's. I'll have to do it when we get back.

The white BMW I bought her two years ago is parked at the bottom of the driveway, same as the last time I came, and she wasn't the only one here then. That tank Damiano drives must have been in the garage. I have to assume he's in the house, maybe not hiding in the bushes this time, or maybe hiding someplace else.

"I'm leaving this in front of the garage doors," I tell Tavie. He looks back at me, too green to hide the fact that he wants to know why. "If someone's parked there, we block it."

"Yes. Okay. Smart."

I put a hand on his shoulder and give him a little shake. "It's going to be all right."

"Are you sure?"

"I am always sure."

"Okay." He gives a sharp nod, convincing himself. "I believe you."

"*Bene.* I'm leaving the keys. Get out with me, but stay by the car. Keep your eyes open."

"I will."

We get out. Tavie stands in the driveway to watch, and I approach the patio. Before I get there, Loretta swings open the door.

"Santino," she says, arms crossed.

In those three syllables I hear an unusual guardedness. As though my name is banging up against a metal shield, making it rattle just a little. Once it was clear I was going to marry Violetta, she and I had to stop fucking, and even then, she didn't put armor around herself with me. She didn't volunteer information either.

"Loretta."

"What are you doing here?"

"Pack a bag."

"It's not a good time."

She tries to shut me out, but I stop her, staring through the space between the wall and the edge of the door. Something is wrong, and she can't say what.

I take out my gun and walk past her, into the house, scanning the familiar living room for danger. I check the corners and closets, exiting to the back patio from the sliding kitchen door, listening for a man in the bushes, the scent of his cologne, or the adrenaline from his pores. All I smell is morning dew.

"You should go," Loretta says from behind me.

I turn to her. She leans against the jamb with her

arms still crossed. I wonder if they're locked that way to hide something besides her heart.

"I haven't seen Damiano in days," she says. "If that's who you're looking for."

"He knows I'm coming for him."

"When you're like this, no one gets ahead of you," she scoffs. Her arms drop to her sides, and she backs into the kitchen. "Come inside, it's buggy out."

Is she saving me from a trap or drawing me into one? Outside is better for me. More options. If men are out here and I go inside, I'm stuck there.

"Sit." I pull out a patio chair for her. "And close the door behind you."

She's so efficient at doing what she's told that I can't read whether this was her plan or not. There's neither satisfaction nor disappointment in her manner.

I do not sit. I stand where I can see everything, with my back to a small, enclosed area with a barbecue and no way to surprise me from behind.

"I'm alone," she barks loudly. "I told you."

She didn't tell me she was alone, so she's not.

"Have I ever lied to you?" When I stay silent, she looks at her lap, and the shield slips. "The way you lied to me for years?"

"I was always honest about what I could be to you." I look over the garden terraces built into the mountain below, sniff deeply for cologne, check for movement in the garage windows.

"Not with your words but with your *mouth*." The last word comes from the bottom of her lungs. It's not loud, but it's still a shout of the heart.

"You lied with your *body*."

I feel no pity, no guilt, nothing. She may be telling the truth, but she's also stalling. Giving me room to locate whoever is here.

"And this is why you sold your body to Damiano? To get back at me?"

She sighs, shaking her head. "Do you have a cigarette?"

I take out the pack and offer her one. She wedges it between her lips, and I use my dented Zippo to light it.

"I heard how your lighter got like that," she says. "You're going on a murder spree, then you're going to have a baby and a happy little family like it never happened."

"There is no baby anymore."

She pulls on the cigarette again, looking at me as if I've done something unexpected.

But the baby is gone, and I can't let her talk about it as if it's going to be born. It's a curse in her mouth.

"*Condoglianze*," she says, then turns over her shoulder to blow out smoke, making a pointed look upward, then at me.

I'm a split second from death. I know it without looking.

With all the energy I have, I straighten my legs and launch myself backward, toward the house and under the balcony, just as a bullet bursts into the tiles an inch from where I was standing. Her eyes widen, but she's too terrified to move.

Without thinking it through, I jump away from a secure position to grab her and pull her into the house, saving her from a second shot.

She doesn't waste a moment.

"Upstairs and in the front and—!"

I yank her behind me and shoot the man coming down the stairs. She growls, and I turn to see what's happening. A thudding sound is followed by a second man falling backward into a table. She's holding a ceramic vase.

I shoot the falling man twice before he has the chance to come back at us. Loretta drops the vase and holds up three fingers, then points toward the front door.

"Stay down," I command, then throw her down because there's another gunshot, and I don't have a moment to wait for her to get out of the way of whatever's coming.

Following the edges of the room, I go to the front of the house. From the bottom of the window, I see a trail of smoke, but no Tavie. Aiming above where he could be standing, I shoot the window. I lean out the jamb to find a car speeding away and Tavie lying on the ground with a lit cigarette still between two fingers.

"Fuck!" I climb out and crouch by him.

His eyes are open, and his breaths come in short *hic-hic* sounds. Calling his name will do nothing, but I do it anyway because he's focused on me, yet looking past me. The front door opens, and light streams over the hole in his chest.

"*Puh-puh.*" A bubble of blood forms between his lips and stays there because he can't get out another syllable. He's trying though. Damn this kid, he's trying. He's living with a weight on his heart, and in a few seconds, he'll die with that weight unlifted.

"Don't worry, Tavie."

"*Dun-duh.*" The bubble pops.

"I won't. I won't do it. I'll figure something out. Do you hear?"

"*Aa.*"

I don't know what that sound means, but it is the last one Octavio Polito will ever make. The cigarette drops from his fingers.

Loretta comes out and stands over us.

"Are there more?" I ask, closing my cousin's eyes.

"Just the three." She steps on the smoldering butt. "It's starting, isn't it? The war for the crown?"

"Yes." I take out my handkerchief. Emilio tried to protect his daughters from this exact war, but he only delayed it and moved it over an ocean. I cover Tavie's face. "*Riposi in pace.*"

I light up a cigarette. I have the feeling I'm going to need to buy a pallet of cartons before this is over.

"How did they know I was coming?"

"They didn't," she says. "They're everywhere. Like roaches. Waiting where they think you'll show up."

They'll be at Mille Luce. And my own damn house. And Anette and Angelo's. And it's confirmation that they've set themselves up with Violetta's aunt and uncle.

"Pack a bag."

"Why?"

"Just do it."

"You bought this house to keep me," she says. "You've told me where to go and where to work. You brought death to my door. Maybe I want to make my own decision."

Fuck this crazy fucking woman for not moving.

"Please. For the sake of every *libretto* writer in the world. *Basta.*" My shout echoes off the side of the mountain, but she does not move. "My wife needs you."

Done hesitating, she goes for her fucking bag.

10

VIOLETTA

The bleeding tapers off. The pain subsides. I curl into the hot water bottle and sleep for twenty-five hours, only getting up twice for the bathroom like a zombie.

The spark inside me was snuffed, along with the hope that Santino and I could ever melt into the world's background and just be together with this child.

Tears don't come when I try to cry it out. Instead, my stomach growls like an angry cat. I need to eat. Opening the closet out of sheer curiosity and optimism, I find my clothes have been moved here. The dresser drawers are full of my things. It's as if my life's been transported whole cloth from Santino's house to my newly claimed family fortress in the mountains.

I shower, line my underpants, and—because I can't bear the thought of being constricted or even seen—I put on a black tank top and loose pants.

My left eyelid is brushed with a web of broken

purple veins and hangs lower than the right. Matching semicircles hover inside a sickly yellow corona.

The wound reminds me of what I've gone through. Santino is alive, but the rest of it really happened. I was kidnapped, drugged, treated like an object with temporary value, and only saved by a miracle. The life seeded in me wasn't so lucky. I'll never know for sure if it was the drugs or the stress or if I would have lost it anyway, but what does it matter?

They were careless and disrespectful with my family and me.

That one broken eye squints to see something it can't when all the light gets in. A shadow behind me and before me. A darkness that's not anger with Damiano and Gia. I do not feel a fiery rage at the thought of them taking everything from me for the sake of an ancient artifact. What I feel is stretched—as if some internal organ has expanded and hardened, or an intangible that I carried inside me has found its shape. It's a feeling given form, and it's the colors of the bruise—purple and yellow—mixed to mud, fired to solid ice, and left to harden in the cracks of my heart.

When Santino saw me in my Z's hallway, I was a child. He saw something I thought was the woman inside me. It wasn't. He saw this calcifying mass of darkness in its shadow form. It fills in my broken places, holding me together, making a shell over the grief and despair.

Now I can say to my reflection what I've been too sick and afraid to think.

"They're all going to die for this."

CELIA SMELLS like basil and rosemary, and it's comforting that no matter how much I change, some things in the world stay the same. In the middle of our embrace, my stomach logs another complaint.

"Let me get you something," she says.

"Just toast, if you can. Where is he?" I ask, sitting in the little kitchen nook.

I don't have to say his name. The pronoun is enough. I need to know how he's planning to kill the people who destroyed my pregnancy. Even if they didn't mean it and I miscarried from stress or the opioids. Even if what they almost got away with had nothing to do with the actual bleeding, it's their fault. I want a list of the plans, the timing, and the amount of pain he will inflict. I want veto power on anything too merciful.

"Around." Celia sets about making the toast on a cast-iron skillet—old school—while I wonder where exactly "around" is in this compound. "It's been a little hectic around here." She touches a corner of bread and snaps her arm back, shaking her hand from the heat. "Men coming and going. And one woman."

She picks up a butter knife and waves it toward the back doors, where rows of tables are being set up. A woman in a green dress unfolds chairs.

Loretta.

"What is she doing here?"

"There are fifty men here." Celia shrugs and slides the toast onto a plate. "I can't do everything myself."

Santino brought Loretta to help? I don't know what

to make of his choices. I find it hard to believe she doesn't still desire him the way any normal woman would. If he thinks he's going to live in some backward paradise where the husband keeps a wife and a mistress under the same house, he has something coming.

Loretta slides open the door and enters the kitchen, seeing me right away. "You're up!"

When she double kisses me, I stay stiff and unresponsive.

"Ah, your eye," she says with concern.

"You should have seen it when they brought her," Celia interjects.

"You put ice?"

"Yes," I say coldly. "It's fine."

"I heard what happened," she says with a glance at my belly. "I'm so sorry."

She can go fling herself off the side of this goddamn mountain. She's lying. She's glad. I can see her face clearly…and I'm wrong.

She's not a liar. I'm lying to myself.

She doesn't look disingenuous at all. She's a woman giving sincere condolences, and I'm a child looking for trouble.

"Thank you," I say.

"You'll try again. You go to the doctor. Get cleaned up. All done."

"You have experience." I hear myself getting sour again, suspecting she lost Santino's child. It's too intimate with him. Too much like stealing something from me. My insides are tearing themselves into pieces.

"I was engaged to Elio Sala," she says, relieving me

of images and ideas I cannot bear to hold. "Santino's cousin. And since I was older, no one expected there to be blood on the wedding sheets." She shrugs. "Anyway. Our baby didn't make it, and neither did he."

"Is that the Elio who...?" Celia stops herself and redirects. "From the baseball field?"

My memory is triggered but still vague. A little boy and his father were early for Little League pitching tryouts and were warming up his arm. When he kicked away the dirt behind the rubber, he came in contact with Elio's buried head.

Loretta sighs, and that's the answer. Same guy.

"Elio was a mechanic. Santino said he was the best he ever had. Elio could marry a Toyota to a Honda and make it look like a Cadillac. I thought, what will the babies look like when he marries me?" Loretta pauses while Celia chuckles. "I found out I was pregnant, and he said, 'Let's get married tomorrow.' So I bought a white dress on Flora, went home, and waited. He was working late, and I didn't find out until the next day. Saturday. When the boy... You know what happened." She takes a deep breath, knitting her brow and shaking her head. "Carlo Tabona wanted him to work in their chop shop. Offered everything. He refused, but he thought even being asked was disloyal. So he didn't tell Santino or anyone. He left himself with no protection."

Her voice cracks. She doesn't have to say she loved him. It's obvious his death left a hole in her life my husband never filled.

Celia puts her hand on Loretta's shoulder. "I'm sorry."

"Me too," I say, hand on her opposite arm.

"Well," she says. "The Tabona family was smaller after that. The king ran through them like a disease."

It will be hard to trust anyone after Gia's betrayal, but Loretta may deserve the benefit of the doubt.

Zia used to say, *Dagli amici mi guardi Iddio, che dai nemici mi guardo io.*

God protects me from my friends, I protect myself from my enemies.

There's no instruction on how to discern between the two. That's up to me. If I'm going to stand beside a king, I have to keep his entire domain in view.

With that thought, I feel him near and turn toward the back lawn. He's standing in the morning breeze, talking to a man who is slightly taller, with the same regal bearing. He's not Santino, the ruler of my heart, but—just in bearing alone—he's closer to an equal than anyone I've seen in my husband's presence.

Santino sees me watching him through the glass, finishes his conversation, and walks toward me. I drift away from Loretta and Celia to open the door.

"My violet," he says, leaning in for a kiss.

The way his lips touch my ear, then the side of my neck right now is something I won't let another woman have as long as I live.

My feelings are intensely private, but there are people everywhere. I feel as if we're in the middle of a piazza. The source of my irritation is back in the house. So I pull him away from the main house to a quiet spot between two buildings on the opposite side of the lawn.

"We have no time to fuck," he says. "And we probably shouldn't, so soon after…" Mr. Tough Guy's unable to say the word miscarriage. God, I fucking love this caveman.

"I don't..." I pause, because when I lay my hands on his chest and feel the muscles there, every neuron in my brain reroutes the current to feeling how hard and substantial he is. "I just... I want you to know that I'm not some jealous little girl. You're mine. Always. If you ever even thought about another woman..."

"Why would I?" He takes my wrists and keeps my hands close to his heart.

"You'd spontaneously combust. *Poof.* Go up in flames."

He raises an eyebrow and fails at taming a smirk. Let him laugh. I have things to say.

"Don't make me explain the science of it," I continue. "It's got to do with the friction created when you rub your dick against the natural order of things. Okay? So I'm not worried about Loretta, *per se.*"

"If you want her to go," he whispers close, "I'll send her away. I want you to be happy."

My husband's face is soft for me, but I see the hardness of a man who has had to make difficult decisions, and the regal indifference he will exhibit when he sends Loretta away.

"No," I say. "It's fine. She's all right. But there's history, and I don't want it to come up in conversation. I don't want to hear about how much you liked tasting *fica* or how rough you were or any shit like that, because I won't take it out on her. I'll take it out on you."

For a moment, I worry that I've overstepped into a serious threat, but he smiles.

"You make me weak. I'm standing here, ready to promise my woman anything and everything to not take her jealousy out on me. Without a single detail from your lips, I find myself afraid you'll take your love away. Who would I be then, my violet? Without you loving me, who am I?"

Before I can explain that's not what I had in mind, he spins me around and—gently but firmly—pushes my back against the wall with my hands over my head. My body is stretched before him, and like an animal, he runs his nose along the edge of my jaw to inhale my scent.

"So I need to know," he continues. "how will you abuse me if you're unhappy, my violet?"

"I'll come into bed naked and suck your dick."

"This is not much of a punishment."

"I'm not done."

He kisses me over and over and says, "Go ahead then."

"I'll take it, but I won't swallow. So when I kiss you, I can wash your filthy mouth out with your own cum."

He keeps his grip on me when he laughs, but lets go when he kisses me, still smiling as he wraps his arms around me so tightly I'm lifted from the ground.

"Violetta," he says into my shoulder, rocking me back and forth as he repeats my name. "I didn't imagine a woman like you existed." He pulls away, brushing my hair from my face with tender urgency. "You won't ever hear a word about the past. I will treat your heart with care... as if it's fragile, when it's not. And I'll love it as if it's my own, because it is."

We kiss again, and the world falls away. We are a

normal couple worrying about normal things, a mortgage, a birthday party, who's doing the dishes tonight. It's as if there's no crown, no war… nothing but us.

"Come," Santino says after a one minute eternity has passed. "Let's get you to the doctor."

11

SANTINO

I park the Alfa Romeo near a field with rows of white tents and signs pointing students toward the first letter of their last name. Registration day at the university. If her life had gone to plan, Violetta would be here with a list of classes, but she stopped asking about it, so I stopped promising it.

She'd be pregnant, but that stopped too.

Everything stops for this war.

In the waiting room of the student clinic, a girl with a nose ring and her mother try not to stare at me with loathing, but can't help themselves. They know I end what other people begin.

"I don't think they like me," I murmur to Violetta.

She picks up a magazine, flips through it, and holds it up to hide our faces. "They think you gave me the black eye."

"*Cosa?*" I ask her *what*, but I am not as surprised as offended. I need to explain to every one of them that I do not, will not, cannot ever harm this woman.

"Violetta?" a nurse calls from the desk.

My wife stands. I stand with her.

"You can go ahead and sit down, sir," she says with a smile so fake it looks painted on. If this woman had been born on the other side of the river, she'd be one of those wives knocking around her husband's business, exacting revenge for petty slights against her children.

I remember why I don't like crossing the bridge at all.

In Secondo Vasto, I am king.

Around here, I'm a diseased fruit on a healthy tree.

"Where is she going?"

"We'll have her back in a jiff." She winks at me, acknowledging that she knows who I am and what I've done.

My skin gets hot. Blood flows to the bruise in my chest, making the pain pound with the hammer of my heart.

She doesn't know the half of it.

They're separating us to ask questions about me. About us. About the bruise on her face and the blood afterward. How dare she try to separate us so they can convince my Violetta that I'm her enemy. How dare they pretend to understand what my wife's been through or put her in the position to have to relive it by explaining. This clinic is owed nothing but the number on the bottom of the bill. They are not owed her story.

"Santino," Violetta says, putting her hand over mine. "On the way in, I saw a vending machine with fruit in it. I'm kind of hungry."

She's giving me a way out of the office that won't injure my ego.

This is meant to soothe me, but leaving her alone in

that room has nothing to do with my manhood. I don't need to save face. My *Forzetta* needs me, and if I leave, I can't be here for her.

"I have it," Violetta adds. "Trust me."

I trust her. She does have it. This is her world. She doesn't need protection here any more than I need to be treated like a plate tipping over the edge of a shelf.

"*Bene.*" I pick up her hand and kiss it. "I'll be outside when you're ready."

"Then we go get what's ours."

I nod quickly to the nurse and leave before I tell her what I think of her suspicions.

The vending machines stand sentry on either side of the elevators. Anette has a bowl of waxed fruit in the dining room that looks exactly like what's in the machine. The apples and oranges are perfect, brightly-colored, huge. The one banana left is more green than yellow because Americans would rather eat an unripe fruit than see a single brown spot.

I never hit my wife, but the entire country would assume I did. I never drugged her. I never hurt her.

That's a lie.

I should have stayed in Italy, where this happens all the time.

The machine rejects my five dollar bill. I punch the clear plastic front, but all that does is make the security guard and the guy waiting for the elevator with his son look at me.

Right now, I hate it here. I want to go home. I should have gone home years ago. Should have stayed in Naples after my obligations died with Rosetta.

I straighten out the corners of the bill and try again.

The slot sucks it in. I clench my fists, waiting for it to get spit out because when it does, I'm going to throw this entire thing right out the fucking window.

But a green light goes on. I punch the numbers with my knuckle as if I want to hit this spiteful box the way I never, ever, even once hit my wife, no matter what they think.

A little box slides across the machine on tracks, picks up the orange as an arm pushes it in, moves it over the slot, and drops it in. A lighted message tells me to open the flap for my prize and pick up the coins that slap into the change slot.

I pick out the fruit and sniff it. Where I expect the clean bite of citrus, there's no smell at all.

I hate it here. They can keep their fourteen quarters.

The orange is still pressed up against my nose when my phone rings. Blocked number. Knowing it would do no good anyway. Good chance the phone will be at the bottom of the river before the sun sets.

"*Pronto,*" I say when I answer.

"Santino." I remember the voice from the era of my first hundred cigarettes, but not the commanding tone it comes with.

"Damiano," I answer, ducking down the hallway and continuing in Italian so I'm not understood. "Where are you?"

"So unfriendly. No *buon giorno?*"

"When you're dead, I'll call it a good day." I back into a less-trafficked stairwell.

"You're killing me now with this drama."

Two women in white lab coats come down the

stairs, chatting amiably. I nod to them and face the fire extinguisher as if that will shut out the world.

"It's not like you, Santi."

I have no time for this bullshit. Violetta will be out soon, and I need to be there for her.

"You tried to have me killed so you could take my wife. Is this phone call an apology for that? Because I'm busy."

He laughs too humorlessly and for too long. He's enjoying this. He thinks he's winning, and I'm still trying to figure out the game.

"Come on, man. It's a courtesy call. Old style. Like my father and his father used to do."

I make eye contact with three people in scrubs. One smiles. This stairwell is too crowded already.

"I got guys everywhere. You know that. You saw it last night. So this is where I give you a last chance to surrender it all to me."

I should laugh, but a call like this requires a serious response. The stairwell door opens, and yet another witness comes through. I can see the obstetrics waiting room just down the hall. Is Violetta out yet? I have to see her.

Catching the door before it closes, I look for privacy in a public space, hissing into the phone, "If you think you can win a war with me, you're mistaken."

"Look, my old friend, here's the thing. We got the Tabonas."

"What I left of them won't follow you."

"Wrong. I'm the one in the golden seat. I'm the one with the power. I'm the one with the future this time. Okay? I have friends. You have none. You're running a town full of people who don't follow you out of love, or fear, or nothing. They follow out of habit, and if you don't have the crown, I can pluck them off."

"You don't have it either."

"You sure, bro? You really so sure? Hey, Gia!" he calls out, away from the phone. "You got that ring with the number in it?"

"Right here, baby." Gia's cheerful little voice comes from the background.

"So like I told you," he says. "This is a courtesy call."

"You come for my wife again, and you will die. I will rip you from this earth."

"Better keep your eyes peeled then because we're coming."

My blood flows faster, hotter, pushing against my veins so something, anything inside me is taking action while the outside stays calm for Violetta's benefit. Standing in the corner of the obstetrics waiting room, facing a plant that could be real or plastic, brow knotted, I put every ounce of energy into staying calm.

"Mr. DiLustro?"

At my name, I turn to find Violetta standing next to a woman in her thirties with a ponytail and a tag that says "Dr. Sanchez." I nod and—with a gesture—ask her to wait before I give Damiano my final answer.

"I'll be ready."

I hang up and go to my wife without fear that I will be falsely accused of violence. The true violence is invisible, silent, painless, and it has already started.

ONE DAY IN LATE AUGUST, the volcano tried to destroy everything around it.

The lava flowed in all directions, destroying foothill cities before hardening to porous, black rock. It was the spitting ash that was deadly, and the wind decided to push it over Pompeii—not Naples.

Every schoolchild learns that their ancestors lived because of the wind, and what any child can tell you is that the wind can change any minute, and rich or poor, young or old, strong or weak—you cannot fight the wind once it's decided where to blow.

Before my mother took me on a climb up the volcano that shaped my horizon, I wasn't that different from any of the other kids. We had nothing, but I wasn't the only one. My mother cleaned the rooms at the hotel and sometimes brought home fancy chocolate. She'd hide it and give me clues to its location. When I found it, I'd insist on sharing with her, and she'd cut it in half with a knife. We tapped them together like wine glasses.

She told me that when she saw me with the other kids, she could tell I was like my father, and that men like him and me had no choice but to rule over others. This was the opposite of everything I experienced outside the walls of our apartment.

When I came home from school that day, Mamma took my books from my bag. She chattered about wrongs done to her by her father. Grandma dying out of spite. When she got like this, I usually ran outside to be with my friends, but that day was different.

"You have a purpose, Santino," she said, stuffing sandwiches and a bottle of water into my bag. "You're meant to be a great man. They won't believe it, but you are. We just have to prove it to them. Go get a pair of socks."

I did as I was told, wondering...socks? Why would she put socks and sandwiches in my book bag? Where were we going?

Giovanna—the most popular girl at school—was making a black and red *scubidù* for my belt. The twist of two plastic strings was going to be three inches long, one inch for every year we'd been friends, which should never have happened since she was always so sparkling and beautiful and my clothes weren't always clean and never fit right. She hadn't ever made one for a boy before, and she said she'd be done by that night. If Mamma wanted to prove I was special, all she had to do was wait for Giovanna to be done with her gift.

"Will we be home for dinner?" My question was timid, and I avoided Giovanna as the reason I wanted to get back. I was eight. Maybe nine.

To this day, I don't know what triggered my mother. I just didn't want it to be me.

She shrugged. "It's up to God."

So I prayed.

We got on a tour bus to a parking lot at the base of Vesuvius, which looked a lot like the rest of Naples. The other passengers chatted and pointed out the window. They were on a pleasure trip to a corpse— hiking up the spine of a dead god. My mother looked straight ahead with her mouth set firm. She and I were on a sacred mission to find the source of its power. I held this in my head along with the grumble in my stomach and the setting sun—at the same time, I held out the hope that I'd get home in time to accept the *scubidù*.

When the rest of the travelers trekked to the start of the trail that would lead them point to point up a safe, guard-railed path to the peak, my mother led me in the other direction. Once we were out of sight, she pulled me aside and put my jacket on me.

The sun was setting, and the wind was picking up.

It was January, and down in Naples, nights only got a few degrees above freezing. She told me to keep my mittens on even if my hands got sweaty, because it would get colder up there, and it did.

My mother was not experienced in the outdoors, yet she took the dangerous way, avoiding the paths and trails. The visitor's center. The views. She steered clear. We slept on the ground, tucked into low shrubs. She gave me her sandwiches, and when those ran out, we ate dandelion leaves. My mother cried, and I comforted her. I wondered if Giovanna was going to give my black and red *scubidù* to someone else, but I was too hungry to care.

On the third day, the shrubs gave way to rock and dust, and the climb got steep. In the late afternoon, we stopped. The peak looked close enough to touch. My mother put her head down to rest. She wouldn't get up. I shook her. I screamed. I even kicked her, but she didn't move.

I turned my back on her and ran. My mother, who loved me and believed in me. The woman who hid stolen chocolate like little nuggets of grace and made me find it so I could feel the power of self-salvation.

I left her behind.

MY WIFE and I go to the Alfa Romeo in silence.

The doctor may have been satisfied with the results of the exam, but Violetta is not. She squeezes my hand as if she's afraid I'll let go, which I won't. She avoids my gaze as if I'll see something in her she doesn't want me to, which I might. When I open the car door for her, she thanks me as if I can't hear the crack in her voice, which I do.

I walk around to my side and get behind the wheel, but I don't start the engine.

"Tell me." I try not to sound demanding, but what can I do? I am who I am.

"I'm fine. Clean inside."

"Of course you are." What kind of diagnosis is this? I'm offended on her behalf.

"I mean, there's no extra tissue. My cervix is closing. It's over."

She stares out her window at the ghost town of the rows of empty white tents, each with a card table and two folding chairs inside. A folding sign sits at the head of an unpopulated brick path.

FALL REGISTRATION
LINE UP BY FIRST LETTER OF LAST NAME

"It's so empty," she says. "But tomorrow? This quad? This path here? Going to be full of students staring at class catalogs. They'll see their friends for the first time in months. Size each other up. Who changed? Who's the same? They'll review the same food on the same campus and tell old jokes to see if they're still funny."

As long as she was my wife, I never cared whether or not she went back to school. One way or the other, it didn't matter. Now, suddenly it matters that she gets what she wants—not just what I allow.

"Can you still go?" I offer.

"No. It's too late."

"They can bend the rules, no? I can talk to someone. Convince them."

She laughs, looks up at the dome light.

"You are one hundred percent yourself." She grabs my hand without looking at me. "It's not against the rules. I can walk up here tomorrow and register. I just don't want to."

Of course she doesn't. How could she go to school so soon after the trauma she just went through?

"Next year," I say. She doesn't reply, and we sit for a minute, holding hands in the front seat. Not one person crosses our path in any direction. The campus is holding its breath.

"They thought you did it," she finally says. "My eye. The miscarriage."

"I know."

"I told Dr. Sanchez that if she said another bad word about you, I'd walk out. That no man I've ever met knew how to love me like my husband, who's so good to me I can't believe how lucky I am. But if he—meaning you—ever laid a hand on me like that, you wouldn't be taking me to the doctor. You'd be dead and buried."

Inside, I laugh. It comes out as a smile and a breath. "I believe it."

"I said I was attacked. Robbed. Mugged. Whatever. I said the authorities in Secondo Vasto knew and were looking for the guy, but..." She looks at our clasped hands. "I told her the mugger drugged me and took me to a second location. You found me and saved me. I told them I wanted to know if I was roofied, so I asked for a tox screen. I know they have a little lab in the back for certain things. They did a hormonal too."

She stops, swallows. I want to jump down her throat and pull out the words, because Damiano is still coming for her. He's hovering over this conversation like a vulture, but I cannot say so. I have to bide my time for her.

"I'm going to kill him, Santino."

"Who?"

"Dr. Farina. I don't like that I killed someone in a church or anywhere...but Farina?" Her eyes finally meet mine. They're glassed over with tears. "He didn't just give me an opioid. He gave me misoprostol."

Am I supposed to know what she's talking about? Because I don't. I'm not a nurse or a doctor or a pharmacist. I'm a capo who extracts tributes and breaks bones.

"I don't understand." Even as I say the words, I know damn well what she asked for and why. As uneducated as I am in the ways of medicines and bodies, I know where this is headed.

"It caused my uterus lining to shed." She blinks, and tears drop down her cheeks. "Without that shot, I'd still be pregnant."

It's my turn to look away. No woman could see the murder on my face and still love me the way I need her to. "I will kill him for you. For both of us."

"Why would they do it?" she pleads through sniffles and a wet cracking sound in her throat. "Why, Santi?"

"So I don't have an heir to the crown."

"Fuck that thing," she says under her breath.

The profanity is like a knife slicing me open, exposing the inside of my heart. Fuck that thing. It's not important. None of it is. Everything comes down to Violetta and the home we build together.

We will build nothing in a war. I will spend my time protecting her instead of cherishing her. This is not the life she ever asked for.

I turn so my gaze meets hers. I won't say this without eye contact. She can't think I don't mean it with all my heart.

"You were given to me," I say, taking out a handkerchief to wipe away her tears. "I took you as a prize, but I never had to give myself back to you." Her face is dry, and I drop the hand with the handkerchief into her lap. "But I will. Now I will. Right now. We drive west with the clothes on our backs, and we find your normal."

Her eyes go wide. When she blinks, there are no tears left, and I think maybe this is it. No more war. No more violence. Maybe I can be as decent as she believes I can be. Maybe I can make her happy.

And when she smiles, I believe I can. But then her face breaks apart into a different expression, and I realize her happiness will now take more than being normal.

12

VIOLETTA

"We find your normal."

He says it with as much excitement as I've ever heard in his voice. As if this gift I asked for and he already refused is wrapped in shiny paper and tied with a big red bow. As if I hadn't already chosen him over this fantasy normal.

It's too late. I don't want normal. I want revenge.

The miscarriage changed me, even before I knew it was intentional. But now, I can't just walk away from the people who did this. My skin is laced in a web of vengeance.

I squeeze his hands in both of mine. "You wonderful, crazy, gorgeous, dramatic king of a man. They tried to kill you, and running away meant you never getting shot again. But there's no normal in my future. Not after this."

"*Forzetta*, this is not you."

He'd consign himself to a life of quiet misery because a life without my happiness would be so much worse. I believe him, and it's almost too much to bear.

"You're going to let them get away with it?"

"To protect you, I would." He believes it, but when my eyes narrow in suspicion, he looks away with a little smile. "For a while. When you were settled, I'd come back and bury them all. I'd make it home for dinner."

I smile with him, then see a bulge in his side jacket pocket big enough to open the slash into a bright orange smile.

"You got me something to eat," I say.

He removes the orange. "You're hungry?"

"Yeah." I try to take it from him, but he pulls it back and peels away its overly thick rind. "If we stay, what do you think it means?"

Considering my answer, I open a napkin from the glove compartment and lay it open between us. He drops the peels on it.

"I think it means we're going to take care of Damiano. And Gia. And Dr.—"

"Take care?" He breaks apart the fruit and holds up a wedge for me. "This means what?"

"I'm not hedging." I reach for it, but he taps my hand away with a *tsk*. "It means one of us is going to kill them. Dead."

"So tough, my *Forzetta*. Open." I open my mouth, and he drops the wedge onto my tongue. "You're so eager to lose your soul."

I chew the orange. The sweet juice explodes, and the tart pith shocks. I really am hungry. "Haven't I already? When I slashed that guy's throat?"

He pops a wedge into his mouth, tasting the same sour sweetness but with a different tongue.

"You were kidnapped, drugged." He feeds me a bigger, double-wedged piece. "Not in your right mind. Maybe God can forgive you, but He doesn't forgive sober vengeance."

"That's a theological stretch."

He nods, looking at the white registration tents. What's going on in his mind? Before I figure it out, he shakes his head once as if resetting reality, but doesn't say a word.

"Santino?"

"I don't know how to protect you from what's coming." He gathers the peels inside the napkin. "Damiano's still reaching for the crown. That means you."

Abruptly, he gets out of the car and walks to the trash can. Halfway there, he turns backward to keep his eye on me. On the way back, I notice his attention scanning the corners and curves, the lines of the rooftops, the vulnerabilities of our position. He leans against the car door on my side and talks to me through the open window.

"What do we do?" I ask.

"There will be a war, and I need you someplace safe while I fight it."

"Such as?"

"The house I bought you, here on this side."

"In River Heights?" The house he tried to bribe me into complacency with, that we then tried to trap Damiano inside—I haven't even lived in it a day, and it already has so much history I don't even want to see it from the outside.

"It's safe. I'll visit—"

"No!" I interrupt him, because there won't be any visiting or living separately. "We're in this together, you and me." I lower my voice in case someone appears from the emptiness. "You can't just go into Secondo Vasto and fight while I sit in some house and wait."

"You don't fight." He leans down and puts his elbow on top of the door. "You live in Torre Cavallo, and if you go up there, you stay. That is my final offer."

"You want to lock me up so you can do what I should be doing myself."

"You? You kill one man swinging your arm around like a sleepwalker, and now you're fighting a war with me?"

"We were going to have a baby, and now we're not. I'm not going to let that go."

"You want a family, Violetta? Or are you going to die for what you can't get back? Before this is over, Secondo Vasto is going to burn, and my wife will not be in the fire."

I am not an object. I am not a prized possession. He cannot protect what we have by putting me in a locked box and keeping the key handy. No.

"When Gia shot you…" I speak slowly so he understands every fucking word. "I watched you die. My mind replayed it a hundred times, and a hundred times I was helpless to pull you out of that pool and save you. They took away my faith in myself, then they took away our child. If they kill you while I'm not there to do everything I can to stop it… What you're not getting is that it's over. I'm over." My hands are up now, fingers curved, pleading with him to just hear me. "If we're not side by side, I'm going to go insane."

"But you'll be alive." He takes my wrists. "This is not negotiable as long as you're a target."

He's too definite. This is the man who shoved me into a car and forced me to marry him. The same guy who threw me over a table and told me he'd wait to fuck me until he decided I wanted it badly enough; who shot a man for me; who dies protecting me.

I have reached the limit of my influence over him.

"What if we get the crown?" I say. "Now. Today. Then it stops being my inheritance."

"And what will you expect then?"

"Damiano tries to get it from you." I shrug. "You win the war easily because everyone follows the crown, and we decide whether to stay and make babies or run away and make babies."

"We will get the crown." He lets his fingers slip along my wrists so they can weave in mine. "I'll take care of Damiano." He squeezes my hands and holds them to his chest. "Not you, *Forzetta*. Say it for me."

"You will take care of Damiano." I can say it. I can even believe it. He lays his palms on my jaw, and I put my hands over them before reciting the names he's skipped. "And Dr. Farina. And Gia. Right? All of them?"

"All of them," he whispers as his thumb brushes my lower lip. "I will bring you their heads."

His bloody promise enters my system like a drug. I gasp from the power of it. My cheeks get prickly hot, my heart thwacks against my ribs like a playing card clipped to a bicycle spoke, and my lips are drawn to him as if they're solely responsible for sealing this deal.

He meets me halfway, leaning into the car and folding me into a kiss that defies gravity and reason. It's a kiss of agreement, that when our tongues meet, so shall our minds. We share an idea of vengeance and justice. We sign a contract to trade our souls for satisfaction, for each other, for a thousand more kisses just like this one.

Connected at the mouth, we agree that murder is the way forward.

SANTINO DRIVES the Alfa Romeo east. Our shadow precedes us like dark sentinel, scouting the highway at sixty-five miles an hour.

"When we get it," Santino says, "we go back. You stay at Torre Cavallo, and I will gather everyone at the church."

"The one we burned down?"

He thinks for a moment, smirking. "Probably not."

There's more than one church, and basically, if Santino doesn't think it matters, it doesn't. The process of displaying the pieces of the crown to assure loyalty is steeped in traditions from the other side of the ocean. I don't pretend to understand them.

"Do you really think people are just going to be like, 'Okay, Re Santino finally has the crown, so we'll fight and die for him,' like it's nothing?"

Coming toward us at a low angle, a charter plane

heads into the farthest points of the sky, disappearing into a dot.

"Yes."

"And the Tabonas are just going to give you Damiano?"

"He'll have fewer friends."

I sigh and slide down my seat. I don't believe he's right about this, but it's a nice story.

"Maybe we can have the life you want." He puts his hand on my knee, slowing down for the increased traffic. "At home. Where we live."

"Maybe," I humor him. "How many babies do you want?"

"Three is enough."

"Really?"

"You want four? Four, I can do."

"I figured you for a traditional fourteen or fifteen kid kinda guy."

"You want to spend twenty years pregnant? Or do you want us to enjoy life a little bit?"

"I want to enjoy life a lot." I smile.

"*Bene*. We have a deal."

Is this the first time we've agreed on something without compromise? Is it the first time we came into a life goal with the same idea? We may never agree on where to live or what community to belong to, but the size of our family seems bigger than even that.

"I have a business question," I say.

"You can ask it."

"Have you ever tried to expand your territory over the river?"

"My... What?" He pops his blinker and checks over

his shoulder, and I catch a glimpse of an expression of incredulous disbelief.

"Your influence," I say. "Your kingdom. Is the river really a boundary?"

"No. I kept it small to stay under the radar. To keep from exposing myself. To protect you."

"You don't have to anymore."

Every surface on my body buzzes. I'm aware that I could have lost what I carried for a hundred reasons.

When they gave me that drug, they took something more than physical from me. They stole my autonomy. My humanity. My hope. The hum of righteousness chases away despair, and the risks of our revenge overwhelm the pangs of grief.

The conflicts bind into a new thing—a virus that infects my cells, reproduces and flows into my bloodstream like an invading army. It is weightless. Even as I sit, my spirit lifts to the ceiling of the car.

"*Cosa c'è?*" Santino asks, sensing something is happening with me.

"Nothing." I push the dashboard button that opens the sunroof. "I just need a little air."

The window over us slides open, whipping the wind through my hair. I stick my hands out to feel the pressure of the air. The speed. The resistance.

I am grief, and I am rage, but I am also vengeance. I understand so many of Santino's decisions now because I understand the power of making them.

Unlocking my seat belt, I get my legs under me. The dashboard lights up with danger and angry beeping.

"What are you doing?" Santino asks.

"Everything." I kiss his cheek. "Because of you."

He doesn't understand.

"Buckle in," he commands, but it's too late.

I am lifted through the sunroof.

"Violetta!" he shouts.

But I'm already pulling up through the hole. His voice is lost in the wind. I'm standing on my seat with the edge of the car at my waist. I feel his arm around my legs, holding me still as he drives down the highway. With my arms out, I speed alone, unencumbered, unenclosed, unrestrained but held firm. Trees fly by in a blur of leaves. Their trunks seem to shift like a handful of thrown twigs. But they're not moving, I am, and the broken yellow lines of the two-lane road are the only things guiding my direction. The world is frozen in place, and I move through it. I am the unstoppable force looking for the immovable object.

There's only one way, and it's forward.

This is not freedom. I will never be truly free.

But righteousness has infected grief, and the result is flowing through my veins.

It is power.

Santino pulls on my waistband, and I bend back into the car, sliding back into my seat with rosy cheeks and hair like a haystack.

"What was that?" he asks, closing the sunroof.

"Fun."

"Don't do it again."

"You should try it."

He laughs as he exits the highway, then he pulls me toward him and kisses my head as if he's delighted that I've had a good time. I lean into his shoulder while he drives.

At the red light, he turns to stare deeply inside me. I am clothed, yet raw in his gaze.

"I'm going to pull over and fuck you blind."

"Sorry. The doctor says I'm closed for business this week."

The light turns green. He nods but not in agreement.

"You need more in your belly than that orange. The lawyers haven't confirmed a time. We eat, then we go whether they confirm or not."

I assume what we call "the city" where the lawyer's office is located is tiny compared to New York or Chicago or even Cleveland, but to me, the stone buildings are huge, and the crowded sidewalks are overwhelming.

Santino takes me to a diner with parking in the back, but makes no move to get out of the car. He doesn't even unlock the doors, so I do. He locks them again.

"What?" I ask.

"We need to talk about what it means when you say 'closed for business.'"

"I think it's pretty obvious."

"You're bleeding still?"

"Not really, but that's not—"

"Open your legs."

Glands that have been dormant for days awaken in a rush, sending signals to the rest of my body that it's time to tingle. Time to turn my blood into an electrical current.

He taps the steering wheel, glances at my legs, then back at my face expectantly.

"Doctor's orders," I say.

He leans over and, with a hand on each knee, yanks them apart. Arousal hits my system so hard I can't keep my eyes open.

"Did the doctor say I can't touch you like this?" He presses his hand over the crotch of my pants and makes circles. "Answer."

"She didn't."

He runs a nail down the length of my nub, then the tips of all his fingers.

"Did she say I can't suck on your clit?" He taps it, and every time, it's a mini explosion.

"No." I'm gyrating against him. The fabric between us is damp and warm.

"Did she say your asshole is out of business?"

"No." I grab his hand and push it down my pants.

His fingers flick my clit, pull it, and stroke it.

"This is out of business? It feels too wet for that."

"It is. It…" I arch with pleasure and plateau before I come. "It wants you."

"Remember this. You are always ready for me. If your cunt is busy, you open your mouth. You offer your ass. Your body belongs to my cock."

"Yes."

He strokes circles on just the tip. "Look at you. I'm barely touching you, and you're pushing into me. And you're going to let some doctor tell you to say no to me?"

"No. You're right. Let me come. Please."

"You're so beautiful when you beg."

"*Ti prego.* Please."

"Look at me."

I do it, but I'm too blind with pleasure to see. "My body is yours. Please. *Ti prego.* Let me come for you. *Sono la tua puttanella.*"

"*Siamo d'accordo.* Give me what you want."

He gradually increases the speed and pressure on my clit until my ass rises from the seat and my hand is leveraged against the window. I scream his name, jerking my hips while he modulates his movements to extend the orgasm on and on and on.

But it's all broken by a sharp *pop*, followed by the rumble of rocks grinding against each other. Someone screams. Before I know it, Santino's pulled my head into his lap to get me out of the window.

"What's going on?" I hiss.

I hear people running across the parking lot shouting "what the fuck" and "where was it?" I try to sit up, but Santino pushes me down. I can't see anything but the top of the dumpster and the brick wall of the adjacent building.

"Hush." He starts the car and reverses with a screech of rubber.

The view changes. The sky is nickel-gray, but there's no rain or lightning to accompany the thunder.

Then the sirens. People running by, close enough to the car to touch it. Someone slams into the passenger side before going around.

"Santino!" I say sternly, trying to overpower him.

"Stay still!"

"Get off me!"

"This is not the time to show me you're a modern woman."

Maybe I'm a self-destructive, disobedient monster,

but I have to see, so I fight my way up to look out the windows. A cop car passes us, lights flashing and siren set to eleven. A dark gray mushroom cap rises to the sky. Not gunshots. And I haven't heard another pop.

"You're being paranoid. It's got nothing to do with us."

"Stay down." He pulls my head back into his lap, throws the car into drive, and takes off. "We're going to pass it. I don't want them to see you."

The back of my head is thrust into his crotch when he whips around a turn.

"Can you tell me what's going on, please?"

"I know why they didn't confirm the appointment."

I twist to look up at him—the curve of his chest, the underside of his chin, the bridge of his arms to the wheel. Even with the creeping smell of smoke and the increasing wail of sirens, is any woman safer?

"What does that have to do with it?"

He stops at a light and cranes his neck to look out the passenger window. "Shit."

"What?" I try to get up, but he pushes me down. "Let me see!"

He's strong but must see the futility of trying to keep me down again.

The block perpendicular to us is short, and it's already being cleared. The stone building nearest to the corner is five stories, and black smoke is billowing out of the top two floors. The façade to the front lobby has collapsed, taking a crater of sidewalk with it. A woman with a blood-covered face stumbles out the front door, tips sideways, and is caught by firefighters before she hits the ground.

"Is that the lawyer's office?" I ask.

In answer, Santino pulls me back into his lap.

"We lost the crown," I say, looking up at his chin.

"We did."

The inheritance is a distraction from what I really want—a life and family with him. I should be happy it's out of our hands, but I'm not. I feel violated.

"It's mine," I say.

"And that's why they're going to try to kill you." He looks down briefly before putting his attention back on the road. "They think they have power over me now."

When I feel the car hit highway speeds, I sit up. He doesn't stop me.

"Don't they have power over you now?" I ask. "Over us?"

"My love is stronger than any crown. They're going to die before they lay a finger on you."

His confidence wraps around me like a bulletproof blanket. It's untested until I'm shot at, but I believe it will keep me safe.

13

VIOLETTA

He drives up the mountain in a silence so hard and thick, I'm afraid trying to break it will shatter me. We pass three checkpoints. The guards at the entrance to Torre Cavallo are more serious and more heavily armed than the last time I was up here. Even Santino can't pass without having his car inspected.

He gets out and speaks to them in Italian. I hear relief. Success. He's alive. Half the conversation is lost in the wind. I'm desperate to know all the details, yet I want to run out there and change the subject. Every brain cell needs to be on getting a crown I didn't want to win a war we didn't start.

We're cleared, Santino returns to the car, and the gate opens. When we pass, it clangs closed.

"What's the plan?" I ask in the short space between the gate and the house.

"Find Damiano. Find Gia." Santino stops in front of the house. "Take what's ours."

"Then what?"

Then wipe them from the earth. That's what I want him to say. Fuck the crown. But he doesn't answer. He just gets out and crosses to my side, avoiding the question. He must think my "then what" requires a promise to be normal, but he has to know that's over.

"If there's going to be trouble," I say, "I want to get my family and bring them up here. My Zio Guglielmo and Zia Madeline. Whoever's at their house while this is going on. My Aunt Anna has to be there. All of them."

"It will be done." He helps me onto my feet, and in doing that, he's the man who married me, not the one who promised the earth and stars. Who squeezed my face to get my mouth open wide enough to say my vows. Hard and cold. All business. Even when he kisses my forehead. "You go inside."

He walks away from the grand mansion toward a row of smaller houses built into the side of the mountain. I'm not afraid he won't wipe out the people who did this. I'm terrified of something much more real.

"Wait!"

He turns when I call out, standing ten feet tall with twenty feet worth of impatience.

"Is this…?" There are too many people here. I can't say this halfway across a lawn, so I run to him. "Just tell me, is this going to be like it was? Where you show up in bed sometimes, but not always? Am I an afterthought again?"

"You were never an afterthought."

"Then come home to me at night."

"We'll see."

"You'll do more than see. You'll follow that rule, or you'll win the world and lose me."

Holding the side of my face, he pulls me into him. His lips are soft and yielding, and his tongue is tender. His kiss makes a lie of the stone he's turned into.

"I will not lose you," he whispers with his forehead touching mine. "*L'amore governa senza regole.*" *Love rules without rules.*

"Fuck you," I whisper back, but he lets me go and walks to the little buildings, flanked by men I don't know. "Fuck you," I say to myself. "I love you."

NAKED. Alone. Wet. The doctor cleaned me out, so the bleeding is gone now, but disappointment will flow out of me until my heart decides it's had enough.

Too drained to stand, I sit on the tile ledge that was built into the shower wall, then slide to the floor, putting the bench at my back.

"Damiano Orolio," I say, watching the water spiral down the drain. "Dr. Farina. Gia Polito. Father Alfonso." The bloody face of the woman stumbling out of the building had nothing to do with any of this. Revenge is for her too. "Cosimo Orolio," I add, then start over. "Damiano Orolio, Dr. Farina..."

Without Santino here, it all hits me. The blood-soaked bedsheets. The violation of the drugs. The explosion. The crown I never wanted but now need. The impending war. And remnants of the old sorrows. The horrifying second wedding. The throat I slashed.

Even leftover bits of grief from Santino's death-that-wasn't settle in the corners like dust bunnies.

I don't know how long I sob in the shower, but I cry until my lungs hurt. I'm blind with it. My eyes are swollen. My jaw aches. My throat is sore. I'm thirsty. I'm wrapped in a towel and Loretta is on the toilet, bending at my feet with a pair of pad-lined underwear between her hands. She wants me to step in. She's asked me to do this already, and I heard her, but the words skipped off the surface of my consciousness like flat rocks on a placid lake.

I step in, and she pulls the underpants up under the towel.

"Thank you," I say. "I think..." I have to stop for a last hitching breath. "I think I can finish."

She stands. I forgot how tall she is. How much a full woman. I feel short and girlish next to her.

"There are clothes here." She puts her hand on a pile.

"I'll do it, just...if you could give me a minute."

"We're downstairs in the kitchen." She leaves, softly clicking the door closed behind her.

I stand still for a moment, waiting for the sobs to attack again. They don't, but I haven't beaten them or resisted their advance. My heart just ran out of tears. It is wrung out, swollen, drained, and broken.

Bringing the pile of clothes to the bedroom, I look out the window, over the lawn, and up into the scrub and rock of a mountainside. The sky is not visible without craning my neck.

I sit on the bed with my shoulders hunched and my hands between my knees, then I drop to my side.

Exhausted. Trapped again and again. Freedom is a lie. It's a promise without substance. A light that only casts shadows.

He put me on this side of the house because it's safe from the world, but my heart has an IV drip of sadness and anger. When it is full again, the world will not be safe from me.

14

VIOLETTA

The dark hours of the morning are so dead quiet, I hear murmurs of conversation from the patio on the side of the house. The scrape of chairs. A laugh cut off before it's finished.

At some point, I got under the covers naked. Now I'm wide awake. Most importantly, I am alone. Santino did not come.

I'm pretty sure the proverb "Love rules without rules" doesn't mean he can break them like this.

After I dress and brush my teeth, I try the bedroom door, half expecting it to be locked. It isn't.

Santino could be anywhere right now. All I know is he wasn't next to me when I woke up.

I told him I didn't want to be an afterthought—that he'd win the world and lose me.

But will he ever lose me?

No. He won't.

I follow muffled voices to my right and wind up in the grand dining room.

The last time I saw the dining room, it was empty. Now the room has been opened into a large patio on the side of the house, and both have rows of tables and chairs. A scattering of men grab food from a long buffet and sit in small groups.

The kitchen was never homey, even when the lack of utensils and pots had been addressed. Now it has been transformed into a place to cook for an army, with a stock pot as big as a wine barrel. Celia isn't here, but the door to the basement is open. I smell a hint of sulfur from the coal furnace and hear clanging from the *cucina* below.

Outside, the crickets are still grinding away. I step into the view from my window—the grassy field between the house and the buildings against the mountain wall, with the slash of blackened blue sky above. The windows in the buildings on the mountain end of the lawn are all dark except for one. A dim beam pulses from one side of the window to the other. I walk toward it. Maybe I'm looking for my husband. Maybe I just want something to do before the day begins, and I have to fight tooth and nail for what I deserve.

The building is one of the smallest on this side of the lawn. More of a one-car garage surrounded by narrow, weedy walkways between buildings. Voices reach me, but they're muffled and unintelligible. Gripping the window's edge on tiptoe, I avoid stepping on a tomato plant to look through the frosted glass.

The movement of the pulsing light has slowed. It's a lamp swinging on the end of a chain like a pendulum running out of energy. Someone is weeping. There's no energy behind it. It is a sob of resignation.

In the window, I discover the crack leading to a corner of the pane, and in that corner, a tiny rhombus of glass is missing. I bend a little to look through it and have to hold my breath against the stench coming from that little hole.

The weeping man has a ring of long, graying hair at the base of a bald head and sits on a metal folding chair, leaning to the right with so much weight, the yellow nylon rope that ties his hands behind the chair's back and an ankle to each chair leg is the only thing holding him up. His white tank top is hitched halfway up his big belly, and the shoulder strap doesn't lean with his body, revealing a delicate pink nipple.

It's the tender vulnerability of the nipple that focuses me. The ring of hair is not long on both sides. Only the right side has been grown out so that it can be combed over the scalp.

It's Santino's Uncle Marco. Paola's husband. Gia's father. The man who reluctantly raised his nephew. The man who said he was driving me to the airport to meet Gia, then made up a story about the brooch so he could deliver me to Damiano and put Santino in the way of a bullet.

I can't really see his face, but he doesn't look like he deserves whatever's happening to him. He looks like a sad old Italian guy alone in a room.

Except he's not alone.

From a dark corner, a man appears. He seems to be made of shadows. The sleeves of his white shirt are rolled past his roped, tattooed forearms. Standing over Marco, he reaches up and stops the lamp from swinging. The light reveals brown hair with a lock over his forehead, arched eyebrows, and a profile cut into marble.

When the man made of shadows speaks, his tone is gentle, even if his words are not. "I don't want to ruin another shirt, sir."

"I told you." Marco's voice has no strength. "I haven't spoken to her."

The man crouches in front of the chair, hands dangling between his knees. One holds a phone.

"But you did." He raises the screen to Marco's face. "We're going to find her. You know that. How should we treat her? Like a woman or a whore?"

The answer is sobs.

"You only get to die once," the man says. "Why do it in pain? Knowing you made it worse for your daughter."

Marco shakes his head in denial.

With a resigned sigh, the shadowy man stands over a five-gallon bucket of tools in the corner, considers, then picks hedge clippers from it as if he's plucking daisies. He looks in my direction, and I freeze in terror, because his blue eyes are coldly brutal and his mouth is full and savage, but he's not directing his attention at me. He doesn't even see me as he spins the clippers in a deft tic. He's looking at the wall beneath the window.

Darkness flashes across the glass and there's a bang to my right. I leap back with a gasp, discovering there's a door there only as it slams open and Santino bursts out.

He's stock still in the morning darkness, staring at me. Behind him, the door closes automatically with a soft hiss and click.

"What are you doing here?" he asks. His black T-shirt is stretched at the neck, and there are two scratch lines on his collarbone. His body is real and vulnerable. I want to heal it.

"I went to bed early, so I woke up early."

Stepping toward me, he enters the light from the frosted window. He is conflicted. Pained. Fighting things he cannot control. He is complex and beautiful.

"Go back inside."

"When you're done with him," I say, ignoring his order. "Who's next? Gia? You think you're going to kill her? You won't."

He takes out a pack of cigarettes. The backs of his hands are dirty.

"You think I'm soft."

"I know you're human, and she's your sister."

"This isn't a television show." He chooses a smoke and flicks open his bullet-bent lighter. "This is real. It's too real for you."

He brings the flame to his face, illuminating the pink of his lips and the color in his skin. I was wrong about the backs of his hands. They aren't dirty. They're covered in blood.

The man tied to that chair sold Santino into death and put me on an altar to another man.

"It's not real enough. Why is he even alive?" I ask.

"Go inside, *Forzetta*."

"Is it because he raised you?" The words are spit through my teeth. "You got sentimental and you forgot? I can remind you right the fuck now, he killed you and the baby inside me."

"You think I don't know?" He comes at me so fast I

end up with my back to the wall. He's pointing at me with the two fingers that clip the lit cigarette. "I can see your fucking face right in front of me." He jams the cigarette in his lips and clamps my jaw, turning my head so my left eye faces him. "You want to know what it looks like? Eh?"

"I have a mirror, asshole."

"It's dark, but I don't need light." He traces the curve below my eyebrow, narrating what he sees as if it's new to him. "You have a black arch here, and under your eye, it's thicker and more blue. The yellow spread out around. And the eyelid." He touches it. "Red. Bright red. Like it's about to start bleeding if I look at it too hard." He lets my face go and snaps the cigarette out of his mouth. "It looks like Damiano hit you. He broke what's mine—the only thing I have that's worth treating with respect—and he treated you like garbage. He hurt you, and he's going to die for it. But I have to find him. So you need to go in*side*."

He's yelling by the end, and I'm stunned because I've never seen him like this. Sure, he's been angry, but he's also shaking.

"What if he doesn't know?" I ask. "You're wasting time."

"He knows. And I know my business." He flicks the butt against the wall, and it explodes into orange sparks before settling on the ground to smolder.

"Marco is the only father you ever had."

"Get. Inside."

"You won't ever really hurt him enough."

I'm right. His rage is the tell. He wants to protect me from seeing that he's hurting someone, but he didn't expect me to see his failure to hurt. Now he's juggling what he has to do against who he's doing it to. A man he despises and loves. A man who took him into his house, then betrayed him.

"Violetta, do not—"

"And you're not going to let that guy in there really do it."

As my realization calms me, it increases his intensity. The path before me and the road behind become clear.

"For the last time," he starts, coming closer.

I duck and run to the little door, swing it open, and enter hell. It's boiling hot. The stench of sweat, shit, and piss has a mass all its own, but I don't have time to ask where it's coming from. Before Mr. Shadows knows what's happening, I reach for the five-gallon bucket, grabbing the first thing I touch. A crowbar. Fine.

I face Marco. His nose is smashed, and his eyes are swollen mostly shut…the way mine was not long ago.

"Violetta." He breaks into a bloody smile.

He's relieved. He thinks I'm going to save him because I'm a woman. That's incorrect.

I'm going to break him because I'm a woman.

"This is for betraying your king." I bring the crowbar down on his knee with all my might, and the scream cuts through the thickness of the smell. "And this is for my baby—"

I bring the crowbar down on his head, but it doesn't land. The man of shadows catches my arm mid-swing while Santino's halfway between the door and me. Marco's screaming and writhing as much as the rope lets him. The chair legs tap on the concrete floor from his effort.

"Let me go," I growl at the man.

He smirks, and inside that half smile are a thousand ways to murder me and not a single feeling about it one way or the other. I realize I'm panting as though I've just run as far as I can. I've hit my limit.

Santino takes the crowbar and flings it aside. He starts to say something to me, but thinks better of it and decides to face his sobbing uncle. With his foot on the seat of the chair, Santino pushes it over. The tied man's leg bends in an unnatural angle. I broke it. Compound fracture. Gotta hurt. Don't care. Not after what he did.

"Talk," Santino says, then points at me. "Or my wife will be the one to break Gia."

Mr. Shadows gets between the man on the floor and me.

"You can lead, follow, or get out of the way," he says in a deep, resonant voice with an accent from somewhere in America. "And we already have a leader."

Santino's crouching by his failed father, tapping his cheek in a cross between tenderness and violence.

"Santi," I say.

He turns to me with his hand on the bloody face. "*Forzetta.*"

"I'll wait for you outside."

He nods, then takes out his cigarettes and lighter with his free hand and gives them to me. I take them.

"Go," he says, turning back to the matter at hand.

I back out of the little house. The man with the brutal gaze closes the door, and I'm left standing alone in the half light of dawn with an emptiness in the place where I kept the violence I just released.

With a shaking hand, I open the pack of cigarettes and eventually still myself enough to get one out. I put it in my mouth and—with massive effort and the grind of metal on metal—I open the lighter and touch the flame to the tobacco.

I've never smoked a day in my life, so I cough. The world swims a little. It's not a high that makes me feel ecstatic or even content, but I am physically buoyant. When I take a second drag, I don't cough, and the high disappears. The cigarette does not fill me or bring me any real satisfaction, but I understand why Santino smokes after he breaks into violence.

This will not become a habit, but it's not my last cigarette either.

15

VIOLETTA

Santino doesn't come out of the building. I stamp out the butt, pick it up, and roll it between my fingers as I reenter the house through the kitchen.

"You're up early," Celia chirps, breaking an egg into a huge metal bowl. This side of the house smells like bacon.

"You're awfully chipper this morning." I throw the butt in the trash.

"I'm making eggs."

"Where's the bacon?" I ask.

"The oven."

The sizzle is as loud as a rainstorm when I crack open the door, but Celia slaps my hand away before I can even see if it's done.

"There you are," Loretta says as she enters. She takes the top off of a huge coffee urn. "You weren't in your room. I got worried."

"I took a walk around."

"See anything interesting?"

I saw Santino and a stranger torture Marco Polito, but not hard enough.

I saw my king weighed down with a guilt he didn't understand.

I looked at what a war will mean for my soul and accepted it. Embraced it. I saw it all, and it wasn't interesting. It was horrifying, and I couldn't look away.

"You can see more stars up here," I reply. Only when Celia pours coffee into the urn do I notice the three pots of coffee waiting on warmers.

"Do you want some?" she asks as if I'm a kid eyeing the juice boxes.

"I'll get it." I get a cup for my own coffee. "How did you get all this together so quickly?"

"It was all in the basement." She checks the bacon and slides out the first of three trays. "This won't be the first war this house has seen."

"I never considered you had to feed the guys."

"The women don't sit around wringing their hands," Loretta says.

"And we're ready," Celia says. "But how are you? Do you need something for...?" She indicates my black eye by drawing a circle in its general direction.

"I'm fine." I guess I should help in the kitchen, being a woman and all. I like cooking and working in a team, but I can't help but glance at the buildings outside, where I used a crowbar to break a man's knee. "Aren't you guys scared?"

"Of course." Celia shrugs, removing the bacon with tongs. Her sleeves are rolled up, revealing forearms dotted with whorled skin the size of burning cigarettes.

When I look at the building I went into—the one with the Shadowy Man inside—the door is wide open.

Have they moved Marco? Was he alive when they did it? Or is he still tied to a chair?

A short guy with a leathered face brings a mop and bucket inside the little building.

I excuse myself and run upstairs to the room where I slept. It's just as I left it, but the bathroom door is open, and the shower's going. The black T-shirt with the stretched neck is pooled on the floor, and smoke and the smell of burning tobacco mixes with the shower's steam.

I strip off my clothes and open the shower curtain. Santino has his elbows on the wall and his head dropped between them while the hot water pounds his shoulders. When he looks up, the cigarette between his lips gets spotted with droplets.

"Santino," I say, reacting to the exhaustion in his eyes. "What happened?"

"There was no point fixing his knee. That's what."

I get into the scalding shower with him.

"He had it coming," I say, running my fingers in the same direction as the wet lines of hair down his chest.

"Listen to you. Judge and jury."

"Did he tell you where they are?"

"What if he did?"

"We're going to go there and fuck them up, right?"

"I don't know." He takes one last drag on the wet cigarette before it's too soaked to smoke, then tosses it into the toilet.

"You don't... What?"

"It could be a trap to get me to leave you alone here. Then what?"

"This is a fucking compound."

"I'm aware."

"Okay. So you can take me with you."

He scoffs, hands roaming over my body. "Which is more dangerous? Leaving you here so they can take you again? Or bringing you into the mouth of the volcano?"

"How many times have you left me home and nothing happened? Or the times you went out with me and we were fine? It doesn't matter which you choose. You just have to kill them…or I will."

He puts his arms on either side of my head, backing me against the wall. "Do you have any idea what this life does to a person? First, you lose control of the people you love. Then, you lose control of yourself, and this is happening, right now. You were so pure when I took you. You were clean and innocent. Now, you want a trail of bodies behind you."

"If I changed, it's because of you."

"You think I don't know that?" he snarls in my face. "You're filthy. Ruined."

Oh, fuck him and his dumb chauvinist ideas. I have no time for it.

I push him away. "If you don't want me anymore—"

He pushes me back against the wall, and I'm flooded with desire.

"Are you blind?" He caresses my breast, sucks in a breath when he pinches the nipple. "I want you more than ever. Can't you see that? I've destroyed you, and I should be sorry. I should get on my knees and beg for God's forgiveness, but why? I'll only do it again."

This poor man is going to wreck himself with guilt. He should be proud of how strong I've become.

"I know I wasn't dragged into marriage by an altar boy."

"You're wrong." He tilts his head. "I was an altar boy."

"Of course." I look from the droplets on his cheeks as they drip to his beard and down at the taut lines of his body and reach for the rigid angle of his erection. "Whatever you are or were, it's you I want."

"You're not ready for what you have in your hand."

There are parts of me that need rest, but he's not seeing the full picture. My body has a place for him.

"You think I ruin so easy." I turn my back to him and put one hand against the wall and the other on my ass. "I'm tougher than you think."

In silence, he draws his touch down my back and to my cheeks, spreading them open. I look over my shoulder. His expression is hidden. All I can see is the water dripping from a triangle of hanging hair.

"Go ahead," I say. "Destroy me. I want you to."

He reaches for the shelf of supplies and knocks over the shampoo, the conditioner, body wash, and bar of soap until he finds the cream, then he sits on the ledge.

"You're going to destroy yourself." He drops a line of lotion on his cock, then fists the shaft. "Come here."

I stand between his knees, and he turns my back to him. I feel his slick fingers probing. Two enter my ass, and I groan with pleasure as he stretches and spreads the muscle.

"Touch yourself," he commands, pushing my legs open so my swollen clit hangs ready.

I rub between my legs. He removes his fingers and pulls me down on him, guiding his cock to my ass, then he lets go, leaving me in control.

Spreading my legs to either side of his, I lower myself onto him, gently opening, paying attention to when the pain comes and when it goes away, until he's buried inside me. I wait for a command or instruction, but I get nothing but a groan from behind. I rise, then fall, fingering my clit as I fuck him with my ass, lingering when I push him deep, forcing down with my weight when his head is at the edge, finding a rhythm that matches his grunts.

He doesn't need to tell me he's close. I feel it in the way his fingers curl on my back.

"Come with me, Santi. Can you? Now?"

In answer, he grabs my hair and pulls my head back, as if he can't culminate without controlling some part of me, and that's enough to send a seismic orgasm ripping through my body. My cries echo off the walls, and when they die down, there's just the sound of the water beating against the tiles.

When I lean back, he wraps his arms around me and whispers in my ear, "I love you, my violet. I am so afraid to play this game and lose you."

"You can't lose me as long as you love me."

"*Lo voglio. Per l'eternità.* Even death won't keep me from you."

"Don't prove that twice."

"No." He lays his hands on my cheeks. "Marco told us they're at Vasto Quarry. When we attack it, you'll be afraid. You'll worry about the danger. You'll think I've lost and I'm leaving you. But I won't be. I'll be loving you."

SANTINO and I walk down the grand stairway arm in arm. Men run past the front windows. The door swings open as we step onto the marble floor of the front foyer. Carmine bursts in first, then Vito, a bloody hand over his bicep.

"Jesus." I run forward to look at Vito's arm.

"We rooted out the roaches," he says to Santino.

"It looks like you did *something*," I complain, directing Vito to the nearest chair.

"Sent them to a hotel," Carmine chimes in.

"It's a motel, *stunad*," Vito snaps back, then resists when I try to look at his wound. "Don't worry about that. Just a scrape."

"Can someone interpret for me?" I pull Vito's hand away. A globule of blood bubbles between the shreds of his jacket. I let him cover it again.

"There were Tabonas at your zio and zia's," Santino says to me, then turns to Carmine. "Gone, yes?"

"Dead as fuck."

A few other guys burst in. I recognize Remo and Gennaro among them.

"Where are they then?" I ask, looking out the open door for my aunt and uncle. They're not there.

"They wouldn't come with us," Vito reports. "They don't trust nobody right now. Guglielmo's still on the porch with a *partigiani* Beretta."

"Fuck." I'm cursing because my zio is being a pain in the ass, but also because the blood's started to seep between Vito's fingers. I run into the kitchen and look under the sink, praying for a first aid kit.

My prayers are answered. The white metal box is as small as a textbook. I run back to Vito.

Santino's barking orders to his men. I only hear they are to "get down there," and "secure the block," before he's outside, finishing the instructions, leaving me alone with Vito.

I take out the scissors.

"I hope you don't like this jacket too much." I'm cutting it before he confirms I can.

The bullet grazed the muscle and left on the other side, missing the cephalic vein. Thank God it isn't inside him. I have no idea how to remove it.

"Is this the only injury?" I ask.

"Yeah." He cringes when I lift his arm to check his side.

"My uncle always said one day he'd need that Beretta," I say to distract him, stuffing more gauze under his hand. "It's been in the basement since forever. Pressure."

"It works like new."

"I'm sure it does."

"He didn't want to hurt nobody."

I scoff. Maybe he didn't. He's an uncle by marriage. But Zia Madeline is my father's sister. She probably wants blood, and I wouldn't blame her.

My thoughts are interrupted when Santino storms back in.

"Get back down there and finish the job, Vito."

"He isn't going anywhere," I say distractedly.

"They ain't coming with me," Vito protests. "Two days ago, they opened the door for the neighbor, and Joey and Willie Tabona busted into the house. They been eating their food and watching their TV since."

"Until today," Santino sneers.

"Good thing Carmine and I came slow. Joey and Willie came out to check us over, and the Beretta started popping from upstairs. Gave us a moment to take them down…but now? That door don't open. We tried."

"Wait." I stop the patient from talking further, because it's already clear that besides Tabona soldiers, Zio Guglielmo was involved. Keeping pressure on Vito's arm, I turn to my husband, whose body language is mid-action. "I told you I wanted to go get them."

"And I said it would be done."

"You could have told me." I look away and pluck up a roll of tape.

"If I wanted you to know, I would have."

He's not going to change. Not today. Not preparing to attack the Vasto Quarry, where as kids, we got chased from climbable stacks of uncut Yule marble. Santino is who he is. It may take a lifetime to teach him that he shouldn't make decisions without me.

"They'll trust me," I say, ripping away a length of tape. "If I go, he'll put the Beretta away, and they'll come."

"You're not going anywhere. The whole town's infested."

"Our enemies have the crown." I pat the tape across

the bandage. "I'm not worth anything to them anymore."

"You're worth something to me."

He's right, and he knows it. The argument is over. I can be leveraged as motivation for surrender or consequence for an attack. But they have to catch me first. Not needing me to admit what's obvious to him, Santino goes outside to talk to the shadow man who stood over Marco a few hours ago.

Finished with the bandage, I stand. "Stay off it," I say to Vito.

"Sure." He stands with a smile that acknowledges what we both know. He has no choice in the matter. "They seem like good people, your aunt and uncle."

"They are."

He goes outside, running to the tall building where the men sleep. Probably getting a shirt that's not cut to shreds.

The couple who raised us are good people. They did everything for us. They made my sister and me their own. If I thanked them with every breath I have for the rest of my life and died with thanks on my lips, it would not be enough.

I go outside and find Santino at the side of the house, by the outside door to the basement, with a man whose back is to me, talking, talking, talking. I'll die of starvation waiting for a polite moment to speak.

"Excuse us," I cut in.

"*Forzetta*," Santino says firmly.

But I don't look at him. I'm locked on the dangerous blue eyes of his companion. He's the one from the room with Marco. In the light, he's harder and even colder, and the shadows don't hide the way the tops of his ears end in a straight line, as if God stopped printing them out before he was finished. The man is bristling—holding back some kind of energy that's not necessarily risky to me personally. I get the sense he's used to releasing that energy by ruling over a faraway kingdom.

"This is Dario Lucari," Santino continues. "Business associate from New York. Dario, this is my wife. Violetta."

My name is more than a name. It's a warning that I'm off-limits.

"From last night," Dario says with a hint of a snarl, as if he's still mad about the interruption. "You didn't have to bother. We were going to get what we needed out of him."

"But I got it quicker." I turn to Santino, who's directing a narrowed eye at Dario as if he's trying to decide whether or not he likes where this conversation is going. I put my hand on his arm. "Please, five minutes."

"*Bene*," he says, pulling me away. "I'll correct how he spoke to you."

"Whatever," I say. "He's irrelevant. I have to get my Z's."

"No."

"You can come with me. They know I love you. They'll trust you," I plead, but make no headway. He's still stone-faced. I hold his lapels as if that will keep him still. "When we came, they weren't ready for us. He built a bed for me, and I wouldn't sleep on it for months. I thought it would break some kind of spell, and I wouldn't be safe again." I speak so fast I'm breathless. I have so much to get in before he's pulled away. "And I wouldn't let him pick me up. Not for the first year. Then I did, and he threw out his back. For weeks, he was on the living room floor, on the phone with his foremen and clients. He told them he spent his whole life moving lumber and brick, but this little girl..." I press a hand to my chest. "This little *patatina* had a spirit heavy enough to break him."

"Okay," Santino says.

"Okay we can go?"

"I'll go."

"No," I say. "Take me. Don't leave me here waiting for you."

"Do I have to lock you in a tower?"

"There isn't a tower in the world that will keep me away from you."

"You mean there isn't one that will keep you safe." He looks away from me, then back, changing the light on his face so I can see the dark rings of exhaustion under his eyes. "One trip."

"There and back. Done."

We kiss on it, and I believe him.

16

SANTINO

A man cannot turn his back on a woman, because when he turns around to see her again, she may be gone.

A man cannot bring a woman into his business, because when the net drops on him, she will get caught in it.

But a man cannot keep a woman in a cage and love her at the same time.

Scanning the rifles and semiautomatics, the sawed-off shotguns and long-barreled weapons, I accept there isn't a right answer.

No. There was another option that solved everything, but I refused it.

She asked me to get in the car and drive far away with her. Away from the safety of what's known into the arms of what's not. I could have stayed by her side and protected her without being a target. We could have walked away, but I was too much of a coward to do it before the fire of vengeance was lit under her.

Now I'm stuck with two bad choices. The one I've made and that has failed me too many times—to separate from her and trust she'll stay safe.

Or the one Emilio made that got his wife killed—to bring her into business so she'd stay by his side.

Neither works.

Violetta needs to bring her aunt and uncle up here. They're not safe, and she won't rest until they are. But they won't come unless someone they trust goes to get them, and using force might get one of them killed.

So she goes to get them, or I do, or both of us.

"Hey, uh, Re Santino?" Armando's voice comes from the stairwell that drops from the side yard. The armory was built as a root cellar and is separate from the rest of the basement.

"Mm?"

"Can I talk to you for a minute?"

Reaching to the crates below the gun racks, I pull out a more powerful weapon than what I usually carry. A .45 ACP revolver. I spin the cylinder.

"*Si.*" I don't like this gun. It's a prop.

I choose a stark black Glock 20 and wait for Armando to get to the point. He doesn't start right away. He's nervous. He's going to ask me for something. I slide a magazine into the well.

"I figure," he starts, then clears his throat. "It's an assumption, but I figure you want me to stay here while you all go to the quarry tonight."

"*Si.*" I try to put the gun in the holster I have. It doesn't fit.

"I want to say, I feel responsible for what happened."

"I told you it wasn't your fault." I search a drawer for a different holster. "You did what I told you."

"Right. I know. But…there's a thing you don't know about, and it's weighing on me."

"Spit the toad then." The new holster fits. Good. At least one thing is going right.

"Okay, so. Me and Gia." Another throat clear. A cough. Maybe he really is choking on a toad.

"You want the Heimlich maneuver? Celia knows how."

He waves me away and settles his breath. "I know you're not happy about my thing with Gia."

He's making a big understatement. The only reason he's still in my presence is that I need him, and I still trust him as long as his heart's not involved.

"How long were you going behind my back, Mando?" I shoulder the holster and adjust it.

"Since Christmas."

That's about eight months of sneaking around, but if I'm honest with myself…they were bad at it. In the back of my mind, I suspected something was happening.

"So, when it came to her marrying Damiano…" He rubs his eyes with meaty fingers. "I told her she had to accept it. Instead of being a man and marrying her…I told her, you know, this is how it is. It'd be fine. And she changed. She just…I don't know…went cold." He drops his hands. "I'm just saying it's not my fault because of anything that day, but it's my fault for not doing the right thing and marrying her or even offering. So she did the plan with Damiano."

"I assured him she was a virgin. Was she?"

"No." His eyes are stuck to the floor. God damn his shame. I want to kill him.

I might.

Without thinking, I put the gun to his forehead. "You should have told me, Armando. Instead, you made me a liar."

"I know." He cringes, squeezing his eyes shut. "I'm sorry. But she said she'd handle it."

"All of this... We could have avoided it if you opened your fucking mouth."

Even as I say it, I know it's a lie. Damiano and his father want the crown, and if Gia wasn't available as a way to get it, they would have found another. All routes lead to the situation I'm in right now. I move the gun away, still annoyed at his betrayal in the months before Gia shot me and in the days since.

"You're so protective of her," Armando says. When his eyes open, they're full of tears. "She thought they'd send her back, and she didn't want to go."

"You were afraid for yourself, not her."

"I know. It's true. And I'm sorry for it. I want to make it up."

"There are these little wooden rooms in the church." Unholstering the gun, I pause, letting him think I'm about to use it on him. "Get inside one and let the priest give you your Hail Marys. But setting your sins straight isn't my job."

"Yes, Re Santino, I know. And I know I take care of the house. But I want to go with you to the quarry. I can't let you take care of business for me. Gia's my fault."

"You're going to shoot her?" I say with no little sarcasm.

"No. No, I couldn't, and you shouldn't trust me to. But I can drive. Or watch the back. Or something. Please. You have Dario to stay behind, and he's... I wouldn't fuck with that guy. He ain't gonna listen to me anyway."

"Dario Lucari isn't a bodyguard." I reholster the gun.

"He won't stick his neck out either."

He's right. Good for Armando for saying what's hard to say, even if it's obvious.

"Camilla Moretti had bodyguards," I say, and with the weight of the gun swinging by leather straps, I remember that night. "I wasn't the only one watching. Men like you were too. But in the end, they failed. She couldn't be protected. She was part of her husband's business, and his wife, and the mother of his children. Got her shot."

"Right next to him."

He's right again. Emilio was right there, and he was twice the capo I'll ever be. This is why I keep a guy like Armando around. He's not muscle. He's not even a mastermind. But he loves the truth the way a priest loves God—even when betraying it.

If I can't protect Violetta, she's going to have to be able to protect herself.

This holster fits me, but it's too big for her.

I rummage around a drawer and find an awl.

"Here's what's going to happen." I lay the strap across the table and drive in a new hole. "You're staying here for the hit on the quarry tonight. But there's an errand before."

"Okay."

"Bring the car out of the gate." I make a second hole.

"You got it. Thank you."

Even with a wall of guns at my disposal, I brandish the awl. "I could just kill you here for laying your mitts on Gia without my permission."

He holds up his hands. "I know. I'm sorry."

I have a near physical need to stab his face and—at the same time—I hate seeing him like this.

When did it all get so complicated?

"Fuck this." I toss the awl on the counter and get ready to lie to give my wife what she's always wanted so badly. Independence.

17

VIOLETTA

Remo rushes to me as I come down the stairs.

"Re Santino says to be on the east side of the house."

"You run the same, you know," I say.

"What's that mean?"

"When you were stealing second, you had this way of running like you were skidding sideways. Lydia Lapore swooned for it."

"Yeah?" He's got a smile that takes up half his face.

I find myself wishing he wasn't here. He should be in town, working at the sporting goods shop, flirting with all the girls my age. I hope he lives through this war and quits the life forever.

"Yeah."

"Cool. I gotta go get the Mercedes ready."

"*Sciò* then."

Remo runs off, and I find the east side of the house, which seems to be the more utilitarian. The sheer drop into scrub and trees is bordered by a log fence. The trash bins on the side of the house are a few steps away.

The direction of the wind has changed, and though the birds and bugs still sing, an eerie silence waits underneath it.

Santino strides across the grass like the master of the universe. His leather side holster is over his blue shirt, and another holster dangles from his fingers.

He takes the gun from the second holster and puts it in my hand. It's not like his grandfather's revolver. This one has a thicker shape, with a textured handle that's grooved for a man's fingers.

"What's this for?"

"To protect yourself," Santino says, letting his palm slide away. "We don't have any statues to break."

He's talking about the statue of the Virgin I smashed so I could use a piece to commit murder.

"Broken statues work though." I inspect the gun. Looks easy enough to operate. I wonder how hard you have to pull the trigger to make it shoot.

"Only when you're in reach." From the bin, he grabs a few Coke bottles by the neck and puts one at the top of the fence post. "No one should get that close again. Also." He looks over his shoulder critically. "Keep your finger off the trigger unless you're going to shoot, and when you shoot, you aim to kill every time. No less."

For a moment, I wonder how many times he's pulled the trigger and how his aim was. How many men died, and why?

He pushes me back a few steps, turns, then gets behind me. The bottle is so far away I can't read the brand printed on them.

"You want me to hit that?" I ask.

"Yes. Hold your gun up with both hands."

"That's too far." I raise the gun and close one eye.

"Now what?"

"Line up the notches here and here..." He points them out on either side of the barrel, then the protrusion in the middle. "And the pin with the target."

"Okay. Got it."

"Do you?"

I hold the gun with one hand and pull the trigger. The gun recoils and flies from my grip. The bottle stands.

"You almost killed two people a block away. Pay attention." He scoops up the weapon and gives it back to me. "Don't you watch television?"

"Sure."

"How do they hold it?"

I turn the gun sideways and point it at the bottle.

"*Santo Dio*, no." He pushes my arm down and comes behind me again, close this time, so I can feel his body pressed against mine. He runs his hand down my left arm and places it under the grip of my right, breathing on my neck, running his lips along the length of it. "Like this. The left steadies the right."

"Do I really need this to get my Z's? Or is it for when we go to... Where are Dami and Gia?"

"Vasto Quarry. Dami killed Franco and took his place. Hold it straight. If you can't give this your attention, your full effort, you shouldn't carry it."

In a split second, a defensive wall inside me is built brick by brick—even though he's right.

"My professors used to say that to me when I coasted on B-plus grades."

"There is no coasting." He turns me around to face

him, and I make sure to keep the gun far from him. "Your father had your mother with him every day. As much as he could. And when he wasn't there, me or Dami or one of a dozen other guys watched over her."

My good mood dissipates like the last bit of water in a hot teapot. "How did it happen then?"

"That night, Dami got me tickets to a soccer game, but when I heard they were going out, I worked anyway."

"So you let it happen?" I don't mean to blame him. I don't. But I want to get at any guilt he's left lying in the corners of his heart.

"Yes and no. My point is they had protection. Everything went right. It didn't matter. He wasn't protecting her by keeping her close. She was killed with him."

My mother's purple hat, leaning in a doorway. One shoe off. Me thinking she'll lose it the way Rosetta loses hers. God, I hate my brain. I hate that I was five.

"Something was going on that night," I say. "But I was too young to know what."

"It was just an anniversary dinner."

It wasn't. My mother was turning into a stone version of herself.

If you find yourself dead, that deal is off.

You can only swear on what's yours.

Their marriage had been arranged. I know this in my gut. Things said that I barely remember. Intonations and assumptions. It was the way it was.

"I don't think she loved him anymore." I turn back to the target. "If she ever did."

"We can't correct the past." He kisses the back of my

neck. "We can only do better. When you are waiting, when you are talking, you hold the gun up at your shoulder." He draws my arm up. "This makes you safe from accidents and still ready to shoot in any direction."

"Okay. I'm ready."

"Good. Aim."

I lower both hands. The bottle is so far away. The bullet is so small, and I am just a girl out of her depth, and I hate how hard it all is.

"You know what I'd do? If I were queen?"

"Squeeze, queen."

I squeeze. A bullet leaves the chamber and lodges itself in the fence.

"If I were queen, I'd abolish '*mbasciata* on my first Monday at work. You know what I'd take on on Tuesday?"

"That bottle, right there."

I try again, aiming a little higher. I don't know where the bullet goes, but it doesn't hit the target.

"On Tuesday, this whole 'best murderer wins' rule would be out." I shoot and miss again. "How many bullets does this thing have?"

"Fifteen."

I shoot again. The bottle seems to move a little, but it could be wishful thinking.

"Breathe in." He puts his hands on my rib cage, feeling it expand. "Shoot on the exhale."

Letting the air go, I squeeze the trigger. The bottle definitely moves.

"Don't lose your concentration thinking about Wednesday."

"On Wednesday, all the men will do the dishes." I shoot and miss entirely. Then again, with the same non-result. "This is the most frustrating thing I've ever done in my life."

"This?" he says from behind me. "Out of everything?"

I shoot again. Miss.

"Ugh. Yes. On Thursday, I'd replace all the guns with bazookas."

"You're rushing."

Well, I wasn't, but it's a really good idea. *Crack-crack-crack*. Miss. Miss. Miss. I drop my arms in annoyance.

"You have to *aim* it, Violetta." From behind, he picks up my arms. "Line up the target with the center pin."

"I'm going to learn this, then watch out on Friday."

"Inhale. Exhale and…"

He doesn't finish. I shoot. Miss. Breathe in. Breathe out. Shoot. Hit a lot of air. Scare a lot of birds.

"This is stupid," I say. "If someone's coming after me, I won't have time to hold it this way and breathe and aim or anything."

"Again, *Forzetta*."

"Fine." I double-grip, breathe, shoot, and the bottle spins a little as if the bullet grazed it.

"Better."

"If that was a person, they'd be dead," I say. "That has to be close enough."

"Is this how you studied in school? Close enough?"

"Nursing's easier than shooting."

He moves to the side to look at my profile. "You haven't even emptied your first magazine."

"Is that all I have to do?" Facing him, I hold the gun up to the target straight with one hand and squeeze the trigger. The bullet shatters the bottle into a million pieces. "Happy now?"

Santino laughs as if he doesn't have a problem in the world, then he holds my head the way he does, looking at me deeply and with appreciation. "Good girl."

"Now we can get my family." He doesn't nod or confirm. This should have set off alarm bells, but I am trusting, and in love, and a fool. "Like you promised."

He knows damn well what he said, but he regrets it. I can tell.

"I did not promise."

"If my zio got the Beretta out of the basement, he's not going to go without a fight. He's a stubborn old man and he's going to get hurt."

"He won't."

"Please," I plead. "Please don't send an armed gang for him."

"You're insisting."

"I am."

He slides the gun from my hand, reaches into his holster for a fresh magazine, and slides it into the handle. He releases the slide, then he drops the magazine again.

"You do it," he says, handing both to me.

I take the gun, then the ammunition, and snap it in exactly the way he did.

"Good girl. Put it away."

I tuck it into the holster and snap the flap.

"Wear it all the time," he says.

"Even when you're right next to me?"

"Yes." He kisses me tenderly. It's a short, sweet peck on the lips. "I have things to take care of. Be back here in five minutes."

"Okay."

He's about to walk off when he stops, turns, and holds my head still so he can devour me in a kiss so unexpectedly passionate, my heart melts from the heat of it, leaving me too boneless to match his fervor. Lost in a kiss that unfolds the minutes inside seconds, I don't question his neediness.

18

VIOLETTA

It takes me three and a half minutes to go to the bathroom and brush my teeth. Ten seconds to go down the stairs. I'm at the head of the driveway with a minute to spare.

Santino is not there.

Not a minute later. Not ten minutes later.

He's probably shouting orders at someone. I'll have to take him by the elbow and drag him away. The sooner we bring my Z's up here to safety, the sooner he can finish this war and we can work on getting pregnant again. I smirk at the thought.

But he's not in the garage getting the car out. The Alfa's still there, but the Mercedes is gone.

He must be waiting at the gate… Except he's not.

He's not in the kitchen, or the basement, or back in our room.

"Remo," I say when I see a familiar face. "Have you seen Santino?"

"Just now?" He runs his hand through his hair. "Yeah, he left with Armando."

"Left?"

"Like, out the gate. Down the hill. Ten, fifteen minutes ago."

I've been waiting for Santino to show up and take me to do this one little errand before a war burned down the city...and he was already gone. He left. Slipped away. Gave me a gun, taught me how to use it, and left me behind.

Of all the emotions I can choose from—disappointment, anger, worry—I decide on dumbstruck.

Maybe there's a clue to where he went in his office.

He's not there, but the room isn't empty either.

Dario sits behind his desk, which bothers me, but no one's telling him to fuck off. I'm not sure if that also bothers me or if I'm seeing the results of a well-thought-out plan.

"Where is he?" I demand.

"Not here."

"I didn't ask where he isn't."

"I answered you based on what you need to know. He's not here, and until he is, I'm taking care of shit."

"This is my family's house."

"Look," Dario says. "I know he's got you on a longer leash than what a guy would call standard, but all I'm telling you is he's gonna be back before dinner."

He thinks I'm just going to disappear. His dismissiveness is infuriating. Even at his worst, Santino didn't treat me like this. I put my hands on the desk and lean over.

"Did he go to get my zia and zio?"

He stands, putting his hands on his side of the desk.

"Are you going to be a problem?" he asks, but it's not really a question. It's an accusation.

And I'm guilty as charged. I'm going to be a fucking problem, but not until I know what's going on. Dario is a man who asks for neither forgiveness nor permission.

"Keep talking to me like I work for you, and yeah, I'm going to be a problem." I take my hands off the desk. "Or you can tell me, yes or no. Did he go for my family?"

He comes around and stands over me—too close, but I won't step back. I cross my arms as if that's enough of a barrier...which it's not. The man's heart was chainsawed from a block of ice, and the blood in his veins is cold enough to keep the organ frozen.

"Yes. He went to pick up people for you," Dario says. "And like I said, he's going to be back before the gravy's done. So maybe take your ass to the kitchen and give it a stir."

This is the only concession I'm going to get from this guy, so I turn and leave before I have to see him sitting behind my husband's desk another second.

S󠀠ANTINO AND ARMANDO aren't back in time for dinner. I join Celia and Loretta in the downstairs *cucina* to prepare it amidst the stink of the coal furnace. I'd hoped to have my zia with us by now.

"He'll be back before you know it," Celia says, chopping an onion. "He'll come in hungry and barking orders. I can feel it."

"I feel it too," Loretta adds, rummaging around the industrial refrigerator. "But most of the time, I had a feeling Elio wasn't coming back, and he did."

"What about the time he didn't?" I ask.

"Funny thing about that." She shrugs, closing the fridge door with an armful of cheese. "The future isn't written on feelings."

Celia grumbles, and Loretta pats her cheek and kisses it before dumping the cheese on the counter. Loretta is pissing in Celia's Cheerios, but she's right. Intuition predicts nothing about the world—but it can tell you who you are. Feelings are the weather vanes of the heart. Do these instinctual, predictive feelings force your attention to what you hope for? Or what you fear? Which of those winds blows strongest?

He'll be fine.

He'll come home victorious.

I try to feel it so strongly it becomes a future fact, but I can't. The opposite belief doesn't move the vane either. Inside me, the air is hopelessly still.

MY FATHER IS A GROCER. My mother works at the store. My sister goes to school. I am a child too young to understand what it means when someone asks me how old I am. I will say *quattro* until I'm told to say something different.

If the wind is blowing a certain way, the early morning rumble and whistle of the trains coming into and out of Napoli Centrale wakes me. In the bed next to mine, Rosetta sleeps like a stone right through it all. So I lie in bed and listen until either Mamma comes to wake me or the sun comes up and it's too bright to pretend.

Nonna put us to bed last night. Mamma and Papino were out. So I'm happy when my father's coughing wakes me. He just got back from the hospital a few days ago. He says his lungs aren't clear yet. I imagine them obscured by a veil of snot and green goop. After a loud, throaty growl from my father, I hear my parents whispering in their room.

Without the sound of the trains, I'm bored. Rosetta sleeps openmouthed, dead to the world, even when I poke her nose.

Dragging Raggedy Ann behind me, I pad barefoot across the hall, looking for company. Instead, there's something strange on the other side of my parents' open door. Not dangerous or scary but odd. There's a box on the floor. It's as tall as my toybox but not as long. It's dark, but the wood looks bitten and old. There are metal straps belted around it and all over the edges. Is it for me? My birthday isn't for a long time, but maybe I was so extra good I get a surprise present?

In her pajamas with her hair down, Mamma is sitting cross-legged on the floor in front of the box. The yellow hat she wore to their favorite restaurant—the one where they wheel the menu around on a school blackboard—is on the dresser. Papino's chair is opposite her. He's leaning over with his elbows on his knees, still wearing his day clothes and the shadow of a scratchy beard.

The way they look at each other is frightening and

awe-inspiring. I move behind the wall, watching them in the tiny space created by the door hinges.

"Did you ever wonder," Mamma says, "what it would be like if this thing didn't exist? Who you'd be?"

"I'd be myself." Dad shrugs.

"You'd be the same big piece, eh?"

"Yes. And you'd still be mine."

"Is that all I'd be? Do you ever wonder what I'd be? What I *could* be?"

He slides off his chair and kneels on the opposite side of the box from her, folding her hands into his. She pulls away her hands, but he grabs them back and kisses each.

"Do I not take care of you?"

She yanks her hands back as if he's insulted her. My father must see this as a challenge. He takes the box by the metal handles on each side and snaps his hands away.

"*Cristo santo.*" He shakes his hands and looks at where they touched the handles. "Did you have this by the stove?"

"Idiot," Mamma says, standing. "Send this monstrosity away. Send it so far away, we can't even see it if we want to. It's evil. Even having it here in the house, I can *feel* the horns."

"My brother will kill for it no matter where it is."

Daddy has two sisters in America. Zia Madeline and Zia Donna. They bring us Pop-Tarts and Fritos when they visit from the other side. But a brother? I never saw a brother. Maybe he's in America too?

I'm scared now. I don't want the box, even if it's a special present or it means I have a secret uncle.

"If he grows the stones to kill you…" She looks away with a face turned inward on itself—blank from reading the thoughts it's created as if they're new.

I'm sure I'm hidden, but she stops, frozen, and I realize that though I'm definitely behind the wall, Raggedy Ann isn't.

"Violetta." Her voice is stern and commanding. It's the tone she uses when she's about to get really mad. "Get in here."

I do as I'm told, trying to stay small and far away.

"I'm thirsty." This is the first lie I remember telling.

"Come," Papino says, holding out his arm for me.

I don't move.

"When your father says something," Mamma growls. She is so, so, so very mad.

I'm shaking in terror already, but I can't go to my father. He's right near the box, and the box is not a gift. The box is evil. The box has horns. I am overtired and convinced the box will get Mamma and Papino dead.

There's no way out.

I'm between the anvil and the hammer.

I start wailing, tears falling, breath hitching with sobs as I shake my head no, no, no, no…

THE EARLY MORNING rumble and whistle of the trains coming into and out of Napoli Centrale is not what wakes me. It's the silence. No birds. No bugs. No Santino breathing at my side. Again.

This will be the second day without him. The first

went by quietly. During the evening, we heard pops and cracks from the south. I went to the windows facing down into the city, but it's partially blocked by trees and shrubs.

"He's probably grating them into cheese," Remo says with a shrug of confidence in the king. He puts his hand on my shoulder and squeezes before taking it away. "Don't worry. He has this."

"A lighter isn't going to save him twice."

"Tough people are tough. Like you. I didn't think you'd end up here, but I ain't surprised you're good at it."

"I wasn't tough in school. I wasn't anything."

He scoffs. "Sure. You came right into the boys' gym class and told Mr. Hamlin if he ever called your sister fat again—"

"I'd show him what a pound of flesh looked like." I shrug. "That's not tough. That's choosing enemies carefully."

"And Dina Marchesi? On the basketball court?"

I touch the back of my head where repeated contact with the pavement left a scar. "She won that fight pretty easily."

So many of my brain cells got shattered on the pavement that the memory of the incident is made of the stars in my eyes and Dina's twisted face bordered by sky.

"But you kept coming back. She was two years older and bigger and a lot stupider, but you kept coming at her. That's tough."

"I don't even remember what we were fighting about."

"She said your father died like a Castellano wannabe."

"What does that even mean?"

"No clue." He shrugs. "Figured you did. Anyway. Hold tight. Dario's a big piece in New York. We're safe up here."

"Yeah."

Santino's probably doing the job he does best, and he needs to have faith that I'm holding down the fort while he does it.

I stay out of the way like I'm told, but I won't be able to for much longer.

After dinner, Celia washes the dishes while Loretta and I wipe down the tables.

"He's okay," Loretta says, apropos of nothing.

"This is a feeling you have? Or real information?"

"A feeling."

"I have the same wish."

She's done nothing wrong, but I can't stand the presence of her hopes. They're not real. I need facts, and it's taking all the energy I have not to jump out of my fucking skin.

An engine rumbles. It's not a hum but a high-pitched *reer* interrupted by *put-puts*. Not a truck or train. I can't see where it's coming from, so I go into the hall and climb the stairs to the cupola. The sky is orange on the west side and navy blue to the east.

I know why Santino didn't want me up here. I can see everything in all directions, but I can be seen the same way. With the right gun, I'm a target, and I don't care. I want to find the source of the noise.

"Mrs. DiLustro," Dario calls from the bottom of the cupola stairs.

Sure, I feel protected from outsiders, but not from him, even with the gun pressing against my armpit.

He appears from the stairway. I back up. Just then, in the corner of my eye, I see a single line of light coming up the twisting road, and the sight of it becomes one with the sound.

"It's a motorcycle," I say.

The road leads to one place. Here. Whoever's driving that bike, they're on their way to us. Nothing about the way it's moving is a sign that it is—or isn't—Santino.

"It's a moped," Dario corrects.

"Don't try to get me to go downstairs," I say, distracted by the light coming up the hill. I'm not afraid, and yet... I have a feeling so strong it's as good as fact.

"Good. You finally understand where you belong."

He disappears down the stairs.

"And don't tell me to stay either."

He probably didn't hear that last sentence, but it doesn't matter. I was reminding myself that I can do what I want, for any reason I want.

Santino tried to lock me away so many times and failed. He knows it's not possible or desirable. That isn't his order. My husband knows I can't stand to be sidelined, and at this point, I'm so strung out on constant panic that sitting in the cupola another five minutes would be like a life sentence.

I run downstairs and onto the lawn. Remo runs across the lawn with three other guys, all armed with rifles. I follow them to the gate where Dario waits. Bright security lights illuminate the area outside the gate, leaving those of us on the inside in darkness.

"No!" Dario shouts at me. When I pass him, he grabs my arm. His eyes blaze, lighting up the darkening night. "Inside."

"He'll kill you for touching me. And I'll let him."

"If you get hurt," he says over his shoulder, "he'll try to kill me anyway."

"I won't let him."

He scoffs as if he's met my husband. Which he has. But he hasn't met the Santino I know.

The dim beam of light points upward, cresting the last ridge, and comes straight for us. The man driving it is no more than a silhouette, but he's too big to be Santino. There doesn't seem to be anyone behind him. How much of a threat could he be?

He keens to the left. Rights himself before falling. Comes straight for a bit before swaying left again. This was the struggle to stay in a line on the way up.

Just before the moped enters the circle of light, Dario makes a sound with his tongue and throat. The men raise their rifles. I hold my breath.

The moped comes into the light and falls sideways, spilling the bloody driver onto the dirt.

It's Armando.

19

VIOLETTA

Dario holds me back. I twist against his grip. I punch him. I make threats I intend to keep. But he won't let me near Armando.

"Let me go!"

"He could be wired."

"He could be dying," I snap.

With Dario between the gate and me, he lets me push him off.

"What hap—?" Celia says from behind me, brought out by the commotion.

"Get the first aid kit and sheets." She's already halfway to the house when I shout the last command. "And alcohol. A lot of it."

Celia passes Loretta, who follows her to get the supplies. Dario gives up on me and climbs the ladder to the top of the stone guardhouse.

Armando's on his back just outside the gate. Vito crouches about six feet away from him while the other guys hang back.

"You sure, Mando?" Vito takes a bent step closer. "They didn't plant nothing on you?"

"Something." Armando's booming voice has been reduced to a breathy scratch, and there's something wrong with his speech.

"What kind of something?"

"It won't hurt you."

"Show it to us," Dario calls from above.

"No. It's…" He shakes his head and swallows with difficulty. "Only Violetta."

"They using you to get us to open the gate?" Vito asks.

"Just a message." He's talking as if he's weak and in pain, but even past that, he sounds as if he's talking with a new mouth.

"We ain't gonna let her near you. Not before you're checked. You know that."

"Then check me, *stunad*." Armando groans in pain. "Get to it."

Vito takes a deep breath and scurries to Armando, opening his jacket. "Oh, Jesus fuck."

Dario calls from atop a stone pillar, "Faster!"

"I'm sorry, man," Vito says, gingerly patting down Armando's body.

I've been daring to get closer, but now I'm at the gate, and the angle has changed enough to reveal what upset Vito. Armando's shirt is gone, and his torso is a mess of blood and tissue. His gut has been cut open.

Blood loss.

Shock.

Infection.

I know how to stabilize him, but I'm not a doctor. I'm not even a nurse.

Face covered in nervous sweat, Vito bolts up to standing position. "He's clear!"

The men jump down from the posts. The gate opens.

I rush through. "Armando!"

He kind of smiles. He's missing two teeth, which explains the sudden speech impediment. "Good to see you."

The men pull him up and bring him inside the gate. It closes. They're about to drop him, which means they'd have to pick him up again.

"No!" I shout, and they all freeze. "Inside. The dining room table."

They look at each other like a bunch of clowns.

"Do it," Dario barks, and they listen, making a disaster of the transport—but these are the men we have, so this is what it is.

Unencumbered, I run ahead into the dining room. The table has a candleholder in the center surrounded by shoeboxes of mismatched dishes and silverware. I throw off everything but the tablecloth.

"Here," I say, tossing aside the last box as Armando's brought in. They lay him down. "Hello, Armando, how are you doing?"

Gingerly, I check the damage. The space between his navel and his open waistband is meat. A bullet ripped him open from one side and exited the other. I'm overwhelmed. I don't know how to fix this.

"I have a message," he says. The effort sends a spring of blood upward.

"I found this." Celia drops a red bag with a big white cross onto the table, and I wake up. It's the super deluxe first responder kit, and I have never been so thankful for anything in my life.

"Sheets and towels." Loretta drops a pile onto a sideboard.

"What's the message?" I open the bag and dump it onto the card table. "Open all the gauze. Don't touch it. Rip the sheets into strips. Someone, get me the alcohol."

The guys do exactly as they're told.

"Listen." Armando coughs. "Violetta."

"You shouldn't talk."

"They got him."

The sounds of tearing fabric and shuffling feet get far away as I'm sucked into a sensory tunnel where nothing exists outside Armando and me.

"Who?" I'm not stupid. I know who, and I also know asking this man to say a single unnecessary word is cruel and dangerous...but I don't know how to believe it without his confirmation.

"He's alive, but..." In Armando's eyes, past the pain and fear, is an apology.

Why does he look like a man who's about to console me through his own excruciating pain?

No. Whatever it is, I don't want to know.

The tunnel widens and disappears. I'm in the dining room again.

"I have to get you stable first. Where's the fucking disinfectant?!"

Loretta puts a gallon of Smirnoff on the table. "It's what I found."

"Inside pocket," Armando says. "Jacket."

I unscrew the bottle and hold my hands out to Loretta. They're shaking. "Pour it."

She dumps a stream of vodka on my hands. I rub them together, ignoring Dario, who's rummaging through Armando's jacket pocket.

"They want the crown," Armando gasps. "Even my sweet Gia."

"What happened?" I ask.

"They ambushed us."

"Oh, fuck," Dario says when he takes out what's in the bottom of Armando's pocket.

"Gia... She'll trade his life for it." The wounded man doesn't have the blood flow to sob for his love, but the sadness and disappointment are unmistakable. "For the crown."

"Disinfect, Loretta," I continue to anyone who'll listen. "Where's the gauze?"

Remo has ripped open a blue paper envelope, and he's ready to dump the gauze inside into a dish, but he's stuck in place. I follow his gaze to Dario, who's holding a ziplock bag. The plastic is cloudy with condensation, as if something warm and wet was put inside before it was sent into the cold night.

No.

They didn't. Not for a dumb crown.

"I don't have it!" I yell. "They have it!"

"I'm sorry, Vuh-vuh..." Armando trails off as if he has no energy to continue.

"Don't you dare make those your last words," I bark.

Dario is opening the bag. Nothing I say will make him stop.

I grab a handful of gauze and staunch the bleeding. "Loretta. Hold this here. Someone disinfect Celia. The women are going to hold this man together, am I right, ladies?"

"You need to look at this," Dario says, looking into the open baggie.

"No, I don't. You." I jerk my chin at one of the guys. I'm face-blind with panic. He could be the pope for all I know. "Wash your hands and rip some sheets."

"You have to confirm this is his or not," Dario says.

Or not.

Whatever is in the bag could be a mistake or a trick, and if it is, I'll be able to tell.

Putting pressure on the bleeding, I lean forward. Dario tips the opening toward me. My eyes close because they have a mind of their own...but my curiosity is stronger. I look inside.

It's a finger.

It has a gold ring on the bottom.

"He's not breathing!" someone shouts.

I tear my gaze away and put my ear on Armando's chest. No heartbeat. "Does anyone besides me know CPR?" Celia steps forward. I drop the bag and get on a chair to start chest compressions. "Rescue breathing, okay?"

Celia tilts his head back, and we begin.

"Is it his or not?" Dario demands.

"How the fuck should I know?" I say between counts, then breathe into Armando's mouth.

"Come on, Mando," Celia says, her hands on his face. I never realized how big they are. "We ran out of the cherry biscotti. Please. You have to get more."

Dario holds the bag out to me while I'm trying to save a guy's fucking life.

"These fucking assholes want a crown they stole." I deny everything in the rhythm of the compressions. "They should check the goddamn cupboards instead of asking me, and you tell me if it's his finger and where the crown is because I *don't fucking know.*"

I know. I've had that finger inside me. I've sucked on it. I've watched how it moved with its brothers and sisters. How it made a fist. How it looked tucked in the web between my fingers.

But I don't really know, do I? This could all be a bluff.

"Come on, Mando." Celia's voice is getting hopeless. We're going to lose him.

"What's engraved inside the ring?" I ask.

If it's a bunch of numbers, it's Santino's. But there won't be. It'll be a date with words of tender eternal love. The finger belongs to one of the other guys, and that will be terrible.

"Nothing's happening," Celia says, looking into Armando's glazed eyes.

Dario isn't squeamish about taking the ring off a dead body part.

"Something has to be happening," I say without evidence. "Give it a chance."

Dario is looking inside the ring. I don't want to know. I don't.

"It says…"

"I'm counting!" I shout because I don't want him to finish.

"The bleeding stopped," Loretta says. "That's good."

"No. That's bad," I say.

I keep trying. I'm exhausted. My arms ache. I'm sweating myself into a raisin. But I can't stop. If Armando's dead, and that ring... I don't know if I'll survive if it comes all at once.

"Violetta," Vito says, putting his hand on my shoulder.

"Shush!"

"I think—"

"Did I ask you what you think?" I turn to Dario. "We have to get him to the hospital. St. Anne's isn't too far."

Everyone in the room seems to know it's too far over the bridge, even if I won't admit it. It's too far a distance, and too long ago. He should have been taken there when the moped was at the bottom of the mountain, but he bled and bled to get up it, and now he's gone.

Celia lets her hands slide off Armando's face and puts her forehead to his chin. She weeps. I get off the dining room chair and stand on weak knees.

Dario holds out his hand. The bloody gold ring is in the center. "Do you recognize this? Is it his?"

This cannot be avoided any longer. Closing my fist around the ring, I drop into the chair, close my eyes, and take a breath. I know what I'm going to see.

Goddamn, Armando. You were a good guy. I'm sorry.

"Santino is not your king," I say, eyes still as closed as the fist holding the ring. "He is mine. He is my country. He's my kingdom. He's the earth and the sun to me, and if they have him... If they're using my entire world as leverage to demand something I don't have, I consider it a personal insult." I open my eyes and look at each man individually. "If they have him, I am going to get him. You won't stop me." I linger on Dario's gaze. "I don't need a crown to kill you for trying. I hope you understand that."

"Please," Dario says, unimpressed with my threats. "Read the inside."

I open my hand. Blood streaks the shiny gold surface. Inside, where a loving couple would share a few words about eternity, the blood has flowed into the engraving and dried into the cut shape of a series of numbers.

I close my fist around it.

20

SANTINO

They cut the tape as a futile act of kindness, but I'm still stuck in a basement with no windows. It smells of mildew and old wine. They bricked in the last wall, leaving one space at the top to let in air—just in case they need me. I'll die of dehydration before suffocation.

On my back, looking at the crossbeams for the floor above, I watch the boards creak under the weight of Damiano's soldiers. If this room has a weak point, it's that old wood and the nails holding down the planks. I can pull apart the electrical conduit. Find something rigid and sharp, then break out of the ceiling into a room of guys who will hear the racket and shoot me before I move a single board.

And that's even if I can do it all with one working hand.

It hurt when they did it. It still hurts. The pain goes from my hand to my shoulder, then to my heart, where Violetta lives. My hand hurts because they took away part of it. My chest hurts because they sent it to her, so she'd worry enough to give them what she doesn't have.

If she's smart, she'll fashion a crown out of tinfoil and wrap it around a bomb.

If she's wise, she'll hole herself up and let Dario handle it.

If she's brave, she'll tell them to fuck off and they'll torture her mad before they believe she isn't hiding what slipped through their fingers.

My queen is smart and wise and brave.

Is there a more dangerous combination in a woman?

There is not.

BEFORE THEY BRICKED in the entrance, it was as wide as two doors. They have me in a chair on one side. Damiano stands on the other side. Behind him, Gia's on a green velvet chair. Its plastic covering has cigarette holes through it. I've had too long to digest these details. Between the hours of boredom and the split seconds between getting hit, I see everything.

Where is it? one of the Tabonas asks.

My head's spinning. Past the stars I keep seeing when I'm hit, the faces are no more distinctive than puddles of spilled coffee.

One of them might be Carlo. He killed Elio, my second cousin and a gifted mechanic, when he wouldn't work for them. Elio built from parts that looked like they came off the factory floor, and he loved Loretta.

Where is it?

They keep asking, and I keep answering.

Non lo so. I'm too disoriented to speak English. The entire language has packed up and left.

It bothers me that I don't know how much time has passed. We're in a windowless basement, and I haven't been fully conscious the whole time. When did I tell Violetta I'd be back? Yesterday? Tomorrow? Is she all right up there on the mountain?

Thank God she didn't come.

The whole thing was a setup. The people Violetta calls her Z's tried to warn me when we approached, but I was thick in the head, rushing to get this easy job done so I could move on to finding Damiano at the quarry. I was looking forward to breaking him, taking the crown, then moving on to a life with Violetta.

But my men were dead, replaced by Damiano's, waving me through the blockade without making eye contact, and closing ranks behind. We were locked into that street before we knew what was happening. Armando was shot, and I had a gun to my head.

I could fight, but I'd lose. That was a deal I was ready to accept.

"I want you to know," Damiano said, "I don't need you. I'm happy to kill you. And this time, I'm not going to marry Violetta before I fuck her."

That was how I got here. Surrender. Hands up. Let me live for the chance to protect my wife. They taped my ankles and wrists together. Threw me down a flight of stairs. But I had hope I could protect her.

This time, by turning my back on her, I've done the right thing. She is safe behind a gate for a little longer.

"You've done so much for me," Gia's voice says on the opposite side of consciousness. "So can you wake up, please? So I can do something for you?"

She's shaking me and spraying my face with water from an old Windex bottle. I cough, snorting soap.

"Okay, good. Hi!" She sits cross-legged on the concrete. "You okay? Your face looks kind of messed up. I mean, maybe it's not so bad under the blood?"

"I'm fine."

"Cool, okay, so listen. You need to tell Dami where the crown is before he goes up there to get it. Because if he has to—"

"I told you. I don't know."

"Well, it wasn't at the lawyer's. Not in the vault or any of the safes they had. And let me tell you, we looked."

"Did anyone sign it out?"

She clears her throat, inspecting her fingernails, then shrugs like a teen. "That book got burned up."

"*Cristo Santo*. Gia. Listen to me. You can't be this stupid."

"I am not stupid!"

"Good," I say. "Because the stupid ones get themselves killed."

"I don't want them to hurt you anymore, Santi. I am so sad. I miss Tavie. I miss how we were. How you took care of me always like a big brother. I don't like this, and I don't know what to do. Please. I'm begging you. Before he hurts her."

"Then I'll kill him the way I killed your father."

She shrieks, and the high-pitched wail goes on for hours.

"*Dov'è?*" a man's voice asks a thousand years later, before another punch lands on my jaw.

I don't even try to guess his name. Everything is mixed up. Time is optional. This is a blessing. I don't know how long Violetta's been without me, worrying. I don't know if she's been able to do something brave that's going to get her killed.

"*Ce l'avete voi.*" I tell them they have the crown, but that doesn't make it true. My brain is scrambling time. Obviously, they don't have it, or they wouldn't ask.

"If I had it," Damiano's voice breaks through the haze, "you'd be dead."

A chill shocks my skin and settles in my bones. I'm drenched in winter cold. My clothes and hair are soaked through. Carlo Tabona stands over me with an empty bucket. An ice cube rocks on the bottom corner, and his face—the black moustache and low forehead under a deep widow's peak—snarls down at me.

"Welcome back to America," I say to him. "I still have to kill you for Elio."

He slaps me across the face because I'm duct taped to a fucking chair, and I can't do anything about it.

"That's for chasing me all the way to the other side," he says, then hits the other cheek so hard I see stars. "And that's for the money."

Goffredo Tabona paid for his nephew's life in cash. But really, once Carlo was in Napoli, he was out of my territory. The money came with a promise the kid would never return.

"You know what I had to do to pay it back?" Carlo asks.

"Get fucked in the ass by all your dead bastard ancestors?"

He's about to hit me again, but Damiano stops him.

Carlo tosses the bucket on a tool bench and throws himself onto a mustard couch so old, the first woman to get pregnant on it is probably a grandmother by now. An ice cube settles into the space between my waistband and my spine.

Dami straddles a metal folding chair, forearms resting on the back, thick hands drooping in front. The white part of his wounded eye is blood-filled in one corner.

"Gia's getting bored," he says. He grips the chair back and taps Emilio's crown ring on the metal. That's the fist that hit my wife. The one that changed her forever.

"Am not," she objects. "I think we should just go up there."

"Same thing."

"That's not the same. He killed Papà!"

"There are fifty guys up there!" Damiano yells at her. "You wanna die? You go up first. Wag your ass at them. See where it gets you." She gives him the finger, and he turns back to me. "Look, you're a dead man either way. But if you tell your wife to give it up, we let her live."

In this weakened state, it's easy for a man to lose his shit. Easier when the love of his life is threatened. That's what he wants, but even if I could be manipulated like this, I don't have the fucking crown.

"Dami, use your head. You don't have it. I don't have it. Who has it?"

"You really are tough to crack, you know that?"

"We need to find them," I say.

"We?"

"You can't do it yourself, and you know it."

For a moment, I think he believes me. Either that I don't have it, or that he can't find the third party without my help.

"Nah, nah." He stands. "You think I'm a *stunad*." He leans into my face. "I'm going to give Violetta one chance to give it up."

"She doesn't have it."

"If we're convincing enough, she'll have it."

What are they going to do to her? Everything Damiano promised on the phone, or—with me out of the way—will it be worse?

"You can't make it appear from a wish."

"Wish for what? A crown I know your wife has?" Damiano leans down to look me in the eye. "It should have been mine anyway. My father is the older brother."

Cosimo is the older brother to whom? And why would that matter?

"*Come?*" I ask. My voice sounds like worn sandpaper.

"Half brother. But still." My expression sends a smile spreading across Damiano's face, and he chuckles. "You didn't know? For fuck's sake, Santi. Did you even know about him and…?" He makes a side-to-side motion with his hand, then—when it's obvious I don't know what he's talking about—waves away the rest of the sentence. "Never mind. That nugget belongs to your little missus."

He pats my chest before standing, then stops himself. He reaches into my breast pocket and takes out my cigarettes and bent lighter.

"This is what saved you," he says, inspecting the lighter.

"God saved me."

"Sure, Santi. God gives a shit." He takes out a cigarette and puts it between my lips. The bent Zippo is too hard to open. He throws it on the cushions of the mustard couch and snaps his fingers at Carlo. "Give me yours."

Carlo takes a tiny red Bic lighter and a pen from his pocket.

"Let me see that pen too," Damiano says. Carlo hands them over, and his boss turns back to me. "I don't want you to think I feel good about any of this."

"I don't care how you feel," I say, cigarette bobbing as I talk. "But you're going to be disappointed. Then you're going to need me, and if she's hurt…"

"Yeah, I know. You're going to blah blah."

He lights my cigarette, and I suck on the filter. I don't want the kindness, but for the sake of a deal, I need to accept it.

"You still think I'll come crawling back? Be like," Damiano continues in a falsetto, "'Oh, Santi, please help me find it!' so you can tell me to fuck myself?"

"I will help you hunt down whoever has it."

"You'll never help me. Your face looks like you been bobbing for sausages in the Sunday gravy."

"Part of the job."

"Glad you understand," he says, fanning the pen between two fingers. "Anyway. As a show of good faith, since we got a pen right here, you want to leave Violetta a message or something? Tell her to open the gate? It's taking candy from a baby either way, but if she don't fight, we'll let her live."

There's no chance I'll tell my wife to submit to this man, and there's no world in which she wouldn't fight.

I know what I'm going to write, but I don't know where.

Damiano jerks his head to Carlo, who gets a pair of hedge clippers from the wall.

21

VIOLETTA

The room is filled with silent people.

Armando is dead on the dining room table.

They have Santino.

Well. Not all of him.

His ring is in my fist, and Dario is still holding the baggie with a piece of his body in it. This is offensive.

Santino is mine. All of him.

I reach over the table and snatch the bag away.

I've spent months pissed off, but I don't know how to be *this* angry. There has to be some kind of talent to containing and releasing it. Or a skill to separating it from sadness and grief, like coffee or nicotine passing through a filter—a massive centrifuge for fire and electricity. My pores are too small to fit all the rage through. It's too big for my body. If it would fit through my mouth, I'd scream.

Wait.

I am screaming.

Everyone looks scared.

Good. They should be. Because this monster in my chest isn't made of love and light.

Loretta isn't frightened. She's in front of me, her hands on my cheeks the way Santino does, saying something I can't hear over my own voice.

She hugs me, and I run out of breath. I appreciate her embrace, but I'm too empty to cry. My fist with a ring and the hand with the baggie are folded between us, and I let Loretta hold me as long as she wants—not for me, but for her. When she lets me go, I feel the hard ball of knuckle in the bag, and for a split second, I'm reminded of Zio eating pig's feet. Rosetta and I watching as he dragged his front teeth along the balls of the joints.

The memory is wonderful, but the smile doesn't find my mouth in the tangled route from my heart. Even so, I have to make sure the baggie contains a finger, not lunch. I open it and find a human finger, as promised—bloodless, grayish, with the skin shrinking away and the carpal bone poking out like a branch from the gristle of flexor tendon. Between the proximal and distal joints are lines in blue ink that make two words.

LOVE RULES

"Love rules without rules," I say to my husband as if he can hear me.

He can't. But I hear him, loud and clear.

The feeling of being stretched by an expanding force inside me—of molecules banging against containment—goes away. The anger is still volatile and hot. It doesn't shrink or lessen.

I am not soothed, but I am big enough to hold an exploding star.

"We need to finish this," Dario says. "Tonight."

"How?" I ask, still clutching the bag.

"Don't worry about it," he says dismissively. "You. Gennaro, is it? Let's see what kind of ammo we have. We're going to shoot through this problem and burn everything else. You, what's your name?"

Carmine stammers an answer.

"Locations for every family member, friend, and mistress he's ever had," Dario says.

This man…this stranger, is going to descend on Secondo Vasto like a blanket of fire. There will be mass killing. Maybe we'll find Santino, and maybe we won't.

This is the war Santino was trying to avoid.

We're in it.

Everyone knows it. Loretta, Celia, Vito, Gennaro, all know as they stand in silence, waiting to be told what to do.

If I want control of this situation, I have to take it before Dario does. I have to earn it, and that won't happen as long as I'm sitting here clutching a body part.

I speak up. "I asked you—"

"Ma'am," Dario interrupts, "with all due respect, this has to be fixed before the sun comes up, or it'll go on for a week…and we're not fighting with glue guns and knitting needles."

By rights and experience, Dario should be in

charge, but this fight isn't his. I own this war, and it will be won or lost because of me.

"With all due respect," I say, standing, "this house and the town it protects are mine. The king you're pledged to is mine. The crown they think they're coming for…it's mine."

"The kitchen is that way. Or we can lock you in the basement *cucina* until you cool down."

"That's the only good idea you've had."

We stare at each other over Armando's body. I don't know what Dario's thinking, but I use the time to inventory who's in the room, how physically strong they are, and the depth of their roots in Secondo Vasto.

"Vito," I say, keeping eye contact with Dario. "Gennaro. Would you please escort Mr. Lucari to the basement?"

"I don't want to make this painful for you, Mrs. DiLustro," Dario says. "But I will."

"Sure." I break eye contact and jerk my head toward Vito. "Take the gun and the phone before you lock him down there."

I try to sound commanding, but I hear a voice that sounds small and feminine. I'm sure Vito won't listen to me, and I'm going to end up in the basement, screaming while a war is waged over my husband's death.

Whatever weakness I hear in my voice must be inaudible to Gennaro because he reacts first, coming at Dario from behind and pulling his elbows together. Vito's right after, reaching into Dario's jacket for the gun. Dario fights for a moment, but when Carmine makes three—removing the small pistol from his ankle holster—and Vito bends him over Armando's dead body, he calms down. There's no use fighting this many.

"This is a mistake," Dario says to me.

"Probably. But it's mine to make."

Dario's hauled to the basement and locked behind the door.

The basement has food for an army and a bathroom, but he won't be kept there for long. Now this really has to be done quickly.

BEHIND THE ROW of buildings on the opposite side of the lawn, between the bricks and the rock face, is a few feet of dirt. My shoulders touch wall on one side and mountain on the other, but I just about fit. When I kneel, my hips wedge me in tighter.

Good. This is what I want. A space just for us.

I turn so I can reach my pockets, getting out a gardening trowel. I dig. The hole is narrow and eight inches deep before I can go no farther. I take out the baggie with the zip that won't lock.

LOVE RULES

I don't know how the message wound up between Santino's knuckles. Did he write it, knowing they'd cut it off and send it to me? Or did Gia and Damiano write it there? They're definitely Santino's words.

Love rules without rules.

He's telling me to do whatever I need to do to win, and he will do the same.

There are no rules for us.

I smile. Silly man.

After all he's seen from me, he still thinks I need his permission.

A DOZEN MEN stand around the perimeter of the office. Gennaro and Carmine sit in front of me. I don't know what I'm doing, but I sit behind Santino's desk anyway. It's too big. The chair is too high. I look like a child playacting in her father's office.

I'm prepared for this. I have to use both my power and vulnerability to everyone's advantage.

"I know it's upsetting that Armando's dead. I know it pisses you off to get our king's finger detached from the rest of him. I want to go down there and burn it all down too. But you know why we can't do that."

The men look to me for a plan—but only so they can dismiss it. In the end, at least part of it has to be their idea.

"We don't know where they are. Descending on the city not knowing where to look leaves this compound exposed. It leaves us spread out all over to get picked off." Looking from man to man, I take the temperature of the room. Lukewarm.

"Yeah," Vito says with a nod. "She's right."

His approval warms the room a few degrees.

"They know where we are," I say. "Obviously. And they expect us to come for them. They're waiting for it."

"There's no one at the bottom of the mountain," a man says, stepping into the room. "If you don't mind me saying." He's so cartoonishly deferential, I barely recognize him. It's Fat Lip. The guy I punched the first day of my marriage. "We got cameras on some of the trees, and there's nobody hanging around waiting. At least not there. Could be anywhere else, I guess."

"Good," I say. "Are there cameras all the way up?"

"No. Just where the road goes private. That's how we knew Mando was coming, but we couldn't tell it was him."

"Thank you. Anything else I need to know?"

The negative answer comes in murmurs and gestures. They're not convinced I should be followed, and the benefit of their doubts won't last long. Everyone in this room has been trained from birth to dismiss women, including me. I have to come at this obliquely. Don't tell them what *I want*. Tell them what *we need*.

"They don't want to come up here. If you're uncertain about that, just look at how hard they're trying to draw us out. We're near the top of a mountain. There's one narrow road up to a fortress. Blind turns. A dozen places we can shoot them from. So first, someone's gotta be in the cupola twenty-four hours a day, watching. Yes?" I take their temperature again. No one's abandoned ship yet, but once someone does, they all could follow. "Second, all guns out, loaded, and lining the ridge overlooking the road up." The last thing to do after flexing my muscle is to let them know I'm not trying to be a man. "Celia, Loretta, and I will keep the home fires burning until they come or we figure out where he is."

Laying hard on the last possibility—that we have to

find out where Santino is—seems to go unnoticed. Doubts creep in like spiders under the door. I've left too much to their discretion. I don't have the knowledge I need to give them more detailed instructions. And yet—they haven't come up with enough of it themselves.

I am not Santino. I can't lay out the whole thing. They need to feel as though they're not taking orders from a woman.

"Yeah, but..." The man who breaks the tension is tall and gangly—middle-aged and set in his ways. "I don't like waiting. It doesn't feel right."

Vito turns in his chair. "I don't remember her asking you to have *feelings*, Benny." He says *feelings* as if it's a rotten lemon on his tongue.

Benny whips his hand in a gesture that means both "fuck off" and "never mind."

"Do we have a problem?" I ask. "Please. Write it down so I can share it with Re Santino when he gets back."

"He could be getting chopped into pieces right now, is all," Benny protests. "And we're sitting up here like pussies."

He's driven by loyalty. I appreciate that, but we can't fall into disarray over it.

"You're right," I say. "But how can we do something without risking our position?"

He makes a constellation of gestures—a shrug, another wrist flip, a glance around the room, and a bigger shrug.

"I tell you what," Benny says. "Someone goes down. Maybe me and one other guy... We go before dawn, down into the city. Talk to people. Find out where he is. If we know that, the wait is over. We go get him."

They all look at me.

"I like it," I say as if it wasn't the last part of the plan to begin with. "Good idea."

I CAN'T SLEEP THINKING about Santino.

What is he going through?

Am I actually lying here in our bed while it's happening?

Am I taking a shift in the cupola for four hours, scanning the city, wondering if I'm looking right at him?

Is he in pain while we clear the furniture? Cook the meals? Watch the sun crawl across our slit of sky?

Does he know we're looking for him?

Or—with every hour that passes—am I getting him killed?

22

SANTINO

The concrete floor is like a hammer to the back of my head, but I don't sit up.

The remaining fingers on my left hand ache with the loss of their brother. The pain that shoots all the way to my shoulder is like nothing I've ever felt before. Putting pressure on my skeleton to get myself up is as distant a possibility as tearing down this wall with my bare hands and running to Violetta at a hundred kilometers an hour. But not only am I horizontal, they used quick-hardening mortar between the bricks. And I can't run that fast. I can't do anything.

So there's me, and pain, and darkness, and regret.

A lot of regret, in all flavors and colors. Regret for leaving my mother behind where I saw her last, sleeping on the side of a volcano. For treating Violetta like a doll. For withholding information because I was ashamed. For being given away in marriage. For not taking Violetta sooner. For not taking her later. For the baby we lost and the children we'll never have.

I regret things I've done and things I've avoided. I promise not to do things anymore and to do everything, all of it—without defining what it is—if I can just see her again. I promise God nine more fingers for Violetta's life and offer the whole hand to spend it with her.

There are noises. Creaking floors. Muffled speech. A kind of harmless cracking, clapping, and slamming one hears in life. I don't realize my eyes are open for a long time.

There's some kind of nightlight in the adjacent room. It casts a dim glow through the little hole at the top of the wall. As much as my eyes adjust, it's not enough to see by without giving it full attention.

Deep breath.

Every sin of neglect and harm has been catalogued. Every sacrifice offered. There's nothing else to do but wait for heaven's reply. I have the attention to spend on what I'm seeing and hearing.

I've wet my beak on construction money enough times to know the difference between a property's value and the assessment, but not enough to know what the net of pipes and conduit just below the ceiling are for.

Dim light bursts in through the brick-sized space above. After the scrape of a chair, there's a click and a rattle from above me.

"Santino," a woman whispers from the other side of the wall. It's not Violetta.

If she was on the other side of the wall, it would melt with shame for being the only thing standing between us. But it's one of many things, and I don't know how to tear down the first. I have never felt so helpless and ashamed.

"Santino," she says again, closer. Gia isn't tall enough to see into the hole, but standing on a chair, she can just about put two bottles on the ledge. Looks like aspirin. I need more than that. "I got you…" She stops, huffing with strain as she puts a bottle of water sideways, so the cap looks like a diver peeking over the board. "Water." I hear her dropping back onto the floor. "Are you there?"

"Yes." My head hurts from lying faceup on the concrete. Maybe it's thirst.

"I understand why you did what you did to Papà."

I let that hang in the air without telling her I don't need her to understand, because I'll kill her too, and none of it will matter any more.

"Is it bleeding still?" she asks.

When I lift my hand over my face, the shoulder bones feel as if they're grinding together. "No."

"I found some disinfectant," she says. "And I left you a surprise."

Above me, the floorboards creak and the pipes hiss. The shaking silver tube spanning the ceiling is the diameter of a can of tomatoes. They've all been making a symphony for what seems like hours.

"Where are we?" I ask, getting my arms under me. My skull is made of lead and my brain is made of screams.

"Damiano told me not to say."

"Who does he think I'll tell?" I have to put my hand on the wall when I stand, or I'll spin right back to the floor.

Mafia Queen

"I don't know. He doesn't tell me anything anymore. It's like…" She doesn't finish.

"It's like he doesn't need you anymore."

I reach for the water and pill bottle. I put the label in front of the basement light to read. Advil. Medicine for women's problems. Fine. Beggars can't be choosers. If it's good enough for Violetta, it's probably too good for me.

After popping the cap, I shake some into my hand. One falls in the new space between my pinkie and middle finger. Three are left. I swallow them.

"If I ask you a hard question, can you answer honestly? Even if you think you'll hurt my feelings?"

"I will not protect your feelings, Gia."

The other bottle is white plastic with a pump top. The name of what's inside has worn off. When I spray into the air, I smell the bite of hydrogen peroxide. Disinfecting the wound is pointless. I'll be dead before infection has a chance to set in, but I hold the sprayer over the space where my finger was and douse it.

"Was I a good waitress?" she asks.

"*Cosa?*" The sting hits my open wound and burrows up my nose, clearing my sinuses. I drop the bottle.

"It's that…when I was little, you said you'd always protect me. And you did. You always took care of me… Ciro Sirigu. Remember?"

Of course I do. Gia and Ciro were in school together. They both got a math problem wrong in the exact same way. The teacher—a middle-aged woman who needed her pussy licked more than any woman I've ever met—called them in. Gia denied cheating. Ciro fluctuated between blame and paranoia. The teacher blamed Gia for copying Ciro, and—at the same time—giving him the incorrect answer.

Marco had dragged Gia out by the hair. I asked Emilio to step in before Gia went bald. Like a king, he strode into the school and demanded they both retake the test. My adopted sister got the same problem type wrong again, proving she was lousy at math, and Ciro got it right, proving he was a cheater.

"The customers liked you," I say before draining the last of the water.

"I always wondered if you regretted letting me work at Mille Luce."

"No." The hissing of the pipes above stops, so my denial sounds like a shout.

"Because I liked it. I really did. And I was extra careful with adding up the checks. I thought this morning, 'I'm late for work,' but then I realized…"

"You may not have your job back."

"I figured. Dami's been talking about burning it down, but I don't know if he got to it yet."

I should be sad or something, but I don't care about the café. I don't care about my house—he can put burning that down on his to-do list. I don't even care about having my finger cut off.

A part of my body was used to hurt Violetta. That's what I care about.

"You missed these," she says.

From the brick-sized hole at the top of the wall, a pack of Marlboros and a small, red Bic lighter drop to the floor.

Smoking will make the headache worse, but I light

one anyway. The nicotine clears my head despite the way the smoke puts a knife in my skull.

"Where is she?" I ask. "My wife. What's happening with her?"

"She's up at Torre Cavallo, I guess? I overheard Dami saying he's waiting for all the guys to come down to find you, or he'll go up."

That won't go well. Altieri Cavallo put his mistress there for a reason.

The ceiling rattles rhythmically. The smell of dry, hot air fights the cigarette smoke.

"Santi?" Gia says. "Can you tell her to come down with it? The crown? You could write a note or something. She'd listen to you."

There's no use saying we don't have the crown. None of them believe it.

"I'm not in charge anymore." I flick the lighter, watching it spark. The flame doesn't add much light.

"What if I talked to Damiano? Maybe I could convince him to free you? Take this wall down so you can reason with her and all this could be over?"

It's tempting to encourage her just for the chance to get out of this little room, but she can't deliver on the promise. Damiano will attack Violetta before letting me out to convince her to give up a crown she doesn't have. Gia may as well be suggesting Santa Claus can come through a silver vent the width of a tomato can, drop a hammer and chisel wrapped in a bow right in front of me, and ho-ho-ho his way back up to the fucking reindeer.

That same silver vent has a tiny slit in it, opening and closing like a mouth that doesn't know what to say.

The hot, dry smell is coming through there. Poor Santa would be cooked like a Christmas turkey.

"She has her own mind, Gia. Just like you."

When I bend over to right the folding chair, my headache doesn't protest. When I stand on the chair, the pain stays a dull throb. The Advil must be stronger than I ever gave it credit for.

"Tavie's not answering his texts," Gia says.

Damiano really isn't telling her anything at all.

I touch one of the hissing pipes. It's warm and vibrating as if something's flowing through it. Water. "He's dead, Gia."

"No!"

"He was shot by one of your guys."

"They're not mine!" she protests loudly.

I don't mind. On the other side of this wall, I would have imposed the correct version of the situation on her. But here, on the dark side of the wall, her delusions are her problem.

"If you say so." I move the chair to reach another pipe. "He's still dead."

"Oh, my God, no…" She breaks down into sobs.

The second pipe is cool and still. If the rhythmic rattle of the floorboard is a washer spinning, then Santa's silver vent hose is for dryer steam. There's a way out.

All I have to do is be stronger than any man before me.

23

VIOLETTA

If I'm up in the cupola for meals, I take them as I watch the men at the gate and the town below. I crane my neck toward the line of rock above and downward to the edges of the lawn. I don't look for his face or his body, but a sense of him, somewhere in the world with me. A direction. An arrow pointing to the center of the universe.

The stairs creak. Someone's coming up.

"How's Dario?" I ask, recognizing the pace and weight of the footsteps.

"Polite," Loretta says.

"Should we let him up?"

She stands next to me and looks over the city, watching the streetlights go on. At the front gate, the floodlights drown the top of the road in blazing light.

"He's like a rattlesnake," she says. "He's courteous. He'll rattle his tail to let you know he's going to strike, but you'll die just the same."

"We can't keep him down there much longer."

"Probably not."

"By tomorrow"—I turn away from the valley to look at her—"we're going to need to make him into a friend or shoot him."

"Well," she says with a shrug. A flash of light—fast as a blink—lights her cheek then disappears. "You can't shake hands with a snake, so—"

We're interrupted by a pop in the distance, then nothing. The sky is still glowing orange as a pillar of black smoke rises over the horizon, blooming into a gray mushroom cap at the top.

"The bridge," I gasp. "They hit the bridge."

I run downstairs and out the back door, to the lawn where men run and shout, where the smell hits like a wall made of tar and asphalt and grit, following the flow of traffic to the gate.

A cry goes up from the station atop the guardhouse. I climb the ladder in the back of the structure, scrabbling to the top before anyone can tell me not to. Gennaro is up there already with a pair of binoculars.

The bridge is burning. The dots of flame peek out from the smoke then disappear.

We're trapped.

All of us. Not just those of us on Torre Cavallo, but Secondo Vasto. My church, my school, the pork store, and the playground. They'll starve us all until they have what they want.

I wish I had the crown. I'd shove it up Damiano Orolio's ass.

But that's not what Gennaro is looking at through his binoculars. I follow his sights to a car coming up the hill. It's shiny, black, expensive. Not quite a limousine.

"What is that?"

Gennaro snaps around, not expecting me to be standing next to him. He hands me his binoculars without questioning why I'm here.

I put them to my eyes. The Lincoln Continental has its headlights blazing as if it's on the way to a funeral. The windows are tinted so dark they're opaque, and I wonder, and hope, and pray that Santino is in that car, coming up the mountain in victory.

Then another *pop* comes from the bridge. An explosion. More fire.

"Violetta!" Carmine says from the ground. "Get down! You're going to get killed!"

They won't kill me. Not as long as they think I have the crown.

I take out the gun Santino gave me, holding it ready at my shoulder the way he taught me, and watch the black car make its way to us.

"We should get Dario," Carmine says.

"Get Dario," I reply, "and I'll shoot you myself."

He glances at the car, then back to me. The only reason he's not running to free Dario from the basement is the possibility that Santino is in that car. If that's the case, I'll say "fuck the ladder" and float down to him like a leaf in the toxin-scented breeze—but it's not. If my husband was coming toward me, I'd know it.

They're all looking at me. I can read their minds. They're wondering what this looks like if Santino's in that car. What will it look like to have his wife so exposed? What are the consequences of not taking her down and putting her away like a china doll? What will the king do if his wife is touched? And what won't he do if she's hurt?

They're asking the wrong questions. They need to ask themselves what I'll do if they don't get behind me.

"Vito, behind them." I make a half-circle with my hand.

He returns a quick salute, gathering four men into the brush on either side of the road.

When the car crests the last rise, I point my gun at it. It's a command. A call to action. I'm telling the men to take their eyes off the threat to themselves and direct their attention to the threat we all face.

There's still an indent in the dirt where Armando fell off his moped. This is exactly where the car stops. It clicks into park. The engine shuts. Carmine's men come from the brush and line up behind it.

Gennaro succumbs to his panic and yanks me back. I elbow him off me and glare. "Do not."

He holds his hands up in surrender, apologizing, but I have no time. No one does. Everyone holds their gun at the ready as the driver's door opens. A blond man with thinning hair and a doughy build gets out with his hands up. He's wearing bright white gloves in the August heat, but not a jacket to hide a holster.

"*Occhio, che arriva il Blocco!*" he shouts, announcing the arrival.

The Lock? What does that mean? Another dead man? Is it Santino this time? Or just another part of his body?

If it's a single royal toenail, I'm killing the messenger and putting his head on a pole.

"Nazario Corragio," Gennaro mutters with relief. "He's one of us."

"He needs to be disarmed," I say without raising my voice, yet I'm heard.

Men come to push the driver against the car. They take his gun and rifle through his pockets, then back off. He stands and looks up at me, indicating the back door as if asking if he can open it.

"*Vai!*" I shout, telling them to get the hell on with it. "*Sbrigati!*"

The driver opens the back door. From my angle, I can only see his back as he takes a cane, and the stretch of his shirt across his shoulders as he strains to hoist the passenger to his feet. Then he moves enough to reveal an old man in a suit it's too warm for. He gives the man the cane and reaches into the back seat again.

It could be a submachine gun. A bomb. A body. And all I can do is lower the gun from my shoulder and aim it at the end of my extended arms. I suck at this. If I have to shoot them, I have a better chance of hitting them if I aim at the sky. I can't hit a soda bottle, and I'm just a girl who wanted to spend her summer on the beach.

I've never been so terrified in my life.

From the back, the driver lifts a box the size of a six-pack cooler.

Could be a bomb.

Could be a body part.

Could be a trick to get us all killed.

Turning around, I see Celia and Loretta holding hands on the dining room patio, hanging back as if negotiating a battle between fear and curiosity.

No one's going to die for me today.

I rush down the ladder and reach the bottom, behind the locked gate, just as the strangers approach the place where the gate opens.

"Get back," I hiss to the men who encroach out of a sense of propriety over my safety.

The old man is stooped and slow, bent at the waist in a summer hat and a suit cut for bad posture. His metal-tipped cane is unsure on the ragged ground. The driver does not rush the old man, but walks reverently beside him, holding the box by a handle on either side. No one is rushing them. Especially not me. I don't want to see what's in that box.

They stop at the gate, a few feet away, separated by wrought-iron bars spaced far enough apart to get an arm or a bullet through.

"Speak," I bark with a confidence I don't feel. "Before I let them shoot you."

The driver answers in a boom. "We've come for the daughter of Camilla Cavallo."

I'm the wife of Santino DiLustro and the sister of Rosetta Moretti. But I am also my mother's daughter, and I don't know why that's important.

Il Blocco's face is blotted with a patchwork of brown age spots, and the long, gray hairs of his eyebrows cover dark indents where the floodlights cover his eyes in shadow. His bottom lip sags, but one edge of his mouth turns up in a smirk.

"I am Nazario Coraggio." He speaks Italian. "I was your mother's consigliere."

Mamma? She worked the register at my father's grocery store. She was a wife and a mother. A daughter to my bossy and controlling *Nonna*. She loved my father, who probably had a consigliere—long ago, when this man was just beginning to be old.

He must have advised my father, and now his brain is addled with age. The secrets he's kept all these years are breaking his brain. He may be powerful or rich, but he is also elderly and confused.

"You're mistaken," I say. "My mother didn't need a consigliere's advice."

"Probably not," he says, rocking his cane back and forth. "But she got it anyway."

Carmine and his men approach the consigliere from behind, ready to turn this violent with half a word from me. I should have them grab these two before *Il Blocco*'s dementia gets someone killed.

Except this old man isn't confused.

He hasn't been confused a day in his life.

I take a step back and issue a command.

"Open the gate."

24

VIOLETTA

My mother's name.

It echoes as the gate creaks open.

It's a pretty lemon sour on the tongue. Ice water hitting a sensitive tooth on a hot day. The itch of a healing wound. It's unbearable, and I don't know why.

Turning, I pace to the house and stop in the kitchen. I don't know why I stop here because everyone's going to follow. The men who are doing what I ask of them, and the two invaders at the gate. I should go upstairs to Santino's office. Whatever is in that box should be opened in the place of power, where the tributes to the throne are made.

Celia rushes in. "They're coming."

"Make coffee."

She grabs the pot and turns on the water.

They're coming through the dining room. Box and cane. I should go up to Santino's office now, but his throne is too big for me.

"In here," I say.

The cane clicks on the marble floor five times before the visitors stand on the other side of the kitchen island.

"Bring a chair," I say, eyes on the old man.

"No," he says, inspecting me in the light for the first time. "I stand for Camilla's daughter."

The driver puts the box on the counter. His gloves are still on. They have a silvery shine in this light and an unexpected thickness. Utilitarian. Not fussy. The top of the box is a mosaic of tiny tiles arranged into a mermaid, framed with vines and seashells.

When I turn back to the consigliere, he's still looking at me carefully.

"I know," I say. "I look like my father."

He *tsks* the same way Santino does when he wants to dismiss something.

"You are a Cavallo." He regards me coldly, with an unveiled interest, which is enough to make me uncomfortable. But more than that, there's something deeply unnerving about how he's speaking to me.

"What do you want?" I ask. "We're a little busy having a war here."

Nazario laughs, but it sounds more like a series of heavy breaths accompanied by bouncing shoulders. "You are like your mother."

Am I? In what way? My words? My voice? My carriage? There are moments when I feel as if I never knew her, and this is one of them.

"This a family reunion?" a man says from behind me.

It's Dario. Fuck. Someone let him out—probably

Carmine—and I can't scream about it, or I'll look like a loser to everyone lining the room.

"Don't rush me, Mr. Lucari," the old man says. "Half of New York wants you dead. The other half thinks you're already in your grave. I can tell one where you are or prove the other right. That's up to you."

What would Santino do?

I have to admit I don't know. But I know what I'd want him to do, and that's good enough. Dario isn't my favorite person in the world, but at this moment, he's on my team, in my care, and I don't like him being threatened.

"He's with me," I say.

"Is he?" Nazario asks.

What is it about the way he's speaking to me that seems so disconcerting?

"He is." I cross my arms.

"As am I," Nazario says. "Before you laid a foot in America, I was with you."

When he smiles, his teeth are a wall of white caps sitting too far in front of his shrinking jaw. Under bushy eyebrows, his glassed-over eyes may be green or brown. He is capable of lies, but right now, he's sincere. He sees himself as an ally. Whether or not he actually is remains to be seen.

"You believe him," Dario says from behind.

I turn to face him. "Do you?"

"I don't believe anyone. Least of all the consigliere of a dead man."

The lawyer leans on his cane at his center with both hands, a smile playing on his spotted lips. "When the box is opened," he says to me, "step away from this man. Respectfully." He nods slightly. "In case he's struck down where he stands."

This old Italian person is speaking directly to me, as if I'm the authority here, not the nearest man. That's what's so disconcerting. His respectfully paternal, yet playful manner is straight out of the old country. But I've never seen a guy from the other side direct deference to a woman under the age of eighty.

"Let's open it and see," I say.

"*Bene.*" He nods to the driver, who reaches for the box's metal latch.

"Let me just warn you," I say, putting my hand on the driver's to still it. "If this box has a hair of my husband's head in it, I'm going to rip both your hearts out, put them in here while they're still beating, and send it back where it came from."

"Americans." *Il Blocco* scoffs, then stands up straighter, his chin high. "Violetta Cavallo, I have brought you your inheritance."

Without saying the words to myself, I knew that had to be what is in the box, and yet—when he says it—I'm still surprised.

The driver reaches to the front of the box and opens it.

I expect a few pieces of a broken crown. But it's not that at all.

"What is this?" I whisper.

This thing... It's not a few sections of holy junk. It's not even broken.

And it's not quite a crown either.

"Yours," the consigliere says. "It's yours. Take it."

I don't know if I can trust him. The hammered

silver circle on the threadbare red velvet bed could be a trap. A bomb with points at the front and a thin band around the back. A trick to get me to claim what belongs to someone else. It could be a decoy sent to distract us from the pillar of smoke coming from the bridge.

Santino already told me what to do.

NO RULES

Love rules without rules. But maybe Santino meant to tell me that the lines drawn around my actions and experience really aren't there. I can step over them and take what's mine. Or that could be what I want it all to mean.

I wish he was here with me. He should be…after everything we've been through over this box.

What would Santino want me to do?

L'amore governa senza regole.

He'd say there's no worn path here. This hasn't been done before.

He'd say that the only rule is our love. We write the rest of history.

I touch the metal. It's warm, but it's also August. Everything's hot.

I lift it out. It's heavy, but it's also iron. Iron's a heavy thing.

The crown doesn't shine or glitter. It's a dull gray with an uneven texture, as if ripped from the earth by ancient gods and twisted into shape by hand. Three points spread across the front, with the center one being tallest. The circle completes around the back, where it's held together with a long, sideways T that's covered in rust.

The nail from the One True Cross.

It's real.

It's really real.

I decide right there that I will never touch that part of the crown. I am too mortal. Too fucked up. Too broken to come into contact with that kind of power. So when I put my thumbs on the front to lift it, my fingertips don't go all the way around the back, which is when the size of it becomes clear.

Though the metal is rough hewn, the crown itself is feminine and small.

This does not go on the head of a king.

The *Corona Ferrea* is a diadem. It is meant to be worn by a woman.

I lift it from the shadow of the box so I can see it in the light, and everyone around me shifts. Arms up, I take my focus off the crown to see what has changed.

In a circle around me. Everyone—even Nazario Corragio, leaning on his cane—is kneeling with heads bowed in reverence to a twenty-year-old woman holding up an ancient inheritance.

Santino, I wish you were here.

I need you here.

I'm not ready for whatever this is.

A SQUARE of butter sits in an oily puddle at the center of my pastina, and it's melting so fast I know it's too hot.

I am five. I asked Zia Saveria for the pastina. Now I have to eat it, but she's ignoring me to whisper to some other women I don't know. There are a lot of people in Nonna's kitchen.

Rosetta sits cross-armed in front of the grown-up cappuccino she asked for because Nonna would let her have it.

Last night, I went to bed, and now I am awake at Nonna's house. Mamma's mother. There are so many people. The grown-ups are upset. I don't have my Raggedy Ann, so I am upset too.

"Eat," Nonna says after she blows on the pastina a couple of times.

It works like magic. The porridge is cool enough. I should save some for Raggedy Ann. I want to ask for her, but there are too many people to focus. Nonna with the kerchief and scapular and Nonno with the swagger and beedi smell are here too. They are Papino's parents. It's not Sunday. It's not a holiday or birthday.

"When are we going home?" I ask.

"Never." Rosetta's crabby. She's been like that lately. But she's never seemed so sad and angry at the same time. She's scaring me.

"Is it true?" I ask Nonna from Mamma's side. She's not as free with the candy as Papà's mother, but she's gentle with us.

"Hush, Rosetta," Nonna answers, looking out the window. She sees something—a bird maybe—and whispers to an older cousin.

"I will not hush!" Rosetta slams her hand on the table so hard the spoon rattles.

"You're scaring your sister." Nonna turns toward us with the expression of a wild animal.

"She should be scared." Rosetta spins in her seat to face me. "Mamma and Papà are dead! They were killed. Papà's brother and Mamma—!"

"*Basta!*" Nonna's arm is made of lightning, grabbing my sister by the hair on top of her head.

"Ow!"

"Say only what you know!"

"But—"

"Never, ever, ever say those lies again."

"Siena Orolio told me—"

Nonna slaps Rosetta. I don't know why. It's loud. I cry before Rosetta does, but we're both sobbing now, holding each other under Nonna's kitchen table. I can't make words.

What does Rosetta not know?

That Mamma and Papà are dead?

Or that they were killed by Papino's brother?

We don't have an uncle on that side.

My brother will kill for it no matter where it is.

Our father has two sisters. So if she's got that wrong, then all of it must be a bad dream she had. A bad, upsetting nightmare. So no brother. No murder. Our parents are fine.

There's a secret uncle if they're dead, and I can't let them be dead.

I am five. I collect data and store it in places so dark, I'll never find it.

Nonna and the rest of the adults get called into another room on some serious and probably boring matter.

Red-faced, Rosetta sobs into my collar, a nest of

hair on top of her head. I place a chubby hand on her shoulder.

"It was just a bad dream, Rosie."

"It's not." She snaps her hand back, eyes scanning the room at floor level to see if we're really alone. "It's real. The sooner you learn that, the better."

"Well, but Daddy doesn't have a brother."

She makes her hands into fists on the linoleum. "Half brother."

I never heard of that. Is he cut in half? Long ways or across the middle? Does it hurt?

My two Nonnas come back in. I see their shoes first, then my father's mother lifts the table cloth to find us. I can ask them, but they sit in the chairs and wait for us to come out. When we do, every question I have about my father's family is washed away with the news they deliver.

Rosetta never tells me what she meant by half a brother, and so much changes that I never ask.

THIS CROWN I'm holding up was not meant for me. It was my mother's. It is Rosetta's.

I drop it back into the box and slap the lid shut.

The circle rises. They're standing. Things will be said. I am not ready. All I can think about is Santino suffering.

With a quick turn and a lowered head, I walk away, up the stairs, and—without asking myself why—I go up another flight to the cupola. Knowing I'm trapped by mountains and men, I want to get far away from what just happened.

The glass is spotted with water-diamonds reflecting the floodlights and the moon—cold and damp against my palms. The rain should blind me to the city below, but it encloses us like a cocoon, fights the fire on the bridge in my stead, and falls on everyone equally. Me. *Il Bocco*. Damiano. Santino.

I need to scan this city like a hawk. I need to put my hands on the window and listen for his voice.

"Violetta," Loretta says from the stairway.

"Leave me alone."

When I open my eyes, I'm trapped in a room of glass, looking over my world in three hundred sixty degrees. The rain, the burning bridge, and the country beyond it. My home city in the valley. The lawn and the people scurrying around it. The gate that opened to let the limousine inside.

"Violetta." Loretta's disembodied head breaches the floor, then the rest of her rises.

Santino left me with her when I was a blood-covered American girl who tried to run, but was nearly captured instead. She fed me and gave me a place to rest. She tried to tell me things I ignored.

"What happened out there?" I demand. "Why did you kneel?"

"I don't know." She sits on one of the benches that line the room. "I had to."

"Santino told me about this. It's a mass delusion. That's all it is, and it's distracting. Now everyone's dusting off their pants when we should be getting the hell out of here and finding him. We need to take this entire city apart brick by fucking brick. I'm sick of waiting here—eating, sleeping, pretending everything's okay—while my husband is somewhere getting his fingers cut off. I can't bear it!"

My fists are white-cap tight, shaking in front of my chest, ready to punch through any stone wall that separates us before they pulverize whoever built it.

"I wish he was here," I say, dropping my hands.

"I know."

"I can't...Whatever this is...with the crown...I can't do it without him."

"You have to. You're the queen now, and everyone knows it."

Overwhelmed, I sit on a bench on the opposite side of the room from her. "I'm not. I'm just a regular girl, and I'm scared."

"Sure, you are." Loretta sighs and leans back on the uncomfortable seat. "When I met you, right..." She gets up and points out the window to a house on the side of our mountain. "Right there." She taps the glass twice. "You had blood all over you and a little bit of maybe brain in your hair, and I said right away...*pfft*. 'She is nothing. Poor Santino, with this...nothing. She doesn't even have the sense to be frightened.'"

"You didn't let on you felt that way."

"I was being a bitch, and I knew it. He was never mine." She sits on the bench, closer now. "You learned about the gods and goddesses in school here, yes?"

"Zeus and shit? Yeah."

"Like Athena, goddess of war?" After I nod, she continues. "The Greeks carved Athena's face to look like a man. They put breasts on a man's body. But our war goddess, Minerva...she was a woman. She was fierce, and feminine, and mad as vinegar. That was you that day, and when he took you back, I realized that. I said, 'One day, she will be queen.' And here you are."

She's saying I'm a queen, but queens don't feel small and incapable without their king.

"I didn't think I'd let myself love him this much," I admit, and she nods.

For a second time, light flashes on her face. The sound that follows is not thunder, but a scream.

25

VIOLETTA

I burst into the kitchen, Loretta following close behind. The door out of the kitchen is open, letting in the wind and windswept raindrops.

Nazario Corragio and his driver are in the same position I left them in. Celia's holding a coffee pot, but not moving to pour it or put it down. Gennaro is stock still and Carmine is the same, but shaking his head slowly. They're all looking down, and I follow their gaze.

The crown is on the floor.

"What the hell happened?" I ask.

The consigliere shrugs and turns to Celia, making a *tsk* to the espresso pot. She shakes the bees from her head and pours.

"Dario," Gennaro says, coming back to himself. "He tried to get the crown. Steal it."

I pick up the crown, careful not to touch the nail. The driver watches me, wide-eyed, and makes the sign of the cross.

"What?" I ask, putting it back in the box.

"It's not hot?" he asks.

"Of course not, you *testa di cavolo*." He calls him a dickhead, scoffing and sipping from his coffee cup. "It's hers."

"That's ridiculous." I close the box and latch it. "It's the same temperature for everyone. It's a piece of dumb metal. You all need to stop treating it like it's got magic."

"Tell that to Dario," Gennaro says.

"Where is he?" I ask, suddenly panicked that he's gathering enough men to put me in the basement.

"Ran off," Gennaro says.

"Like a kitten when the vacuum's turned on," Celia adds.

"The rest of the guys chased him but—"

"Why?" I interrupt Gennaro. "Why did he run out like that?"

"When he touched it"—he waves at the box—"he was struck by lightning."

God save us all from stories about God.

"It's fucking *thunder and lightning out*," I growl. "And if—by some miracle—a lightning bolt came through the roof without breaking it, then through the second story of this house without making a hole in the ceiling, the floor right here would be black. So stop it. Everybody, cut it out. This crown is magic, but not the way you're saying. We have the thing Damiano's coming for, and we can trade it for Santino."

The consigliere laughs into his espresso, clicking down his cup. "More of this, please."

"What's funny?" I ask.

"Do we have a place to talk privately? Or is it all"—he waves at the room with distaste—"gossiping?"

He means *women's space*, but I let it slide because he's old and he brought me the crown.

"If you can get up a flight of stairs." Maybe I'm not letting it slide as much as I think.

The driver cuts in. "He can."

THE CONSIGLIERE HOLDS his cane against his chest and between his knees as his driver—whose name is Sam—carries him up the stairs and places him in a chair facing Santino's desk. Sam and Gennaro take opposite corners of the room.

I place the box on a side table and sit where my husband usually sits. The chair is still too big for me, but I don't feel as small. On the desk to my right, an ivory-faced teak clock with Roman numerals and brass feet ticks away my luxury.

With his cane planted in the carpet between his feet and both hands resting on the brass head, Nazario looks at the old box on the side table and sighs. "I am done."

"I accept your resignation. Anything else? Because I have to find Damiano Orolio and give him that crown."

"No," he says, facing me. "You will not do that."

"If it gets me my husband back, I will."

"It will reject Damiano."

"I don't care," I say with dead seriousness, letting him anthropomorphize the crown just for the sake of argument.

He sighs again. "You're the first one who can truly use it to rule without being subject to a man, and of course...you want to trade it for your husband. *Che ironia.*"

My Italian isn't great, but I know irony when I hear it. Outside, lightning flashes and—three seconds later—thunder rolls. Santino is under the same rain, suffering in ways I can't imagine. I don't have time to pick apart the paradox between my desires and his superstitions.

"You wanted a place to talk," I say. "Not gossip. We're doing neither."

"Capo." He smiles at me like a proud father, calling me a boss in the traditional, non-mob sense. At least, this is what I believe.

"You brought the crown to me. I'm grateful. But I can't sit here all night waiting for you to tell me what you want out of me." I flip the clock around to face him. "You have ten minutes."

Instead of blurting out his intentions to fit it all into ten minutes, he pauses. There's a light knock on the door, and Celia comes in with a tray of coffee. He wastes two full minutes waiting for it to be poured.

"*Signora,*" he asks her, "do you want Damiano to have the crown?"

She hesitates. "It's not my place."

"You can tell him," I say.

"He killed Armando. A good man. My friend. He shouldn't get rewarded for that." She glances at me. "Sorry."

"It's fine."

She nods, turns on her heel, and leaves.

"She has a sense of justice you lack," Nazario says.

I remind myself that he doesn't know me or what I've become since I was stolen from my home and forced to live a life I didn't ask for. I'm different in ways I haven't had time to name.

"The summer I was ten." I lay my hands flat on the desk. "My uncle took my sister and me to the Signorile Oxbow Lake, where San Vitus Boulevard ends. There's a dock you can dive off. He set up a picnic, and Rosetta and I went out on a blow-up raft with a horse's head. He packed Zia's *granita al limone*—my favorite. All I wanted was to spend a few minutes in the lake, then go back and eat it before it got mushy. But there were boys on the opposite bank, and Rosetta was fifteen, so she found this more interesting than her little sister. Her and one blond kid were—I don't know what you'd call shouting across an entire lake."

"I think it's called flirting."

I smile at him and continue. "She paddled us into the center to meet him. I was smaller, so I couldn't fight it. I couldn't do anything but scream louder and louder that she had to stop. I was making a racket. And she turns to me, with all these raging teenage hormones, and says, 'Swim back if you don't like it.' I thought…yes. I could do that. I was an okay swimmer. It wasn't *that* far away. I was going to get off this thing and swim to the dock. And so I stood, grabbed the horse's head, and froze because I realized I wasn't leaving the safety of the blow-up raft thing. I'd rather be miserable watching my sister flirt with this stupid boy than go to the effort of swimming back."

"So you ate mushy granita."

"It was worse… liquid." I wrinkle my nose. "I was mad, but I never questioned my decision. I always did the easy thing, even if I was miserable. Until Santino took away all the easy choices. Being in his house was hard. Accepting his kindness was hard. Obeying him was impossible. Loving him… It changed everything. So before you say I don't have a sense of justice, you need to know that Santino DiLustro is my only justice. Before him, I was nothing. I dreamed, and I worked, but I wasn't alive. I was asleep. The walking dead. I stayed on the raft, and if he hadn't pulled me off, I'd still be floating around, protected from my own life. So fuck the crown. It's a raft in a lake. I'll jump off and swim to him. I'll give the crown to whoever returns my king to me."

The old man blinks slowly, and with a groan, he turns the desk clock around to face me. The ten minutes are almost up. He drops onto a seat with the sigh of easily-emptied lungs.

"You are worthy," he says. "But you know that."

"I don't want to be worthy of anything but him."

Leaning on his cane, Nazario Corragio gets up with cracking, grinding bones. Sam holds him straight. I stand with him.

"Santino DiLustro," Nazario says when he's upright, "is in the sub basement of a nightclub. Under a laundry room."

Hope is a fuse that—once lit—can set a soul on fire and consume every last breath of reason.

"How do you know?" My voice cracks.

"It's my job to know."

"Is he all right? Who's guarding him? How many?"

"No, Violetta Cavallo, my job begins and ends with the heads who share the crown. You are the last of a line of women sold to men for it and the first able to wear it without a man to tell you not to. Use its power to get the DiLustro boy."

"It doesn't have power. There's no such thing."

"Power is belief."

Power doesn't come from one's own confidence or certainty. This, I know now. It comes from the belief of others. That's what Santino always said, and he's always right.

"I am done here." Nazario turns his back to me.

Sam helps him to the door without my dismissal. His last statement is more than an excuse from the room. Nazario's done with the meeting, and he's done with life.

The door opens and Remo stops just short of knocking over Nazario, stammering. "I'm sorry... sir. Ma'am, but...they're coming."

"Good," I say, opening the crown's box. "Good."

26

SANTINO

I am not strong enough. At first, I blame myself for having a suicidal survival instinct since this escape plan is as likely to kill me as to free me. Then blame goes to the missing finger. Then the pain with a home base in my shoulder. It's hunger. Thirst. Desperation.

It doesn't matter whose fault it is. The gas pipe was built not to break. Not from the weight of one man. Not from all his strength, his will, or his fear. Not even his love can bend it enough.

"What are you doing?" Gia says from the other side of the wall.

She fell asleep when she was done sobbing, and I decided I didn't have time to wait for her to get the hell out of here. If she stuck around looking for salvation from me, she deserved to die in a gas explosion.

Now she's up.

"Get out of here," I say, straining to bend pipes a plumber would be able to just cut.

"I can't see!" She's standing on the chair again, but she's no taller. Her fingertips reach the hole as if she's trying to pull herself up.

"Gia!" I shout, releasing my hold on the gas line. "If you want to live, walk out now. I'm not responsible if you don't."

I hear her drop back to the floor. I wait, hoping for footsteps on the stairs and a slammed door. But she doesn't leave.

"Gia! Go!"

"You care," she says. "I don't know what you're doing in there, but you still care about me."

"Don't think I won't kill you where you stand," I say to a woman behind a freshly-built brick wall.

"Let me help you," she says. "Please."

"Like you helped Armando?"

"I didn't know they were going to do it!"

"Now you do, so you should go away."

"Give me a chance to do better than I did."

"Why are women so stubborn?" I mutter.

"Please. I read about what it feels like to die without water. It can take a week or even more. Your brain shrinks and you go blind because your eyes get sucked into your skull."

I hear her get back on the chair. I expect a bottle of water to appear in the little hole, but of course, something that welcome and simple would never occur to a woman with no hope for me. Instead, a gun is laid there.

She says, "I know where to stand so you can't shoot me through that hole, so—"

"Shooting you wouldn't help me." I take it down. It's loaded.

"But you can end it if it's bad."

"That's sweet, Gia. I'm sure St. Peter will look favorably."

"If I could let you out, I would, you know."

I close my eyes and sigh. There's nothing she can do. This room has no windows to open and no door with a key she can steal for me. All I have are silent water pipes and gas lines I cannot break. The room on the other side of the wall has a couch, and chairs, and bloodstained hedge clippers.

With my left hand, I clench through pain to make eighty percent of a fist. The plan I'm trying to execute will probably get me killed unless I can cut a pipe on the other side of this wall.

"You want to help me get out?" I ask.

"If I could—"

"What if you could?"

There's a pause. I'm sure she's rethinking this, and I'll be stuck in here with a gun and nothing to shoot besides myself.

"Tell me what you need," she says after a deep breath.

"When this is done, I still have to kill you. I've never killed a woman, but I've never met one who earned her death with such enthusiasm."

"I know."

She knows. Nice to embrace natural laws men are sworn to uphold. It's almost enough to make me trust her, which I don't…but that leaves me in a windowless, doorless room, slowly starving while my wife is hunted like a dog. Inaction is not a choice.

"Look around the tool bench behind the couch. Tell me what you find."

27

VIOLETTA

My spurts of competence are replaced by a single hum of panic. I have to get out of here. I have to find him. I'm not going to stay trapped behind a gate, waiting for messages or threats, when I know where he is.

This is the third time since Santino left that I've been warned someone is coming up the mountain, and it's the first time I'm prepared to do something about it. My skin tingles, and my muscles throb. I'm enflamed with the possibility of finding him, touching him, hearing his voice. I have never wanted anything as much as I want him back.

I walk out of the office with the box under my arm. All the men—young and old, experienced and green, the tough guys and the softer soldiers—all of them watch me go down the stairs and past the kitchen, waiting for me to tell them what to do, but not getting close enough to ask. How did Santino manage so many of them?

They hang back as if they're too afraid to approach me.

Celia has no such apprehension, following me onto the lawn where the crickets have taken over the night's song.

"Violetta," she says, catching up. "Where are you going?"

"I know where Santino is."

"Thank God." She makes the sign of the cross. Habit demands I do the same, but the box is under my right arm, and prayers are for the powerless. "Are they going to get him?"

"I am. No one's doing for me what I have the authority to do myself."

"Take me," she says. It takes me a moment to understand that Santino's cook wants to join me on what could be a suicide mission. "Santino took me in when no one else would. He kept me when my father demanded me back to marry me off."

My gaze falls to her exposed forearms and the cigarette burns her father gave her when she disappointed him.

"I owe him my life, and I'm tired of sitting back and waiting for the right things to happen," she adds.

"They're coming for us," Loretta calls when she's halfway between us and the house.

Celia's eyes go wide. Obviously, word hadn't gotten to the kitchen yet.

"They want to trade Santino for the crown," I say.

"You guys"—Vito gets the courage to approach—"they'll be at the gate in a few minutes. You can't stay out here."

"I know," I say. "How many are there?"

"Looks like seven cars."

"Is Santino with them?"

"No way to tell. It's night, and the windows are dark, so there could be six guys to a car or one. So you all need to just stay inside until we know. Come on." He tries to wave me to the house, where he'll lock us up safe.

That's what Santino would want. I'm sure he'd rather die than find out I put myself in danger to save him. Too bad. He's not here to tell me not to come for him.

"Does Lasertopia have a sub basement?" I ask Loretta.

"There's a boiler room. The bouncers turned it into a hangout."

I ignore Vito and pace to the gate. "Remo!" I call over my shoulder. "Get out the Alfa."

Loretta and Celia follow me.

Vito runs past them to walk next to me. "Please, Mrs. DiLustro. You can't just drive away. They won't let you by."

"I'm not going to pass them, Vito. I'm going through them."

We leave him behind. Celia is to my right, and Loretta is to my left. In front of me, a line of soldiers stand between us and the gate.

"I'll show you the sub basement," Loretta says. "You won't find it otherwise."

To my right, the garage doors open, and the Alfa Romeo's headlights flash when the engine starts. I stop a few feet from the gate and drop the box between my feet to address the men strapped here with me.

"We have about five minutes before they get here, and we start shooting at each other. If we wait, more than half of you are going to die. I don't want that. Santino's not here, but if he was, he wouldn't find that acceptable either. You will not die to protect this crown."

"If you give it to them," Carmine shouts, "they're gonna shoot us all anyway."

Maybe. Probably. I don't know the codes or traditions of this kind of confrontation, and I don't care. They're all changing if I survive this, and if I don't, there's nothing I can do about it.

"There won't be a trade," I agree with a voice that echoes from the mountains and over the sounds of the night. "Once Damiano has it, he has no reason to let Santino live to challenge him."

The Alfa approaches from behind me, casting the line of men in unforgiving light. They're scared. I don't blame them because this plan puts them in front of a rain of bullets with nothing more than a woman with a piece of metal on her head to protect them.

"We cannot trade for what was always ours. Tonight, we're not going to make any concessions. We will save our king."

Then I explain to the soldiers of the Cavallo family exactly how I'm going to lead them.

Four cars quickly line up behind me. They'll follow us to Lasertopia while anyone left in Torre Cavallo will take care of the Tabonas if—and only *if*—the first part of this plan works. If the first part bombs, we're fucked.

Outside of their own mothers, I've never seen the men of Secondo Vasto do a woman's bidding unless she made it sound like his idea. If the influence of the *Corona Ferrea* is a mass hallucination, it's more powerful than any documented case.

When I'm done, there are no questions. They line up as I explained. The plan must be so simple a child could understand it because all I can see are the list of things that can go wrong.

Remo gets out of the car, and Loretta gets behind the wheel.

"We'll be right behind you," Vito says, leaning down to speak to me through the open back door. "And the guns above." He flashes a look toward the ridge overhead.

"Just hold until we know if Santino's with them. There's no point to this if we end up killing him. For me, at least."

"For any of us." Vito taps his phone. There's rarely any signal up here, but he doesn't need it.

"Good." The gate creaks open.

"I'll be on the speakers." He shows me his phone. Bluetooth connected to the Alfa.

He closes the door, and I'm left with Loretta and Celia looking back at me from the front seat. The reality of three women in the lead car hits me.

"This is nuts," I say, trusting they know exactly what I mean.

"Is it?" Loretta asks. "We come from a land of abundance, and it always comes down to the women. Always."

Celia makes the sign of the cross again and passes through the gate as soon as it's open wide enough. When she makes the first turn, cutting off the view of the gate and Torre Cavallo, I breathe for the first time in days.

I am free, but I have a purpose that's as forceful as saving my own life.

Santino. His life. Our life together.

"Okay, Loretta," I say, holding the box in both hands.

She presses a button on the left armrest. The sunroof slides open.

"Around the next turn," Vito's voice says from the speakers.

I take the crown out of the box and stand, putting my head and arms through the sunroof. The tight curve is up ahead, so I hold tight as the car makes the turn and nearly smacks into a black Chevy Suburban driving too close to the center line. Five more are in the opposite lane behind it, screeching to a halt in quick succession. The last car stops gently but across most of our lane.

Through the sunroof to my waist, I hold the crown so tightly the edges hurt, but I stay still.

I don't have long to wait. In the hard light of headlamps, the car doors swing open. Men get out with guns. I press the fear to the bottom of my heart. So many men. Twenty. Thirty. More gun barrels than I can count are pointed at me. Each is an endlessly deep void.

This is it. We didn't count on this many. The cars behind need to stay behind or it'll be a slaughter.

How did I get human adults to go along with this ridiculous idea?

Santino would never have approved. He would have laughed at me. Kissed me. Called me *Forzetta*.

I hold up the crown—then put it on my head.

Counting on another mass hysteria event is the dumbest part of a dumb plan.

I love you, Santino.

Thank you for teaching me how to be brave.

I spread my arms. "Bring me Santino, or shoot me and take it."

I wish I could have been smarter for you.

Crowned like a homecoming queen, I wait to find out that whatever power this thing has doesn't work under a waxing moon, or extend past the Torre Cavallo gate, or influence men who pledge loyalty to another family.

I'm sorry, my king. I am so sorry.

A barrel jerks, then another, and I'm sure my time before death is splitting and splitting infinitely, and I'm going to see bullets fly through the air in slow motion, unable to move before they shatter through me.

But that moment doesn't come. The bullets stay cold in their chambers. The guns are lowered, and the men holding them look at the ground before bending their knees.

"They're doing it," I say to Loretta and Celia in the

seats below, not expecting them to actually hear me past the roof of the car or even the thrilling heart thrum of the enemy's mass submission. "Go!"

I smack the roof. I don't know how long the impulse to show fealty to a piece of metal actually lasts. There's no time to enjoy it or understand it. We need to go. But though Loretta drives forward, we don't get far. The last Suburban has left little room for us to get by, and no one's kneeling near its closed doors.

We stop. If we try to pass, we could get rammed into a cliff face. As it is, I'm still a sitting duck to get shot from behind a tinted window or from behind when the guys we passed snap out of whatever trance they're in.

And Santino might be in that car in front of us.

I take out the gun he gave me, holding it in two hands as he taught me.

I couldn't hit a bottle this way, and now I don't even know what I'm aiming at.

Until the passenger door opens and a man gets out. He has a thick black moustache and dark widow's peak on a low forehead. No one is in the driver's seat. He was alone in the front. His hands are up and he's blindfolded himself with a long black scarf, as if he's been prepped for his execution.

"No!" Loretta shouts.

"What?"

"Violetta DiLustro?" The blindfolded man's knees bend, but he manages to keep upright.

"Carlo!" Loretta screams from below me.

"What is it?" I ask.

There's a scuffle up front, making me shake a little against the edges of the sunroof.

"I have something to deliver to Violetta DiLustro," he says.

"If it's another body part, you can keep it."

"Turn over the crown and we—"

The rest is lost in the rev of the engine beneath me. Inertia that bends me in two as the Alfa thrusts forward, hitting the man, then pinning him against the Suburban and pushing it so hard it tips onto two wheels.

"What the fuck?" I cry.

The car stops. The Suburban rocks back into place.

Carlo is practically torn in two.

I slide down into the back seat. Loretta's bawling against the steering wheel with Celia resting her hand on Loretta's back as she stares at the bloodied windshield.

"What just happened?"

"He killed Elio," Loretta roars into her hands.

To think I was worried that she still loved Santino.

Now is the moment we're supposed to drive down to Lasertopia with four cars behind me, but the road's blocked, and there are so many people. They all need me, and there's one man I need.

I get out of the Alfa and run to the Suburban, then I open the back door.

No Santino. There was no trade. We planned for that, but there are too many people. I keep saying it to myself because I don't know what to do about it, and I don't know how long their delusion will cow them. If they all wake up at once, we're fucked.

Loretta's crying because she just killed a man, and that changes a person. Celia's staring at the carnage. I crouch by Carlo Tabona's mangled body. An internship in the ER did not prepare me for this many compound fractures or a dying man's screams. People shouting. No gunshots. Not yet. And I don't need Santino any less.

Without apology, I reach into Carlo's front pocket, praying it's the only one I'll have to search. My prayers are answered when my fingers find the car's fob.

Leaning into the driver's seat of the Alfa, I use the Bluetooth to ping Vito. "I'm going alone. Take care of Loretta."

I rush around the Suburban. The driver's door opens with the glow of the dome light, and the standard monotone dings...as if the passenger door isn't pushed into the seat like a freeze frame of a train wreck.

I get behind the wheel, and with some back and forth, I separate it from the Alfa. Carlo flops to the road, and I head down the mountain alone. This is what it should have been from the beginning. Just me, speeding to him.

"Hold on, Re Santino. I'm coming for you. Finally."

Finally, finally. I'm going to apologize to him for taking so long. For letting myself get stuck up in a tower. If he's alive, I'll beg for his forgiveness.

At the bottom, where the street is more level, a rain-drenched man appears, straddling the centerline. The light washes out his features. He is upright, tall, and utterly still. There's no room to pass without wrecking the car, and when I consider stopping, I realize that at this speed, on a rain-slick road, I won't. I hit the brakes, swerve, and let God decide his fate. The man raises his arms in front of him. By the time I see the gun he's aiming at me, it's too late to duck.

God will decide both our fates.

28
SANTINO

Science lab. Ninth grade. Sal Renzi shook the test tube over a burner. He wasn't supposed to, and I don't remember what was in the tube, but I remember *il professor Campi* grabbing his wrist and saying, "A little science is more dangerous than complete ignorance."

I should have stayed in school, but I failed more than *il professor Campi's* biology class. Over Zia Paola's objections, I stopped going. Complete ignorance seemed like a reasonable choice for me. Gia and Tavie finished school. Tavie's dead. Gia will be soon.

But not today.

The rusty hacksaw blade she found in the back of an otherwise empty drawer wouldn't cut all the way through the pipes, but it would open one just enough.

After stamping out the cigarette, I told her which pipe to cut on her side. I said the fumes would kill her if she didn't leave as soon as she smelled it.

She thought I was trying to end it all by gas inhalation instead of a bullet, so she did it, and she ran away when it started to smell.

"Goodbye, Santi," she said at the steps as the pipe hissed. "I'll see you on the other side."

"Sure, you will."

She ran up. I lit a cigarette, took a drag, and after a minute of guesswork, I threw it through the hole in the wall.

The explosion knocked out a section of the exterior wall, and the debris protected me from the flames that would have killed me.

Stumbling on the street, I barely remember what happened next. I have a brick in my right hand, and when I drop it, spots of burned skin stick to it. The cool night air brushes over my body where my shirt's been singed away.

The gun is in my back pocket, and my ears are ringing like a scream.

There's no traffic on the streets, so the sirens from the volunteer fire station pass quickly, a block away. That has something to do with me, but I can't find the will to care.

If we're convincing enough, she'll have it.

In all this pain and confusion, the map of the town has been erased from my memory, but I walk toward the mountain, toward Torre Cavallo, toward her. When rain clouds my view, I follow streets that slope upward.

If she don't fight, we'll let her live.

At a point I can't define, my ears stop ringing, and the rain turns to mist. Still walking, I take stock of the situation. My shirt is made of a back and sleeves. My right palm has a splatter pattern of raw skin. The pain where my finger was removed is like an old friend. My head hurts. The headache is the worst because it blinds me, and I'm afraid that when I get to her, I won't be able to see well enough to protect her.

It's taking candy from a baby.

In front of St. Paul's church—the one I burned down so no other man would try to marry Violetta in it—is a makeshift shrine with candles and flowers. A concerned citizen of Secondo Vasto left a bowl for offerings to rebuild the church. I scoop the money out onto the ground and drink the rainwater. The headache stalls. My mind clears. The rain slows to a fog.

I've been making my way to her like a sleepwalker, but now that I'm awake, I run.

The streets I've lived on all these years reveal their secrets, sloping upward at increased grades with every block. I know where to go, and I won't stop until I get there. The turn up the mountain is right ahead. The slope will increase, and there's not enough energy in my bones to get me to her, but I don't stop running on the empty avenue, following the yellow centerline as if it's an electrified track, and I'm on metal wheels.

The lights ahead are tiny. Then bigger. It's a car, and unlike the ones parked all over town, this one's already running. I need it to get up the mountain.

29

VIOLETTA

A web of cracks explodes across the windshield. A hard little breeze—warm as a man blowing in my ear—whooshes against the side of my head. A part of me says I need to take my foot off the brake and just mow him down, but my body's been driving without the help of my mind for too long, and I stop. My head bops against the steering wheel, hard enough to throw the crown onto the dashboard but light enough to keep my wits about me.

Someone is on the road. He shot at me. That's all I know. Could be one of my guys trying to stop a Tabona, or a straggling enemy who knows I'm behind the wheel.

With my right hand, I reach for my holster while the left pulls the door handle. It's wrenched from me, and I tumble onto the pavement with enough presence of mind to hold the gun at the man standing over me.

In a millisecond, I make a decision not to shoot him until I know who he is.

He pushes my hands aside. The gun goes off, releasing a bullet into the bushes. He falls on me, putting his weight on my throat and wrists.

"We gonna do this easy?" he asks with a voice I'll never forget. "Or we gonna do this hard?"

"Easy," I say, knowing that's the only answer that'll shift Damiano Orolio's weight.

"Where is it?"

The stupid crown. It gets men to kneel before you. He can have it.

"Car."

He wrenches my gun away and stands, looking at me with his barrel leveled at my chest.

"Better be." He tilts his head slightly, as if he's seeing something new about me as I lie in the street. "Has anyone ever told you that you look just like my father?"

"Where's Santino?"

"Starving. Dead." He throws my gun to the side of the road, where the SUV that must have brought him sits in the shadows. "No one's gonna find him." He looks in the Suburban, but the crown isn't in the seat where he must expect. "It better be in here."

With his next movement, I'm sure he's going to shoot me. Instead, a slight jerk of his shoulders turns into a full spin, and it's only then that I hear the humidity-muffled *pop* of a gunshot. My eyes have frozen mid-blink, squeezed shut against the news of my own death. My singular failure. My complicity in the murder of the only man I've ever loved, and who loved me in a way no one had before or will again.

At least I had that, even as I die now.

A thud and grunty *umph* happen instead. I still feel

the drizzle on my face and the hard earth against the curve of my head, but there's no pain from a bullet.

A voice I know and love reaches through the rush in my ears. Something I've lost twice and not had a moment to grieve for either time is found again.

"*Forzetta!*"

My heart is struck by lightning.

Had it even been beating since he left? No. It had turned to frozen meat in my chest.

I twist into a crouch. He's leaning over me, and the relief on his face mirrors my reprieve from despair. I was dead without him, but now I live again.

"Santi," I whisper. "You're…"

You're here. You're alive. You're mine. All of them swirl up my throat and get caught on the sob squeezing its way out of my lungs.

"So are you," he says.

So am I. We are here. Together. Only now do I realize that I'd assumed he was dead and I'd never see him again.

He grips my arm and pulls me upright until I'm standing face to face with my husband—my heart pumping and my eyes finally open. He looks like shit with dark circles and sunken cheeks, and he is the most beautiful sight in the world.

Forgetting where I am and the danger we're in, I kiss him. Rain drips off his cheeks and hair into the seam between our lips. It rests on our tongues and I taste the sky, the earth, the salt of the sea. Barbed wire stubble scratches my mouth, but we press each other closer because we're never separating again. We promise it with that kiss. Never.

The scrape of metal on the pavement breaks the lock we have on each other. We are standing on a street in front of a man trying to kill us.

Santino wraps one arm tightly around me and looks past me at the man on the ground. I turn inside my husband's protection. Damiano's trying to raise an arm attached to a shattered shoulder, but the gun only scrapes the asphalt.

"Say a prayer, Dami," Santino says.

"If you kill me..." He leverages his good arm to get himself into a crouch. "My father's coming after you. Hard."

"That's a wish. Not a prayer."

"He'll kill you." Damiano's useful arm takes the gun from the dangling one. "And then his own—"

Santino doesn't wait for him to finish. He raises my gun—the one thrown to the side of the road—and hits the other shoulder. Damiano's gun clacks to the ground. Both arms are useless now.

I can't hold back another second. Santino's here, alive, in my embrace. The taste of him and the rain is on my lips. My heart is thawed. All I want is to spend days in bed with him, telling him how much I love him.

I bury my face in his chest, letting him hold me up —still so strong after everything he's been through.

"We're not done," he says softly. I shake my head against his bare skin, but I know he's right. We're not done. "Kick his gun away."

Letting Santino go takes more strength than I feel, but there won't be days in bed until I do what he says, and I trust he knows what to do. But when we separate,

I feel the pang of want and the safety of the ties that keep us together.

With a breath, I take a few steps toward the man with two flopping arms.

"You think being with him makes you something," he says. "It doesn't. He doesn't give you any power."

"I know."

Using the side of my foot, I send his gun skittering over the wet pavement.

"Now pick it up," Santino says, keeping Damiano in his sights.

Santino takes nothing for granted, but I do because I'm looking at him when I bend for the gun. His competence. His grace. His shredded shirt. The way the rain plays over his face and body.

"Shit!" Santino shouts, and before the whole word's out of his mouth, the gun is swiped from under me. "Gia!" He aims at her, then Damiano, then her again.

"Stop it!" Gia cries, snotty and bloodshot, aiming the gun at me. "Please. Can you all stop?"

"Put it down," I say.

"I can't stand it!" She's shouting now, raising her voice to a shrill scream. "No more killing. No more fingers. No more pain. It's too much. Do you understand? It's *too much to take!*"

Her hands get tighter around the pistol, and I'm a dead woman.

"Gia!" Santino roars.

That will be the last word I hear. Her name in his mouth.

With a jerky motion, she aims over her head and

with a long, primal scream, takes five shots into the air. She runs out of energy and tosses the gun at my feet.

"Fucking Gia," Damiano mutters, kneeling, knuckles dragging, held in check by the threat of death.

"Shut the fuck up," Santino barks.

I pick up the gun.

"Shoot me," Gia says. "I don't care. Just end this. It's not what I wanted. I hate it."

"On your knees," I say, aiming at her.

She complies, palms upward.

Will Santino stop me? Will Damiano beg for her life?

"Do it," she pleads. "Please."

Is no one willing to stand up for this sad, weepy little bitch? I look at Santino.

"You're a queen now, *Forzetta*," he says. "You choose what to do with her."

What does he mean? Is he seriously giving me authority in his kingdom?

No. He's not. He confers nothing. This isn't a gift. I already have the power. He's just stating a fact.

"I'm sorry, Violetta," Gia says, stressed and uneven, somewhere between screaming and insisting. "And I'm not sorry. I don't know why. I think there's something wrong with me and I can't take it."

"Wee wee wee, all the way home," Damiano mocks, an asshole to the bitter end.

"I can't live with it all. Tavie and Papà. It's my fault. Do it. Please. No one will blame you."

I don't care if anyone blames me. Santino's right. I'm the queen, and her life is my choice.

When I kill Gia, I won't be sorry either. But I'm not

afraid of my brokenness the way she's afraid of hers. How different are we? Both of us fought to be free, and we are. The only difference is she lost everything in the process—her family and her lover—while I gained everything.

I squeeze the trigger. A bouquet of broken asphalt spurts right in front of her.

"You are not cut out for this life," I say, then watch her flinch as I shoot the space in front of her again.

"And you are." She points at the hole in the ground as proof. "Just do it."

"I am, and I'll do it when I feel like it."

I pop another bullet around her—and another, and another—intentionally missing her over and over until there's a firework finale of rock exploding so close, she has to cover her eyes.

"Run, Gia," I say, eleven bullets later. "Don't stop. Just the clothes on your back. Run as far as you can. When you find what you think is normal—a life you're cut out for—live it, and never come back here again."

She takes her hands away and looks around as if the world is new. At me, then Santino, then Damiano, who is sitting cross-legged on the wet road.

"Go!" I shout.

Gia snaps out of it and scurries downhill. She gets smaller and her footsteps get quieter. Damiano fills the void she leaves with a sound that could be laughing or crying.

"Did I do that right?" I say, turning to my husband.

"There are no rules."

Of course not. That is plain now. He and I are the rules, and his best friend is waiting to hear our verdict.

"You should be the one." I point at Damiano, who's trying to back away on his knees.

I can list every wrong that justifies me pulling the trigger. The full force of Damiano's fist in my face. The forced marriage. The death of our baby. And even that doesn't come close to what he did to me when he hurt Santino.

"We will do it." Santino waves me closer, puts the gun in my hand, and positions himself behind me, arm to arm, hand to hand, his mutilated left fingers breaking my heart just enough to make me more angry.

Damiano's almost to his feet, but he's wobbly without his arms to leverage, and his shoes slip in the rain.

"I'm your brother," he says to us.

"No," Santino says into my ear, his body arched against mine. His cock is erect against the curve of my ass. I'm wet for it. For him. For the freedom of bloodshed.

"Not yours," Damiano shouts, slipping again.

Before Damiano can utter another word, Santino's hands squeeze around mine, and his arms absorb the recoil. Damiano falls back onto the street with a hole in his forehead.

I hold my breath.

He doesn't get up. The rain drips in his open eyes and rinses the life from them.

Santino's erection is hard and thick against me as he squeezes our hands again, pulling the trigger to hit the fallen man's chest.

It's over.

It takes me a few seconds of leaning against my rock-hard husband, watching the rain hit Damiano's dead body, to fully realize that my king is with me again, and it's over.

I feel as though I've been holding up the entire world, and now that he's here, collapsing seems like the only reasonable response. But my knees stay steady, and my shoulders do not drop. My arms lock around him and my lips taste the rain falling from his.

Santino is all right. This isn't a dream. I'm not between life and death or in a delusional state. He's with me, standing, breathing, telling me how completely alive he is.

How alive we both are.

And how dead the man who hurt us is.

My brain fires a million miles a minute, flooding with dopamine.

"You're here," I say, clutching what's left of his shirt.

"I'm here." He drops the gun, takes a fistful of my hair, and forces me into a kiss that's not meant for a sweet reunion, but a demand. "Pull your pants down so I can prove it."

They're soaking wet, so I can't get them down fast enough to satisfy my own lust. When they're around my thighs, he pushes me into the Suburban's open door. My back is on the seat and my head against the gear shift. He pushes my legs up, and with my legs still bound by my waistband, he gets out his cock and shoves it in me.

As he drives and thrusts, he rips off my pants, pushing my legs apart so he can split me in two, proving to himself that he's killed a man but is still alive.

It's a victory screw. A murder fuck. It's blood and gunpowder and a rush toward the sharp edge of death.

I slap his face. "You left without me." I slap it again. He drives into me so hard the pain is exquisite. "Don't do that ever again."

"I'm not sorry," he growls, laying his right hand on my throat to keep me still.

I slap him, and he tightens his grip, pounding hard enough to break me, and I want him to. I claw at his face to rip him apart. Taking a man's life took me to an edge, but not all the way. It's not enough. I'm still cracking from the inside, and Santino needs to shatter me until the life drains out.

"Kill me," I cry, scratching his chest. "Kill me with it."

"We go to death together." He squeezes my throat until his face is at the end of a long, dark tunnel. "And come back."

As the tunnel closes and my senses shut down, my body explodes in pulsing electricity.

I am dead. I'm sure of it. No one can feel this much pure pleasure and live.

My lungs take in air as Santino cries out, coming inside me while I'm still inside my orgasm. Gradually, the sound of pattering rain enters, and reality returns.

He's here, above me, eyes half-closed with release, and it's a better reality than I ever hoped for.

"We won," I say, caressing the face I just slapped.

"I found you." He kisses my throat. "My queen."

"My king."

He pushes himself away as if reminded of something. He puts his dick away. "Get in."

Grabbing my wet pants, I scoot to the passenger seat. He walks away to stand over Damiano's body, then crouches by him. A minute later, Santino strides back, hands together as he puts my father's ring back where it was meant to be.

30

VIOLETTA

We are together in our castle. What happened last night is like a dream—if a dream could transform me into who I was always meant to be. I look the same, but I feel different at a cellular level. My atoms are vibrating faster. The firing of my brain is hotter, but my blood runs colder.

Santino sleeps.

I don't think I've ever seen him at rest before. I can't help staring at his black eyelashes and the crease in the center of his lower lip. I want to touch it, but I don't want to wake him. He's earned a few hours of sleep.

When we got back, he threw a blanket over my naked legs and carried me into the house. Gennaro got right to business, reporting our losses as one bullet graze and an attack of pre-battle vomiting. The Tabonas, caught off guard and trapped by the guns on the ridge above, woke from their crown-induced haze and dropped their weapons.

I demanded they call Dr. Aselli to take care of Santino's hand, and while we waited, I told Santino about Dario, who hasn't been seen since a bolt of lightning struck by chance or heavenly design just as he was attempting to steal the crown. I told him about my plan to rescue him from Lasertopia and Loretta's vengeance of Carlo Tabona for Elio's death.

When the doctor came, I was still tending the first and second-degree burns on Santino's torso as he caught me up on his story of his eternity behind the brick wall.

Now, with the late morning sun finding its way into our slit of sky, there is peace. The crown is out of its box, sitting on the dresser like a piece of costume jewelry.

Santino put it there with his bare hands.

Last night, before he started the Suburban, my husband picked up the crown from the dashboard. He'd never really seen it up close under anything as bright as the car's dome light. He turned it around to the back, where the nail connected the diadem's U-shape, and let out a long exhale.

"This is it?" he asked.

"Yes." I tried to take it from him, but he wouldn't let go.

"How did you get it?"

"It's a long story with a crazy ending." I let go, and he tossed it back on the dashboard to start the car. "Was it hot? The metal. Did it burn when you touched it?"

"It's cold out. Why would it?" His brows knit as if he didn't understand the question.

Why should he? It didn't burn him because he

didn't expect it to, proving the crown is just a random antique, and its power is a crowdsourced effect.

This is what I believe, until I remember a thing I never understood.

Rosetta's upstairs, stuffing Mamma's old lipstick into her overnight bag so she can try it at Nonna's. I packed my favorite pajamas with the roses and kittens.

When I come downstairs, my mother is still wearing the purple hat with a black ribbon. She looks good in hats, and she looks good now, but I remember the moment before I went upstairs. Her flat features. The waxy never-aliveness across her face for that split second before she shooed me away with "*Sciò!*"

She's fine. Alive. Round with a new baby brother. Smiling at me.

"Is Papino still mad?" I ask.

They were fighting last night. Whenever Mamma is mad at Papà, I feel as if she's mad at me, but when he's mad, it feels as if the world is going to end…and he was very, very mad last night, barking into the phone about America. He seemed very serious.

"He is mad, my little chicken." She tickles my belly. "But it's our choice to care or not."

How can anyone not care?

One day, I was hiding in one of the many little storerooms in the back of the grocery. It was a perfect place to hide from Fiori when we played *nascondino*, but only when the door was open. Once I was tucked between two boxes of canned olives though, the door closed. I could only see two men's feet. One was Papà. I stayed frozen between those boxes because I wasn't supposed to be there. So I never found out who the other man was. All I heard was his voice pleading with Papà not to be mad, and all I saw were his shoes, bent at the toe as he kneeled, begging.

"You don't care?" I ask.

How can Mamma not care if Papà was mad when a grown man was reduced to weeping over the same thing? Aren't women weaker?

"Violetta." She crouches to my eye level and squeezes my arms. "When a man won't let you be who you are, you stop caring."

"About Papino?"

"About anyone."

For my five-year-old self, this revelation is not about a marriage. It's about a family.

"What about Rosetta and me? Do you care about us?"

Had we let her be who she was? Had we stopped her? She seemed frustrated with us sometimes, and she yelled or cried. Was that who she wanted to be?

"I'll always love you both. More than life itself."

Papà comes in then. His call is done, and his footfall is heavy with whatever disappointments he's lugging around.

"You ready?" he asks.

Mamma stands and nods, barely looking at him.

"Don't cause trouble," he says to me, following her out.

I promise myself I won't cause any trouble. I'll be

good. Mamma might stop caring about me, and if she does, she'll be her most unalive.

IN THE NEWSPAPER PICTURES, the purple hat was a few feet from her body, leaning against the half-open door of the restaurant. The pool of blood under her head crept toward it, but in the pictures Rosetta showed me, the blood didn't quite reach.

I wanted to ask for the hat because I was sure I'd look good in it too. Just like Mamma. But I didn't have a chance. We were sent running to a new normal.

"What do you look like that about?" Santino asks.

I don't know how long he's been awake. Could be half a second. Could be the entire time.

"Your hand." I pretend to mean the left hand with the missing finger, but I'm really thinking about the way the crown was cool to his touch, and how it would feel if I stopped loving him the way my mother stopped loving my father.

"Don't waste your time feeling sorry," he demands. "I'll still fuck you the same. And I punish you with the right hand anyway."

"Keep promising me a good time." I reach around him and take his left arm, pulling it forward. He lets me see his hand in all its bandaged glory. We won't see it again for a while. The wound was a mess. An abomination. A hole in the universe. "Does it hurt?"

He scoffs. "It hurts. *Fa molto male.* But when I thought of losing you, the pain was nothing. It was better than morphine."

This bravado thing isn't going anywhere. He is who he is, and he'll never admit to weakness or pain, but I can admit to it for him. From the finger, I knew they didn't even get in the joint space where there's no bone. They just cut the proximal phalange above the socket, leaving bone splinters and raw tendon gristle. But seeing this mess attached to him and not in a disembodied part buried another seed of rage in the fertile soil of my love.

"I'll get the codeine." I start to get up, but he pulls me back onto the bed.

"I'm fine."

"That's up to Dr. Aselli." I straddle him while he holds my wrists.

"It was a good thing there's a doctor left you don't want to murder."

"You want Farina's dick shoved down his throat as much as I do."

"We're going to kill them." He lets go, and I drop to put my nose next to his. "You and me. For everything they did to keep us apart."

"*Come, come? Cosa hai detto?*" I ask him what the hell he's talking about, then kiss him and pull back an inch to find his eyes meeting mine. "You left without me."

"I am not sorry." He runs his hand over my ass and pinches it. "Not even this much."

"You know what I think?"

"No." He smirks. "I do not."

"I think I should put that crown on and see if you fall like a Tabona."

"That crown can be in the box or on your head." He plants his lips on mine, then rolls us over until he's on top of me and my legs are wrapped around him. "When I tell you to suck my cock, you'll get on your knees and open your mouth just the same."

In our bed, late in the morning, kissing him with more feeling than I thought existed in the entire universe, I realize how happy I am.

"Are you all right?" He kisses a tear off my cheek.

"I didn't think I'd ever let myself love you this much."

"Love rules without rules, my violet." With a kiss to my jaw, he moves to my throat and then my collarbone. "Even when you rule."

"Do I?"

"Yes." His lips brush between my breasts and down my belly.

I groan at his attention, turning to the dresser where the crown sits without glory or protection. It's not harmless. I may never know if its power comes from shared belief or Heaven above, but it's still a mindlessly evil thing that I do not need to rule.

"I want something," I say.

"The world?"

"It's bigger than that."

If the community defers to a piece of metal, nothing will change. It's a hollow victory. My partnership with Santino was earned in blood, but it won't be recognized by our subjects with a simple statement.

"What is it?" He kisses between my thighs.

"I'll tell you after you make me come."

He pauses to look up at me from between my legs. "Maybe."

"I shouldn't have called you *Forzetta*," he says.

"No?" Is he going to imply I'm not as strong or powerful as he thought?

But he smiles and lowers his head to lick where I'm soft and wet.

"You are a *il Ducetta?* " He gives my clit a quick suck.

"No. That makes no sense. But you are a little Mussolini—without the moustache."

I laugh, then he makes me squeal with delight.

31

SANTINO

In the next three days, Violetta starts turning Torre Cavallo into a home. Our people are here. Our family. She prefers to have meals cooked in the upstairs kitchen. She tells everyone she prefers the food stay far from the smell of the coal furnace, but her presence above is a strategy. It is where she can be seen, and where she can overhear things she cannot when she's sitting beside me.

As merchants and priests come up the road to swear loyalty, she hears whispers about the crown. They don't believe. They think I'm *schiavo della fica*.

"Pussy-whipped," she translates with her feet on the short edge of my desk. Her chair faces in the same direction as mine. It's late, and I'm pacing.

I wave it off. Doesn't matter.

"Maybe I should give you English lessons now," she says.

"You take this too lightly. They only fear you because they fear me."

"Let them think what they want."

I swipe her feet off the desk and put my hands on the arms of her chair, leaning into her beautiful face. "Letting people think what they want without consequences... This is an American problem. It rots from the inside. By the time you see the black spots on the skin, it's too late."

"So what do you want to do, Re Santino?" She puts her hands on my face.

I could kiss her now. I could fuck her on this chair again and again, but that would do nothing to impress on her how important this is. "Show them the crown."

"No." Her hands slip away, and she sits back. "They kneel or they don't kneel..."

"I'll cut their knees from under them if they don't."

"All that means is my partnership with you is contingent on an artifact. An inheritance from my parents. Their respect will rot just the same."

I stand straight and cross my arms. I am going to fuck her. I've decided. I'm already hard with the thought.

"I have a better idea," she continues, getting off the chair to reach for my belt.

"Say it first." I grab her hand. This needs to be solved. "Then I fuck you."

"Trying to prove you're not *schiavo della fica?*"

"*Mia Regina*, you miss the point. I am a slave to your pussy, and your mind, and your heart. But even a slave can resist long enough to hear his queen's strategy."

"Fine." She falls back into her chair. "We call a meeting at the café."

She tells me the rest of the plan. It is as brilliant as it is brutal.

AT MILLE LUCE the next afternoon, Violetta and Celia serve two dozen leaders of Secondo Vasto and their wives. They treat Violetta with common deference. The wives try to help. She does not let them. Everyone needs to see her serve them.

When everyone has been attended to, she sits to my right.

"You ready?" I ask.

"Yep."

I rise, tapping the crown ring on my left pinkie finger against a glass. The space where my wedding ring used to be is still red and raw, but it's healing well. I wear the gold band on the right side now.

"*Amici miei*." I call them my friends, then wait until they're all eyes and ears. "It's been a week since the bridge that connects us to the rest of the world was cut off. Today, it has been reopened."

They applaud. I put up a hand to stop it.

"Alvise Galdano and his sons used their boats to move supplies over the river." I raise my glass. "*Grazie*."

They all drink, and those within reach of Alvize and his sons click glasses with him.

"The threat to us is gone... for now. The men who caused this won't trouble us again."

By mutual agreement with my wife, I'm eliding the full truth. The men I'm speaking about are either dead —like Damiano—or have switched loyalties from

Tabona to Cavallo. Cosimo lives, and as long as he does, complete safety cannot be guaranteed.

"St. Paul's will be rebuilt," I continue. "Lasertopia, God willing, will not be."

The laughter dies down before I go on. Everyone here deserves a good laugh.

"There will be changes." I take a bit of amaretto and put down the glass.

At this point, I wanted Violetta to take out the crown and wear it, but she convinced me it was a bad idea, then proved it by sending Vito out to gather information about how the story has changed in the past week.

They've heard about the crown, how men kneel before it, but the story got twisted in the retellings. Now, they say I am the one who stood through a sunroof wearing it. Sometimes the story says it's Dario, who hasn't been seen since he tried to steal the crown. But no one believes it was Violetta. Even the men who were there don't speak too loudly, or they claim it was too dark to see, or they were too overcome with its power to notice whose head it was on.

This is not acceptable. They will not defer to a piece of metal, and I will not accept such a hollow victory. Violetta's and my partnership was earned in blood, but it won't be recognized by our subjects with a simple statement.

"There will be changes," I repeat, taking my wife's hand. Our rings click against each other. "Neither my wife nor I will bless another 'mbasciata."

I preside over a confused silence of glances and knotted brows. The end of arranged marriages is one thing, but the thought that my wife could even bless an *'mbasciata* in the first place is another.

Sweat gathers on her palm.

I lean down to whisper in her ear, "You wanted a bike, now pedal."

She nods decisively and stands. "That is not to be petitioned or questioned. Your daughters are not for sale."

Now the resistance is audible.

Tommy from Lasertopia stands. "I'm sorry, Re Santino, not to question you, but the Lanzonis and us already have a thing you blessed back in April. It cost us a tribute so…uh, I'm wondering if you're gonna honor it?"

"Your tribute will be returned," she says. I know her. She's nervous. She shouldn't be. "And no. Your *'mbasciata* is no longer valid."

"I'd like the money back as much as the next guy," Giulio Lanzoni says over the ensuing murmurs. "But Joe and his girl?" He jerks his thumb at Tommy. "They kinda like each other."

"Have them come to me," she says.

The murmuring turns to shouts about profanity and blasphemy, as if God himself recoils from my leadership.

"All marriages," I add, and the noise dies down into shock. "Every single one, if you want to remain here, will be blessed by Violetta. So you aren't making any under-the-table deals. I know my people." I let my gaze sweep over the most stubbornly traditional, then I raise my glass. "She is the queen, and you will go to her the same way you come to me. Now, drink to it."

Some make sidelong glances, and some take false sips like men crossing their fingers behind their backs.

"What about the crown?" a voice rises from the noise. It's Violetta's Zio Guglielmo. Suddenly, there's silence, and all eyes are on him. "Show it to them, so they believe."

Violetta predicted this would happen, but she did not predict her own uncle would demand a viewing of the crown to protect her.

"No," she says.

"No," I repeat. "That isn't necessary."

I squeeze her hand and look at her, asking if she's ready, because this is it. There's only one way to prove her power isn't contingent on a crown.

She meets my stare and lets go of my hand. I sit, leaving her alone on her feet.

"Dr. Martino Farina," she calls. "Show yourself."

Heads turn. Gennaro and Carmine get into position, in case anything goes wrong.

Farina stands, buttoning his jacket. He's been laying low. Vito delivered the invitation to come here, with the message that the morphine hadn't harmed Violetta. There was no mention of the drug that ended her pregnancy, so he assumed we didn't know.

That was my idea. The math of whether to come or not had to be hard enough to think about, but Farina's equation had to reach the conclusion that forgiveness was possible.

Now, standing at his table while everyone else is seated, he looks like a man who wishes he'd checked his work with a calculator.

"At Damiano Orolio's order," Violetta says, "you gave me morphine."

"*Signorina*," he says with his hands out in a kind of half-shrug, "I knew—"

"*Regina*," I demand, gently but firmly.

"*Regina*," he says more loudly, his chin up. He doesn't fear Violetta. He should. "It was known that Re Santino was dead. You had no husband, so when Capo Orolio called from the other side and ordered the marriage with his son, it was my duty to make sure you complied."

"You were told I was pregnant."

"Of course. As a doctor, I can assure you, a single dose of this drug does not cause adverse effects. We can discuss further if you like. Perhaps as part of an internship if you make it through nursing school? I don't want to bore you with complicated medical terms you're unfamiliar with."

"What about the misoprostol?"

He swallows so hard I'm sure his entire spine just went backward down his throat.

She waits, watching him squirm, keeping everyone in the room in suspense. She's giving them a minute to suspect he did something unacceptable, so the shock of his punishment will be absorbed in that suspicion.

"It seemed..." He spreads his arms, looking at the faces of his peers before turning back to the queen with his hands folded in front of him. "Just a precaution. Surely no woman would want to enter into marriage with the possibility that another man's baby—"

"The king... Re Santino's baby."

"Of course." He's now too afraid to defend himself

further. Good. I don't want to hear another word out of him.

"That second drug you gave me worked, doctor. I lost a baby I wanted very badly."

It sounds as if the entire room—even the flatware and furniture—lets out a gasp.

"Vito," Violetta says, "take Mrs. Farina outside."

The tension in the room rises to a fever pitch, but no words are spoken. The leaders are afraid. Their little betrayals, no matter how slight, and their acceptance of a new rule may come to sit heavily in their laps.

They've already been forgiven for all that, but they need to understand that though things will go back to normal, they'll also change.

As his wife is led out, Farina stands in shock, yet he's not afraid—as if he thinks he'll be able to walk away because Violetta is the one standing. Maybe he expects humiliation or a dressing down—and that will be shameful from a woman. It would make him an angry man…maybe a dangerous one.

With a wave, Violetta has two men bring Farina to the front of the room. I am both surprised and proud of how natural she is at this. This is who she is. Who she's always been. The moments I fuck her and she submits to my will are more precious with every ounce of power she takes for herself.

Dr. Farina's pushed to his knees in front of her. He sighs, resigned to the degradation.

"*Regina*," he says, looking down, "I am sorry."

"I'd have Father Alfonso come over and forgive you," she says, taking her gun from its holster. "But he died of a heart attack when his church burned." When he looks up in shock at the murder of a priest, the barrel of a gun is waiting for him. "So make your apologies directly to God."

This morning, I offered to do this part of the job for her. I said I'd do it at her command, with obedience, in front of everyone. That would send a message.

She refused. I knew she would. It's the right decision.

We joked about making sure she had enough bullets, in case she missed at close range.

But she doesn't.

32

VIOLETTA

The evening after Mille Luce, I'm up in the cupola, smoking a cigarette. My family is coming to live up here for a while and enjoy the retreat from the stresses of war.

The town below, the lawn behind, everything side to side belongs to Santino and me. It's my birthright through the Iron Diadem and the nail that connects it into a crown.

So much of this is clear to me. Greed. Lust for power. Loyalty.

But so much more is muddled.

"Here you are," Santino says, coming up the steps. From behind, he puts his arms around my waist. "Queen of the world."

"Please don't kneel." I turn to face him.

"I'll kneel when I want, and you'll kneel when I tell you."

"Really?"

"Before another hour passes, we need to be clear

between us." He pushes me to my knees, a shock of arousal flooding my body. "Out there, we are equals. One and the same. But when we're alone, I rule you. Your body is my kingdom, and it obeys."

Looking up at him, I see him as ten feet tall, effortlessly in command.

"Yes," is the only word I can make.

"My cock is waiting for your mouth."

I unbuckle, unbutton, unzip, remove his bludgeon of a dick, and without hesitation, put it in my mouth.

"Such a queen," he says, arms crossed, letting me do all the work. "Shooting the man who hurt you. Didn't even blink. Didn't ask for forgiveness. And here you are, on your knees, sucking my dick like you're starving." He takes a hard breath. "Put your hands behind your back. Good. Nice. Now, slow. Take all of it."

I open my throat and push forward, taking his entire length.

"You're in charge," he says. "Let me see what you do with it."

He's making sure I know he's the king. He can't live without his dominance over my body, and he needs to know I can't live without it either.

Leaving him to be still, I'm the one who does the work, pushing him down my throat and halfway out until I need to breathe, then doing it again. I'm ready to swallow what he releases when he says, "Stop." I pull away, spit dripping down my chin.

"Take off your clothes."

Heart pounding with anticipation, I strip down to my skin. He does the same.

We're naked. I hope no one's looking up at the

cupola at that moment, yet I hope that if they are, they understand that this man owns me.

"You're doing very well," he says.

"Thank you."

"Get on the floor and show me your cunt."

The words alone make me dizzy with heat, but the act of getting on my back and spreading my legs for him is the mightiest thing I've ever done.

He crouches on the balls of his feet and slides two fingers of his left hand inside me. The empty fourth place sends them deeper than they've ever gone.

"No matter who you kill or who you rule, I rule your body." He removes his hand and flicks my clit.

I squeak with a burst of pleasure.

"You do as I say." He puts his palm against my nub—barely touching it. "Make yourself come."

Jerking slightly, I rub against his hand. He doesn't move it as I grind again. He holds still, watching me use him for my pleasure, arching and bucking myself to orgasm, just as he commanded.

Then he's on me, flipping me to my side, spreading me open and thrusting into me like an animal.

"Don't you ever forget," he growls.

"I am yours," I gasp. "You own me."

"And you love me."

"Always. I love you always."

I come a second time, and he explodes inside me.

It's right afterward, as he kisses my shoulder tenderly, that I realize love might be the key to it all.

My parents had the crown between them in their bedroom the night I overheard their conversation.

What it would be like if this thing didn't exist? Who you'd be?

You'd still be mine.

Do you ever wonder what I'd be? What I could be?

Do I not take care of you?

A few months before their deaths, Papino had missed the point entirely. Twice. Through the hinge-wide space between the door and the jamb, I'd watched my mother fall out of love with him.

And then the handles were hot.

There has to be a perfectly unmagical explanation for the heat of the crown and its case, but that doesn't mean history isn't trying to tell me something. The possibilities of power had made Mamma hungry for it. She resented the disappointments of her station, and they turned her against her husband.

The coal rocks burn bright white, shimmering with heat inside a hot metal box. We're having this stinky coal furnace taken out as soon as possible. Then we're scrubbing this shit out of the floors and walls and plastering all of them over with peppermint and lavender sheetrock, and if that doesn't get out the smell, we're sealing off this section of the basement behind seven layers of lemon-scented cinder block. Zio Guglielmo says none of those materials exist, but I can dream.

But I've proven to everyone that I am Santino's partner and equal. That day, I set myself free of any desire for vengeance. I'll never kill anyone again. That's his job from now on.

We aren't saints, but we're home, living in a place

that feels more right to me than St. John's or the Leaky Bean or anywhere across the river ever did. I have a place with him, here.

Between us, he rules me with love, and my love for him rules my life.

Santino comes to the basement of Torre Cavallo with the crown's box under his arm. He grips the bottom with his left hand, which is now only partly bandaged.

I meet him at the bottom step and kiss him. He hands me the box. I place it on a red milk crate I've set in front of the open furnace, between two metal folding chairs. We sit in reverent silence for a moment.

"Do you remember the night my parents died?"

"Yes."

"Do you know who did it?" I ask.

"Nobody knows."

"You said you had the night off, but you went anyway."

"Emilio planned a last-minute dinner, so…"

"It was her. My mother. She sprung it on him. I remember. And she said if Papà died, she was in charge."

His eyes narrow as if he doesn't know where I'm going with this.

"Santi, she didn't love him. She'd been getting harder and harder for months, but that morning, she went ice cold."

"Wait. You think she planned it? Camilla Moretti?" He's practically laughing.

"Camilla Cavallo. And yes. I think she planned to

have my father killed, but she got the wrong guy to do it, and he shot her too."

"This is why you brought me down here?" He shakes his head. "They loved each other, *Forzetta*."

"Look at me. Everyone says I look like my father, and maybe I do. But listen to everything that never made any sense. Emilio had a half brother who felt entitled to Camilla, to the crown."

His head tilts. He's getting it, but not yet.

Not quite yet.

"I asked Zia Madeline and Nazario—who's, like, never leaving. They told me everything. I don't look like my father." I pause. He can't see it, but Nazario says he will. "I look like Cosimo Orolio."

Santino's eyes scan me as if for the first time. He doesn't have to tell me he sees a man I've never met. It's all over his face.

"He never forgave Mamma for hanging him out to dry after Papà was almost assassinated the first time. I was little, and I was his, but she wasn't ready to fully betray her husband. So the second time, he did the hit, but he shot the both of them."

"My God."

I can practically hear things clicking in Santino's head, observed moments I'm confident he'll tell me about during calmer days. But he knows I'm right.

"Damiano was going to marry his half sister." His face contorts in disgust. "An animal."

"It was because of this." I point at the box. "It made him an animal"

Santino is still shaken by the revelation, but my brother's fate isn't my point. "And it made my mother wonder what she would have been without her husband. It made her feel like he was keeping her down…and he was, but she was part of a world where she wouldn't have even had a choice without the crown, and her choices were taken away because of the crown too. But what locked her into a life wasn't a piece of metal. It was expectations. Assumptions. And they had no reason to change any of that because of this thing…" I tilt my chin toward the box. "It fucked with all their heads. I don't want that. Ever. I don't want to wonder what I'd be without you. My life with you is the only one I want."

He nods, knees to elbows, tenting nine fingertips. "You don't have to do this."

"I know." I open the lid.

"It's what brought us together."

"But it's not what keeps us together."

Last night, Santino argued to have the crown sent to a museum, but there's no provenance, no chain of ownership since it was stolen during Mussolini's regime, then stolen again by the *partigiani* and left to rot in a warehouse of artifacts the *camorra* was selling to finance a mob war.

"Do you not want to?" I ask.

"No, no." He *tsks*. "You're right. It causes too much trouble. It's already broken too much."

I take the crown out of the box. "Do you feel the compulsion to kneel?"

"Put it on your head. Let's see."

"I don't want to know."

"Maybe I do."

"No."

Before I can change my mind, I toss the crown into the white-hot furnace. It sits on the bottom of the coal box, implacable at first, as if nothing can touch it. The tips and edges blacken, then turn bright hot.

Santino and I grab for each other's hands, holding on for dear life as the object that brought us together in marriage loses its shape and melts into bubbling lava.

"It is done." He closes the door and latches it. "Do you still love me?"

"I will always love you."

He puts his hands on my thighs and gets down on his knees, resting his head in my lap. I bend over him and put my cheek on his back. We remain like this for a minute before Loretta's voice comes down from upstairs.

"They're here!"

"*Patatina!*" My zia rushes out of the car, and we meet in the middle of the yard. Her eyes are red-rimmed and her round cheeks sag. When she throws her arms around me, I feel her grief against my chest. It awakens mine with the hum of a shared language.

"I'm so sorry," I say into her collar. "I hoped to bring you up here days ago."

Telling her what was sacrificed in my failure to get her—what lies were told and consequences felt—won't help anyone. I leave that for Sunday dinners in the undefined future.

"We're here now." She rocks me back and forth, tighter and tighter. "That's all that matters."

I hold her at arm's length, smiling at the sight of her, while the car empties of her sister, Donna's family. Her husband Angelo, Antonio, Elettra, and Tina.

"Where's Zio Guglielmo?" I ask.

She doesn't have to answer as my zio gets out last, carrying his old Beretta *dei partigiani* in a holster like a dare. He greets Santino as my husband comes out the front door to welcome his extended family.

Zia watches with me and shakes her head. "We saw when they took him." She stops herself and makes the sign of the cross to ward off the devils in her thoughts. "And we heard what they did to his hand."

Santino pats Zio Guglielmo on the back with a bandaged hand. A few days ago, Dr. Aselli sent his assistant to live up here and continue the work on Santino's hand. Dr. Aselli is too busy to stay himself. As of yesterday, he is Secondo Vasto's only doctor. We'll have to get another.

"It's going to be all right," I say.

Santino's body will heal, and so will our little corner of the world. There is an uneasy peace in the valley below. Our enemies are being rooted out, and loyalties are shifting. But there will be an end to it.

"You've been through so much," Zia Madeline says. "And you look like my beautiful niece, all grown up."

Santino slides his arm over my shoulder, resting his fingertips on the back of my neck, and gives Zia Madeline a kiss on each cheek.

"She is the queen. My queen."

The family I brought up has formed a receiving line. We greet and double kiss, hug, and cry. They're here, and I didn't even realize how much I needed each of them.

Everything's on the way back to normal. Thank God.

"So this is the famous Torre Cavallo," Zia Donna says to my king and me. "It's beautiful."

"Thank you." I greet her with a hug, then see my uncle's mother. "Welcome, Nonna Angelina." I take her hand and kiss each papery cheek. The last time I saw her, Santino was shoving me into a car after a walk around the block. "You can stay as long as you want."

"I knew you'd come to accept it." She squeezes my hands, and I remember how unfazed she was by my screaming on the day Santino stole me away.

"I accept *him*, Nonna." I pull him close. "But now I have the power to change everything else."

"And she might," Santino says.

I look up at my husband, who has utter dominance over me, and who I rule with the same power. The unstoppable force and the immovable object, in harmony.

By some unspoken mutual agreement, we kiss, but we have to break apart, laughing, when Tina rushes in to hug my legs, throwing me off balance for a moment. Elettra follows her sister, and I drape my free arm around them both.

For the first time—holding these girls—I have no doubt that it was all worth it.

EPILOGUE
VIOLETTA

With my family in Torre Cavallo and our rivals either dead or shifted to our side, I thought we were done, but Santino always knew better. I have a sense of his rhythms now. The way his attention shifts too slowly because a doubt holds him up.

"Tell me," I say in the dark of night when we're both supposed to be sleeping. The moonlight glints off his eyes when he opens them, and though his doubts pump the brakes on his reply, they do not stop him.

"Dario Lucari," he says. "He sent a message today about our deal."

"He didn't exactly live up to his end."

"He only promised to help with Marco."

"Being an asshole, and trying to steal the crown, puts him in the negative." I get up on my elbow and lay my hand on Santino's bare chest. Our men weren't an abstraction to me any more. They have names and families. "He owes us, and we shouldn't send him anyone until he pays up."

"Don't get drunk with power, *Forzetta*." This is not a reprimand or instruction. It's a warning, and he's right. For the moment, he knows the rules better than I do. He's my partner but he's also my mentor.

"How can we trust him with our guys?" I push over him, arms straight, one leg over his hips. "They're our family. You're sending them to fight what you've basically described as a mega-mafia family—"

"It's not a superhero movie. They can be beaten if he says they can."

"That doesn't make me feel better."

He takes my face in his hands and draws me closer.

"We cannot say no without causing another problem, and a problem like that? We don't want it. Trust me. If he beats the Colonia and comes for us with their power and their men, we may win, but we will lose all of our normal."

With a tick of his attention out the window, he indicates all of our world, from mountain to river and back again.

Our normal. I don't want to lose it after a few days of earning it.

I get up on my knees and straddle him. Neither of us is pretending to sleep now.

"What if we just send him the dumb ones?"

He laughs, then quiets, considering the curves of my body. I'm a little sore from his attention a few hours before but not too sore for another go.

"And what if…" I pause, wiggling against him. "After we send Dario his payment, you and I take the honeymoon we never had."

"Where do you want to go?"

"What if we just got in the car and drove?"

In the time it takes a heart to beat, Santino goes from tenderness to dominance, rolling me over and pinning me to the mattress.

"This again?" Santino kisses my neck and chest, his lips working down my breasts and belly with the urgency of his mind. "Just drive west until we're eating fried chicken and saluting football?"

"Just be away and do nothing but try to make babies. And try and try and..." The next try falls into a gasp as he kisses between my legs, soothing the soreness into soft warmth.

"There's no trying, Violetta. Only doing." With that, he makes me come with my arms outstretched and a cry from the depths of my pleasure.

"Let's do it then. We drive into the sunset and come back good and knocked up."

"I like this plan. Now open your legs." He pushes my knees apart and up before I can comply, leaning on my bent legs so he can drive inside me. "We start tonight," he says when he's so deep our minds connect. He moves slow, always mindful of when I may be sore from an earlier fuck. His eyes close and his head turns. I know him now. He's close.

"Violetta," he whispers. "You are everything."

"Santino," I reply as his motions arouse me as if he just hadn't given me an orgasm. "Take me."

I don't clarify whether I'm asking for him to take my body or take me away into the sunset because I don't have to.

TO OUR SOLDIERS, Santino explains the mission, its dangers and benefits, then asks for volunteers. The half dozen men required step forward, including Vito, and Remo, who wants to see New York. Surprisingly—and privately—Gennaro offers to go.

And then, after we send them east, Santino and I slip away for the honeymoon we never had. We get in the Alfa and drive west.

I don't know what I expected, but I have never seen anything like my country.

It is truly vast. Santino retracts the roof as we cross through the southern tip of Indiana, and the immensity of the sky, its clarity, its everywhereness creates a vacuum so powerful, I fear I'll be sucked upward and into it—a tiny speck of a woman, lost forever. I grab his hand to keep me on the earth, even as the ground moves under me.

"You all right?" he asks, shouting over the wind.

I'm overwhelmed by the size of the world, the limits of my knowledge, the inconsequential impact of my body and mind.

"I'm fine." I squeeze his hand.

We've passed through Colorado, Utah, Wyoming, and Idaho, avoiding cities in favor of the open road and unbroken horizon line. I am in a new world, away from the natural boundaries of mountains and river. Unenclosed. Limitless. Free, yet humbled into amazement. The sown fields go on endlessly, barely taming a few inches of soil depth. Houses are built low and wide as if they respect the sky too much to challenge it. I understand why indigenous people revered the majesty of the heavens and the regenerating life of the earth.

Every single thing a person could observe around them was a miracle, worthy of its own prayer.

"You're doing that thing again." He takes his hand off the wheel to make a circle with his three fingers to define what I'm doing.

"What thing?"

He *tsks*. "Come on. This." He waves in my direction, as if that explains what he sees.

Santino can be lazy and would rather use a gesture or a vocal tone when words fail, which lead to assumptions, which can lead to misunderstandings. I want to know exactly what he means.

"I'm quiet?"

"You're closing your eyes with your eyes open."

I love him so much. He has all the words he needs.

"Doesn't it all overwhelm you?" Now it's my turn to gesture toward the vastness I cannot describe.

He scoffs. "The only thing that overwhelms me is you."

"Wait until we have our fourth child."

"Did we say four?" he asks. "Is that all?"

I have to look at him for a few seconds to be sure he's joking, and even then, I'm not one hundred percent convinced.

"We need to have an Armando and a Camilla," I say.

"I want a Tavie." He puts his arm behind my seat, and I lean into him. "He was a good kid."

"That's three."

"As long as I fuck you enough to have ten children," he shrugs. "How many is up to you."

I turn my face upwards, pressing my nose into his scruff. He smells of the wind and the widening horizon line. He's the road narrowing to a point in the distance, farther and farther with every mile under the tires.

He's Secondo Vasto. Our forever home. Our normal.

I take a deep breath of him, drawing in the sweet scent of freedom.

LA FINE

THANK you for going on this journey with me.

Take a deep breath, and read on, because though Santino and Violetta have found their happily ever after, Dario has some work to do.

YES. My next dark mafia series belongs to the dangerous, shadowy figure of Dario Lucari. His first book is called *Take Me* .

SARAH'S KIDNAPPED *on her wedding day, held by a man who wants vengeance on her father, married to him against her will, and thrust into a world of betrayal, lies, and deviance she's lived in her entire life...but never known.*

All she has to do to escape is destroy everything she's ever loved, and love a man she must destroy.

TAKE ME IS AVAILABLE EVERYWHERE.

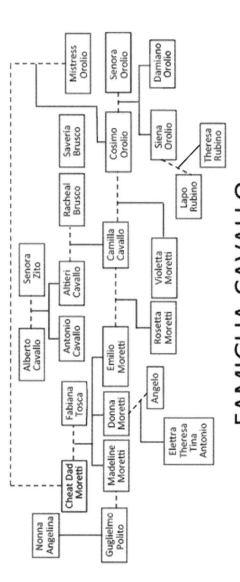

FAMIGLIA CAVALLO

ACKNOWLEDGMENTS

Gentle reader, welcome to the space where I acknowledge my mistakes, shortcomings, and facile assumptions. I am sure this list is incomplete. Should any other oversights come up, it will get longer.

1. The Roman goddess of war was Ballona, but if Loretta said that, your brain was going to say either "she's wrong" or "she's right," because we were all taught it was Minerva. For fuck's sake—half the damn internet says it's Minerva. I thought it was Minerva myself, but God forbid I don't triple check a thing before typing it. Anyway, it's my job to get pulled out of the story by humble details…and it's also my job to make sure reality doesn't pull you out. In this case, to keep from distracting you, I chose common knowledge over facts.
2. Regarding Marco—torture doesn't really

work if the person being tortured is withholding information about things that are really important to them. It feels like it should, but it doesn't. It's a narrative convenience and trope convention. Do I feel great about using it? No. But it does a lot of heavy lifting to express both main character's development. If you call me lazy, I won't fight you.

3. We can talk endlessly about Neapolitan *camorra* hierarchy and how it compares to the Sicilian *Cosa Nostra*, but we'd be wasting a lot of time with things that don't matter, or that have changed, or that the English-speaking world has internalized from movies and books. Let's not, because my next Mafia series (beginning with *Take Me*) will loosely borrow from the 'ndrangheta, and I don't want to hear anyone say it's wrong because it's not the Sicilian mob.

4. The last student clinic I visited was USC's in 2003, because I thought I was pregnant... and I was! Was there an OB right there, on staff? Maybe? Maybe not? Is it common to have one hanging around the clinic, ready to take appointments in the 2020s? No clue. But did you believe it as you were reading it? I hope so.

5. On another student clinic note... misoprostol in the blood would not be caught by a simple, back-of-the-clinic tox screen, so I fudged for the sake of narrative

convenience. If you know of a more realistic way she'd catch it at the clinic, drop me a line and I'll fix it.

6. When I needed to know how hot a fire had to be to melt an ancient iron crown, I called my friend Leonidas Moustakas from Adam's Forge. He's a blacksmith, which is ten shades of awesome but he's also an scientist, which meant quick answers weren't coming. He thought it would be wise to make an iron crown and destroy it in a coal-burning fire to test the exact temperature and time. I thought if he was into making a crown, it would be best to put it on the cover and skip the whole testing part.

7. Is the *Corona Ferrea* actually magical? Or were the men who kneeled before it and the men who swore it was hot to the touch experiencing mass hysteria? I have no idea. I couldn't commit to adding magic into the story any more than I could commit to traditionalist men choosing to bow to a woman's power. Both are equally unlikely.

8. I got the Zippo-beats-bullet idea from the original Hong Kong version of *Hard Boiled*, directed by John Woo—which you should totally watch. In checking to find out if the bullet-blocking abilities of steel lighters was possible I wound up here, here, and here. Now, are these stories apocryphal? Maybe. Does the effectiveness of the Zippo lighter as a bullet-stopper depend on the angle and the

firearm and blah blah blah? Sure. Do I care? Nah.

9. Can we talk about guns and gun safety? My editor, Cassie Robertson at Joy Editing, noped Santino training Violetta at all because they're romantically involved and double-noped him getting touchy/kissy with her while handling live weapons. She's obviously right about all of it. I kept it all because I needed it all, and it was cute where the story needed something lighter, not because I think it's a better way. Everything I know about handling firearms, I learned from movies. Everything she knows, she learned from experience. So, though it seems too obvious to mention, I will anyway. Please, for the love of God, don't take any of the activities or behaviors around guns in my books as an example to follow.

10. You've asked where exactly these books take place. It's a good question. The answer is… nowhere. I built Secondo Vasto out of my imagination. I wanted it to be possible anywhere in the landlocked United States. As I got to the middle of *Mafia Bride*, the story needed the terrain to be more precise, so I honed in on a particular state and region. I've left clues to it in this book. If you figure out the general area, I salute you, but don't waste time looking for the river or the university. The specifics are made up, map and all.

ALSO BY CD REISS

The Edge Series

Rough. Dark. Sexy enough to melt your device.

He's her husband but he's rougher and more dominant than the man she married.

Rough Edge
On The Edge
Broken Edge
Over the Edge

The Submission Series

The *USA Today* bestselling Series

Monica insists she's not submissive. Jonathan Drazen is going to prove otherwise, but he might fall in love doing it.

One Night With Him
One Year With Him
One Life With Him

The Games Duet

The *New York Times* bestsellers.

He'll give her the divorce she wants on one condition. Spend 30 days in a remote cottage with him, doing everything he commands.

Marriage Games

Separation Games

The DiLustro Arrangement

Twisted. Dark. Gritty. Will knock you off your feet story.

An epic mafia romance trilogy that sets a new bar for just how dark a hero can get.

Mafia Bride

Mafia King

Mafia Queen

PAIGE PRESS

Paige Press isn't just Laurelin Paige anymore...

Laurelin Paige has expanded her publishing company to bring readers even more hot romances.

Sign up for our newsletter to get the latest news about our releases and receive a free book from one of our amazing authors:

Laurelin Paige
Stella Gray
CD Reiss
Jenna Scott
Raven Jayne
JD Hawkins
Poppy Dunne
Lia Hunt

ABOUT THE AUTHOR

CD Reiss is a Brooklyn native and has the accent to prove it. She earned a master's degree in cinematic writing from USC. She ultimately failed to have one line of dialog put on film, but stayed in Los Angeles out of spite.

Since screenwriting was going nowhere, she switched to novels and has released over two dozen titles, including two *NY Times* Bestsellers and a handful of *USA Today* bestsellers. Her audiobooks have won APA Audie Awards and Earphones Awards.

She resides in Hollywood in a house that's just big enough for her two children, two cats, her long-suffering husband and her massive ego.

To find out when her next book is coming out, sign up for her mailing list here or at cdreiss-dot-com.

Made in the USA
Columbia, SC
11 February 2022